Praise for earlier Cram mster

"I found myself quickly wrapped put it down until it was done!" *Me & My Books*

"A fun read with humour throughout..." *Crime Thriller Hound*

"An excellent novel, full of twists and turns, plenty of action scenes, crackling dialogue - and a great sense of fun." *Fully Booked*

"A good page-turning murder mystery, with a likeable protagonist and great setting." *The Bookworm Chronicles*

"A highly enjoyable and well-crafted read, with a host of engaging characters." *Mrs Peabody Investigates*

"An amiable romp through the shady back streets of 1960s Brighton." *Simon Brett*, **Crime Writers' Association Diamond Dagger winner**

"A highly entertaining, involving mystery, narrated in a charming voice, with winning characters. Highly recommended." *- In Search of the Classic Mystery Novel*

"Part adventure story, part politically incorrect comedy, this is a fast-moving and funny book. I would recommend it as a light and satisfying read." *Northern Reader*

"A romp of a read! Very funny and very British." *The Book Trail*

"Superbly crafted and as breezy as a stroll along the pier, this

Brighton-based murder mystery is a delight." *Peter Lovesey,* **Crime Writers' Association Diamond Dagger winner**

"It read like a breath of fresh air and I can't wait for the next one." *Little Bookness Lane*

"By the end of page one, I knew I liked Colin Crampton and author Peter Bartram's breezy writing style." *Over My Dead Body*

"A little reminiscent of [Raymond] Chandler." *Bookwitch*

"A rather fun and well-written cozy mystery set in 1960s Brighton." *Northern Crime*

"The story is a real whodunit in the classic mould." **crime author M J Trow**

"A fast-paced mystery, superbly plotted, and kept me guessing right until the end." *Don't Tell Me the Moon Is Shining*

"Very highly recommended." *Midwest Book Review*

"One night I stayed up until nearly 2am thinking 'I'll just read one more chapter'. This is a huge recommendation from me." *Life of a Nerdish Mum*

"I highly recommend this book and the author. I will definitely be reading more of this series and his other books." *The Divine Write*

"Bartram skilfully delivers one of the most complex cozy mystery plots I've read in years." *Booklover Book Reviews*

The World Cup Mystery

A Crampton of the Chronicle adventure

For " The Hound "

The World Cup Mystery

A Crampton of the Chronicle adventure

Peter Bartram

with best wishes,

Pete

Deadline Murder Series Book 6

THE BARTRAM PARTNERSHIP

First published by The Bartram Partnership, 2021

ISBN: 9798482906804

For contact details see website:
www.colincrampton.com

Text copyright: Peter Bartram 2021
Cover copyright: Red Nomad Studios 2021

Text and Cover Design: Red Nomad Studios.
www.rednomadstudios.com

Chapter 1

Taormina, Sicily. 19 July 1966

The lizard had a mean slit of a mouth and a dark green fretwork pattern down its back, like an artist had painted ribs on the outside of its body.

It sat on a stone step and basked in the last rays of the evening sun.

It flicked an insolent lid over a dark beady eye and stared at us.

"Colin, why is he giving us the evil eye?" my girlfriend Shirley asked.

"He thinks you're sizing him up as a pair of lizard-skin shoes," I said.

"Wouldn't get a sandal strap out of that critter."

"He doesn't know that. He wants to know what's going to happen next."

"That makes two of us," Shirley said.

She was right. Here we were in Taormina, a town perched on the cliffs above the Ionian Sea. Me, Colin Crampton, crime correspondent, Brighton *Evening Chronicle*. Hot-shot reporter and trouble magnet, according to my news editor.

And Shirley Goldsmith, proud citizen of Adelaide, Australia. Have toothbrush, will travel. Photographers' model. Totally gorgeous, whether glimpsed through a camera's viewfinder or across a crowded room.

We were sitting on a step in the town's ancient Greek amphitheatre. A tall bank of stone steps, bleached white in the sun, swept in a long arc behind us. Moss grew in crevices where the stones had crumbled. In ancient days, townspeople would have sat on these steps. They'd have wept over a two-hanky tragedy from Aeschylus, who died when an eagle dropped a

1

tortoise on his head. Didn't even get to write a play about it. Or, perhaps, they'd have laughed themselves silly at a ribald comedy by Aristophanes. He invented the dirty joke and the smutty innuendo. And gave centuries of busybodies something to tut-tut about.

But there was no show tonight.

Only a play we'd make for ourselves.

And I didn't know whether it'd turn out to be a comedy – or a tragedy.

The slanting rays of the sun lit Shirley like a spotlight. Her blonde hair shone like polished gold. Her blue eyes sparkled with fun. Her wild lips parted in pleasure.

She was wearing a yellow shift dress, with black trim. Eight guineas from a boutique in London's Carnaby Street. And who cared if the dressmaker had skimped on the silk so the dress ended four inches above Shirl's knees? Not me.

The lizard scurried closer for a better look.

I couldn't blame him.

Shirley glanced at me and winked. "So, just remind me, big boy, why are we here?"

Why, indeed?

How do I get myself into these things?

I'd brought Shirley to the most romantic spot I'd ever found on Earth to ask her a question.

Will you marry me?

Shirley had tagged along because she'd promised to answer it.

Yes. Or no.

She hadn't yet decided.

What had become our own Greek drama had started a month earlier. We'd been having a drink in a pub when the subject of love and marriage had come up. When I'm with Shirley, the idea of love is never far from my mind. But marriage? Well, we'd never discussed it.

But it was just after I'd written a story for the *Chronicle* about a pirate radio station. It had turned out to be a front for communist spies. The radio station. Not the *Chronicle*.

Shirl and I had been through a lot together. Not least, escaping narrowly with our lives.

And then I'd passed a jeweller's and seen just the perfect engagement ring in the window. I had it in my pocket now. Gold with a big emerald-cut diamond. Smaller shoulder stones on either side. Impulsively, I'd bought it. And there, in the pub, I'd pulled it out and asked Shirley to marry me.

It wasn't like the last reel in a Hollywood weepie, where the girl falls into the hero's arms. No, Shirley took one look and told me she wasn't sure.

And so, that's why we were in the Greek amphitheatre. We waited for the moment when the shadows lengthen and twilight falls. When the stones darken and the moon casts a silvery light over the Ionian Sea. When the scent of romance is carried on the evening air like fragrant bougainvillaea.

The moment when men are bold and women weaken.

Or, at least, that's what I'd heard. And if I were impressionable, I might have believed it. But anything's worth trying once.

I'd told Shirley I would go down on one knee and ask her to marry me. And she'd promised to give me her final answer then.

So, here in the amphitheatre, now was the moment.

And it was nothing like I'd heard.

My heart was pumping like a steam engine's piston. My skin felt clammy and hot. My eyes viewed the scene through a kind of mist. And it felt like a herd of wildebeest had started their annual migration in my stomach.

(And where the hell was that damned bougainvillaea scent?)

I was about to learn just how the rest of my life would turn out.

3

The lizard flicked his tail, like he didn't care.

Shirley grinned. "So, are you going to do it?"

"Do what?"

"The one knee thing."

"Of course."

"Anyway, what's that all about?"

"It's a mediaeval tradition. You know, knights and their ladies. It was a way for the guys in their armour to show how much they honoured their women. You said that's what would get you here. Me down on one knee."

"Yeah! Now I'm not so sure."

"You mean you're not going to accept my proposal?"

"You haven't made it yet."

"But if I do?"

"Having second thoughts?" Shirley asked.

"No. But haven't you made up your mind about your answer?"

"Not yet. I want to see what I feel when you actually ask me the question."

I kicked the dust on the ground. The lizard scurried into a crevice between the stones.

"Now you've frightened the poor critter," Shirley said.

"Too bad. Two's company and three's..."

"A sex orgy. Yeah, I know the joke."

I looked at Shirley. She grinned at me. I raised my gaze to the sea. It was that kind of impossible blue. But where the sun's rays slanted across it, there were streaks of gold. In a few moments, they would be gone as the sun sank below the summit of Mount Etna.

When I'd suggested the trip in the pub, I was convinced the sight of all this beauty would have fired up Shirley's mind.

Now, I wasn't so sure.

I looked back at her. She'd folded the fingers of her hands together. She stared intently at me.

"I'm doing it now," I said.

I took the ring box from my pocket and flipped it open.

I dropped to one knee.

Yeeeeooooow!

The cry came from behind one of the pillars in the amphitheatre's backdrop.

Yeeeeooooow!

It came again. The cry of a soul in pain. Of someone who looks into the future and sees only a black empty space.

The cry echoed off the pillars, bounced off the steps. And then rang in my ears. I shivered. Felt my whole body tense.

I looked at Shirley. Her mouth had dropped open. Fear filled her eyes.

Yeeeeooooow!

The cry came a third time. I sprang to my feet. Shirley jumped up. She shot me an alarmed look.

I closed the ring box and thrust it into my pocket.

Now deep gulping sobs echoed from behind the pillar.

The sobs of a woman.

Shirley and I hurried towards the sound.

The woman behind the pillar was slumped on the ground. Her back rested on the stone. Her knees were pulled up under her chin. Her face was buried in her hands. Each sob was so deep it shook her body. She gulped for air.

She had long raven hair and, as far as we could see, a complexion so white it could have been dusted with flour. She wore a cream blouse which was torn on the right sleeve and a simple fawn skirt. She had a pair of old canvas shoes on her feet. There was a ragged hole in the heel of the left shoe.

Shirley knelt down beside her. Put her arm around the girl's shoulder. Whispered something softly in her ear. I couldn't hear what it was.

But the girl turned, parted her fingers and looked through them at me.

5

"It's my father," she said in English.

"What about your father?" Shirley asked.

The girl whimpered into her hands. "He died… He's dead."

"We're so sorry," Shirley said.

The girl cupped her hands more tightly around her face. She gulped back another sob.

"I think he's been murdered," she cried.

As soon as we'd landed at Catania airport earlier that afternoon, I should've known there'd be trouble.

We were held up in a queue at immigration for half an hour while an old guy in front argued about whether he should've had a visa in his passport.

Then, when we went to pick up our luggage, a vanity case Shirley had brought with her had gone walkabout.

I said the case was probably too vain to ride the carousel with the other baggage.

Shirley told me I should take it more seriously. She stomped off to make a complaint to an official in a blue uniform with enough gold braid for a Ruritanian general.

He waved his arms about a bit. Shirley waved her arms and stamped her foot.

And the vanity case finally developed some humility and turned up last on the carousel.

So, by the time we arrived at our hotel in Taormina, it was the middle of the afternoon – and we both felt frazzled. But some sandwiches and a bottle of *Asti Spumante* revived our spirits.

Shirley relaxed in her chair and looked out at the street as a girl on a Lambretta sped by.

"So, when you gonna do the dirty deed?" Shirl asked.

"If you mean the proposal, I don't look on it as a deed and certainly not a dirty one."

Shirley grinned. "Listen to you. Sound like some kind of old fogey."

"I want it to be special. That's why we've come to Taormina."

"Could have done it on the end of Brighton pier," Shirley said.

"Too frivolous."

"Or in the Royal Pavilion gardens."

"Too regal."

"Or high up on that Devil's Dyke hill behind the town."

"Too public."

"You sure are Mister Particular."

"I want to knock you off your feet, so you'll say 'yes'."

"More likely to give you a two-fingered salute if I'm lying on the ground."

I slumped back in my chair.

Shirley was in one of her difficult moods. I put it down to tiredness from the journey. Or perhaps she was nervous about the proposal. Maybe she wouldn't accept.

And where would that leave her? Or me?

We needed a diversion. Something to occupy our minds until evening, when we'd go to the amphitheatre.

"Let's go for a walk," I said.

"Where?"

"The main street here is called the *Corso Umberto*. Apparently, it's got a lot of interesting shops."

Shirley grinned. "Sounds like my kind of street."

"Wow," said Shirley. "Just look at all these flags. They must know you're in town."

We'd climbed the steps to the *Corso Umberto*, a cobbled street flanked by old stone buildings. They crowded together so close, like they wanted to be friends.

The place was strung with red, white and green bunting. Shops sported signs which read: *Forza Italia!*

"All this show is for the World Cup," I said. "Italy are one of the strongest teams. They hope to win it."

"And what do those signs mean?" Shirley asked.

"*Forza Italia!* It's like shouting 'Come on, Italy'. I expect there'll be plenty around town yelling it this evening. Italy play North Korea. They have to beat them to stay in the competition."

"I didn't know you were a football fan."

"I'll be cheering England when they play."

"Hey, what's this over here?"

A shop window had caught Shirl's eye. A jeweller's.

"No girl would think twice of turning down a guy with that in his back pocket," she said.

Shirl had her nose pressed up against the window. Inside, a blue velvet stand revolved slowly. The stand held a gold box with a single ring. A hoop of gold with a rock the size of an asteroid mounted in it.

"There must be a zillion carats in that diamond," Shirley said.

"Any guy with that in his hip pocket would be walking around with a limp," I said. "Could rupture a buttock if he sat down."

"Rock that size - no guy would hold on to that for long. Any gal would have it on her ring finger in a trice."

"I thought size didn't matter to you," I said.

Shirley winked. "What are you talking about now, big boy?"

"The same thing as you, I think."

"Sure, the size of the ring doesn't matter. It's what it stands for that's important. But there's no reason why a girl can't dream."

"You want me to trade in the ring I've bought for another?"

"No, of course not. You couldn't do that here."

I pointed at a sign in the window: *Compriamo buoni gioielli.*

"We buy good jewellery," I translated.

"Yeah! And sell it at twice the price," Shirley said. "I bet the guy who runs this joint is a pirate. You stick with the ring in your pocket."

She tore herself away from the window and twirled around in the street. "I've decided I love this street. I love the cobbles and the grey stone. I love the shadows and the light – and these mysterious alleyways that lead off on both sides. Let's go up that one over there and see where it leads. An adventure."

"We'll be having an adventure in the amphitheatre later," I said.

"That's not an adventure. It's a transaction."

"We don't know where those alleys lead – or who lives up them."

"You think it's the Mafiosi – and you're a scaredy-cat."

"And with good cause where the Mafia is concerned. Let's walk on. I think I can see an ice-cream parlour further up the street."

But before we could move, a woman shot out of the alley we'd looked in.

Her face glistened with sweat and her breast heaved with deep breaths. She was young – barely twenty. She had a trim figure, like an athlete's.

She turned and bent forward to rest her hands on her knees. Took a couple of deep breaths. Straightened up and screamed at someone further down the alley.

"*Mi hai picchiato una volta di troppo. Mai più, Brando.*"

Shirley stared at me and raised an eyebrow.

I translated. "You've beaten me once too often. Never again, Brando."

The woman turned and ran – away down the *Corso Umberto*.

But before she'd covered fifty yards, a burly man shot out of the alley. He was built like an ox with a big head and a mop of jet-black hair. He had dark deep-set eyes. He peeled his lips back in a grin that bared teeth like tombstones.

He opened his mouth and yelled in a deep rumbling voice after the fleeing woman.

"*Torna indietro, Rosina. O non ti batterò. Ti ucciderò.*"

"Her name's Rosina and he wants to kill her," I said.

Shirley's eyes flashed with anger. "I'm going after Rosina," she said. "You stop the brute."

9

Shirl's shoes clacked on the cobbles as she took off.

I turned towards Brando.

He gave me a look like he wanted to barbecue me and feed me to wild dogs. But he knew I'd understood him. And there were other people in the street giving him the hard eye.

He scanned the street. The kind of look I've seen before.

Are there are any cops about?

I sauntered up to him. Played the lost tourist. *"Puoi indirizzarmi all'ufficio postale?"*

The old can-you-tell-me-the-way-to-the-post-office ploy. Never fails.

He curled his upper lip, all the better to give me a view of his faultless dentistry.

"You are English," he said. He made it sound like a bad habit.

I nodded. *"Sai quanto costa un francobollo per l'Inghilterra?"*

"I do not know – or care – about the cost of your postage stamp to England."

He sucked in his cheeks. Gobbed a huge flob of saliva onto the cobbles. Charming.

I said: *"Pensavo ti fosse permesso uccidere tua moglie solo nel fine settimana in Sicilia."*

"A proud Sicilian may kill his wife whenever he wishes," Brando snarled. But at least in English. *"Ma forse ti ucciderò invece io,"* he added.

"We rather draw the line at killing anyone in England."

Brando pulled back his shoulders and squared up to me. Looked like the old can-you-tell-me-the-way-to-the-post-office ploy was going to fail me. For the first time.

From the corner of my eye, the curtain at the back of the jeweller's window twitched back. A delicate hand reached in and took the monster diamond from its place on the velvet platform.

"Killing me will have to wait," I waved my hand at the jeweller's window. "I see my purchase is being made up and the armed guard that accompanies me will be in the shop putting it into a locked case."

So there would be no mistake, I added: *"Lo faccio all'interno del negozio in modo che quando esce, sia facile per lui prendere la sua pistola."*

I added in English. "He likes to keep his gun hand free in case of street trouble."

I looked down the *Corso*. Rosina – and Shirley – had vanished.

"Troverò Rosina e la ucciderò. E lei, signore," Brando snarled.

"You'll never find Rosina," I said. "And, if you come to kill me, try to avoid Sundays. I have the day off."

Brando growled something at me. He turned and stomped into the alley.

I called after him. "If you want to kill me in Brighton, you better do it when Detective Chief Superintendent Alec Tomkins is on duty. Never been known to catch a killer."

I strolled off down the *Corso*. I had a feeling Shirley would not have caught the fleet-footed Rosina. Instead, Shirl would be lying in wait for me in a bar.

I hoped she already had another bottle of *Asti Spumante* on ice.

I badly needed a drink.

Chapter 2

In the amphitheatre, Shirley and I gawped at each other with open mouths and wild eyes.

Shirley knelt down beside the girl. Reached out a hand for hers.

But the girl buried her face deeper in her hands.

"My father's been murdered," she moaned.

"Come on, give me your hands," Shirley said gently. "Then we can dry your eyes and talk about your troubles."

The girl dropped her hands and looked straight at Shirley.

"No one can solve my troubles," she moaned.

"Strewth!" Shirl sounded like a girl from the Aussie Outback when she was shocked. "It's the girl from the *Corso Umberto*."

"The girl who was running away from that brute of a bully?" I asked. "Is your name Rosina?"

I stooped down to look the girl full in the face. Her eyes were misted with tears.

"Yes, I am Rosina," she said with a spark of fire in her voice. "And the brute is Brando, my husband."

"Did he murder your father?" I asked.

"No. My father is in England. But he is dead. The police tell me on the telephone. I think he is murdered. But the police will not say how he died. Even though I am born in England and have a British passport. They treat me like I am an Italian – like I am a foreigner and a nuisance."

Shirley wrapped her arm around Rosina's shoulders. "Why don't we go and sit on those steps over there? You can tell us all about it."

We helped Rosina to her feet. She walked slowly towards the steps. She sat down on one that caught the last rays of the sun. A dark shadow had descended across most of the amphitheatre – like the show had come to an end.

I felt it was only beginning.

Shirley and I sat on either side of Rosina. Shirley gently stroked Rosina's hands.

I said: "Tell us about your father and how you heard of his death."

Rosina gave me a searching look – like she wasn't sure she wanted to share her dark family secrets with a stranger. Then she shrugged.

"I have no one else who will listen to me. At least, not here. Not Brando. Not his friends. And I have no friends. Brando does not like me to mingle with other people."

"Sounds like a little charmer," Shirley said.

"Brando is a brute," Rosina spat. "He beats me because I want to go to my dead father. He says: 'What's the point?' I tell him I have to know how my father died."

"Who is your father?" I asked.

"His name is Sergio Parisi."

"Italian?" I asked.

"But he lives in England. He owns a small café in Crawley."

"That's near Brighton," I said.

"Where we live," Shirley chimed in.

"I know Brighton," Rosina said. "There are many smart cafés and restaurants there. Not like my father's. His is a transport café."

"For working people. Nothing wrong in that," I said.

"Perhaps not for the working people. But my father is not like that. He wants to have money – and there is not much profit in a plate of egg and chips. I know he does other things to make money."

"Illegal things?" I asked.

"I won't say. But it is why he wanted me to marry Brando. He told me Brando came from a good family in Sicily. A family with plenty in the bank. I did not know that the bank was somebody else's and Brando's family planned to rob it. But the police here know when to look the other way. Because Brando's family is... connected."

Shirley and I exchanged worried glances.

"To the Mafia?" I asked.

"You do not speak that word around here. Not if you want to keep five fingers on each hand."

I said: "Do you think your father has been killed by the Mafia? They have connections in Britain."

"I don't know."

"But you want to find out?"

"Yes. But all the policeman would tell me over the phone was that they are looking at all the possibilities."

"Did the policeman give a name?"

"Yes, I wrote it on a piece of paper."

Rosina rummaged in the pocket of her skirt. Pulled out the crumpled paper and read.

"He said he was Detective Chief Superintendent Alec Tomkins. He said he would clear up the case."

I said: "Tomkins couldn't clear up the cups from a kids' picnic."

"You're saying he's incompetent?"

"I'm saying if he had to put a crook behind bars, he'd first have to find the bars."

Rosina wiped her eyes with the backs of her hands.

She said: "This is why I want to go to England. I need to find out how my father died. I need to arrange his funeral."

"What about your mother?" Shirley asked.

"She died when I was two. She was hit by a lorry while riding her bike. She had bought a chocolate cake for me at the baker's."

I leaned towards Rosina. "Why doesn't Brando want you to go to England?"

"I told him I wanted money to buy a plane ticket, but he said he couldn't spare any. I told him he had much money that he hides from me..."

"And he hit you?" Shirley asked.

"You didn't see that," Rosina said. "Brando lets no one see what he does to me."

"That's what guys like Brando do. Their brains are in their fists."

"Yes, I ran from Brando in anger, vowing I would never return. Even though I snatched my key as I rushed from our apartment. And now I don't know what to do. I have no money – and nowhere to go."

"It's worse than that," I said. "We stopped Brando. He told me he'd find you and kill you. But he'd have said that in anger."

Rosina shook her head furiously. "No, no. no. When Brando says he will kill, he means it." Her voice dropped to a whisper. "I know he has killed for money. I cannot say who paid him."

"The Mafia," I said.

Rosina shot me a worried glance. But she gave the tiniest of nods.

I looked at Shirley. She knew what I was going to say. She nodded, too. But not like Rosina. Not a reluctant crick of the neck. Shirley's was a determined tilt of the head – with one of her flashing smiles as a bonus.

I turned to Rosina. "We could get you to England."

"Sure, we had nothing special planned," Shirley said. "Only a marriage proposal."

"But how can we do that?" Rosina said. "Brando knows I want to get back to England and he will be looking for me – even at the airport. And not just Brando. He has powerful friends, too."

I stood up and looked around the amphitheatre. Eerie pools of darkness had appeared between the pillars of the theatre's backdrop. Between them, the colour of the sea had turned from blue to black. Tiny white flecks showed where waves broke. Above us, bats had started to circle, hunting for food.

I thought about the mission that had brought us here. Wondered whether we would ever return. Wondered whether

I would ever get to propose to Shirley. And whether she would ever accept.

I looked at her now. She had her arm around Rosina and was whispering something in her ear. Rosina nodded her head gently. Shirley took Rosina's hand and squeezed it.

Shirl looked up at me. "Well, big brain, what do we do next?"

I pulled back my shoulders like a bloke who knows what he's doing. I could see from her face that it didn't do much for Shirley. But it encouraged me.

"We need a plan," I said. "But first we must get Rosina to a safe place."

Shirley gave me a hard look and said: "Before you dazzle us with your brilliant battle plan, Clausewitz, perhaps you could tell us where we're going to find the cabbage."

"Cabbage?" I asked.

"Money," she said. "We spent most of our cash on paying for this dump of a room in advance. We're gonna need ready money to buy an air ticket for Rosina."

We were in our room at the *Hotel Bella*. The name may have been chosen by a hotelier with a sharp sense of irony.

On our return from the amphitheatre, Shirley and I had waltzed through reception. We'd made like a couple intent on a night of passionate love-making.

Then we'd scooted round to the back and let Rosina in through a fire exit - while no one was around. We'd ordered room service sandwiches – some kind of fatty meat. Looked like something left over from a dissection class. Rosina had hidden in the loo when the waiter had brought in the food.

"There is another problem," Rosina said softly. She had perched on the bed and rested her back on the headboard. "I do not have my British passport. It is in the top drawer of my dressing table."

I breathed out deeply. Problem. Big problem. In fact, huge

problem.

I said: "Let's deal with the problems one at a time. We need money. We don't have enough, but we do have a valuable asset."

I looked at Shirley and raised my eyebrows. I couldn't find a way to put the question into words that wouldn't hurt her feelings.

But she'd picked up the message. "The ring? Yeah! You must've emptied your piggy bank to pay for that. Guess we've got no choice. But where are we gonna find a buyer at this time of the evening?"

I said: "The shops around here stay open until nine, sometimes later. They're shut most of the afternoon. And we know the jeweller's in the *Corso Umberto* buys items."

"The pirate," Shirl said.

"We have no other choice," I said.

Rosina said: "No amount of money will get me a passport in time."

"Where do you live?" I asked.

"Brando and I share an apartment above the *Trattoria Garibaldi* on the road to Castelmola. When we married, he promised me a house on the beach. He was talking sandcastles in the air. Like he usually does, when he's drunk."

"He drinks much?" I asked.

"Every night in the bar at the *Trattoria*. Sometimes at the *Bar Mazzini*, nearby. But you cannot get into my apartment without going through the *Trattoria*. There is a door leading to stairs just inside the *Trattoria's* entrance. Anyone in there could see you. And the bar is crowded every night. Often with Brando's friends."

"I think there might be a way," I said. "Tell me, do the *Trattoria Garibaldi* and the *Bar Mazzini* both have television sets?"

"Of course. All Italian bars have them." She shook her head. "But you can't get my passport by watching television."

"I won't be. Tonight, the bar will be packed with football fans watching the World Cup game between Italy and North Korea."

"Brando will be there," Rosina said.

"Only if the television's on."

"It is always on. Especially for football."

"Somehow I've got a feeling that tonight there's going to be a transmission fault. Just at a crucial point in the game. When the *Garibaldi's* TV goes pop, the whole bar will head down the road to the *Bar Mazzini*. There'll be nobody around to see me enter your apartment. Especially as you'll be lending me your key."

"But why should the TV screen suddenly go black?" Rosina asked.

"Because I'm going to turn it off. Now, I need you to tell me exactly how your apartment is laid out. And where I can find your passport."

Rosina shot Shirley a confused look.

Shirley rolled her eyes. "Tell him what he needs to know, kiddo. But let me give you a piece of advice. If a guy says he wants to propose marriage to you, make sure he hasn't got anything else on that day."

Chapter 3

An hour later Shirley and I stood in the shadow of the doorway of an old tenement building opposite the *Trattoria Garibaldi*.

We'd just come from the jeweller's in the *Corso Umberto* where I'd sold the engagement ring. For little more than half what I'd paid for it. Shirl had been right earlier. The man who ran the joint was a pirate.

But at least we had enough cash to buy Rosina a plane ticket.

Now we needed to snatch the passport from her apartment.

Which is why we lurked in the shadows and watched the *Trattoria Garibaldi*.

The place was lit by red, green and white neon, like it was carnival night. We could see through the windows the place was crowded. Everyone's gaze was fixed on the television.

"We should have brought Rosina with us," Shirley said. "She'd be able to find her passport faster than we can."

"Too dangerous. Especially if Brando is in the bar. Much better she stays in the hotel room with the door firmly shut."

"With that crowd in the bar, it doesn't look great for us," Shirley said. "Are you sure this is going to work?"

"Look, let me run over it again." I glanced at my watch. "The Italy-North Korea match kicked off in Middlesbrough at seven-thirty British Summer Time. Not that Middlesbrough actually has much summer time. That's eight-thirty here. And it's ten past nine. That means there'll be half-time in about five minutes. A great time to cut transmission. The fans can roll down to the *Bar Mazzini*, which also has TV, during the half-time break."

As we looked, a groan went up from inside the *Garibaldi*. Some fans shook their heads in despair. Others buried their heads in their hands. The wise ones ordered another drink.

"It looks like North Korea just scored a goal," I said. "They must be leading. Look at those guys. They couldn't be more distressed if their home had just disappeared down a sinkhole."

Shirley's elbow jabbed me in the ribs. "Cut the cackle and tell me how you're gonna kill their TV. You can't just walk into the bar and announce you're switching to the other channel. They'll lynch you."

I pointed to the *Garibaldi's* roof. "See the TV aerial behind that neon light?"

Shirley twisted her neck to get a better look.

I said: "If the TV set is in the left-hand corner of the bar, the aerial wire will run down the back of the building and probably pass through the wall via a small drillhole. All I need to do is cut that cable and – *phut!* – no more TV tonight."

"And no doubt you're planning to gnaw through it with those sharp teeth of yours."

"Nope, I'm going to saw through it with that nail file you always carry in your handbag."

Shirley's elbow jabbed my ribs again. "That's a beauty aid."

"Some beauty aid! The thing's like a dagger. You could fight off an armed commando with it."

"If he's a commando, I might not want to fight him off," Shirl said. But she rummaged in her handbag. She grabbed the file. Handed it to me.

"So that's one nail file you owe me - alongside the engagement ring."

"I'll ask my secretary to make a note. Now, this is important."

"Yeah! I rather thought it might be."

"When I've cut the aerial cable, it will be like the last days of Pompeii just met the charge of the Light Brigade in there. Some of the guys will try to get the TV working again. The smart ones will head for the *Mazzini* so they can get the best seats. But eventually, they'll all realise the TV is kaput and follow their mates. When they've all gone, I'll sneak back to this side of the building and wait for a signal from you that the place is empty."

"What kind of signal? I didn't bring my semaphore flags with me."

"The mirror in your compact. Open it up and let the light catch it briefly twice in quick succession."

"And what if one of those goons sees it and comes to check me out?"

"Then act like you've decided to freshen up your lipstick."

Shirl rolled her eyes. I ignored it.

Instead, I said: "When I see that sign, I'll scoot down to the main entrance, sneak in, and use Rosina's key to enter the apartment. You wait here and I'll re-join you when I've grabbed the passport."

"What! And you expect me to hang around here like a street walker on the lookout for some passing trade?"

"Hang around, yes, but turn down new business tonight."

That earnt me another elbow jab in the ribs.

I would have complained. But another groan rose from the fans in the *Garibaldi*.

"I have to cut that cable. The TV must go dead just before the first half ends. It will pile real pressure on the fans to find a new way to watch the second half."

I leaned across and kissed Shirley on the cheek.

"The great romantic!" Shirley mumbled. But she reached out and squeezed my hand.

I let go of hers and slipped silently like a wraith across the street. At least, that's what I hoped I looked like.

The back of the *Trattoria Garibaldi* wasn't as flash as the front.

No red, white and green neon. A backyard was enclosed by a low wall. The yard was lit by a couple of bulkhead lights screwed to the wall. A hazy yellow gleam made the place look like the set for a silent movie.

I passed a couple of windows with frosted glass. No need to wonder what lie behind them. A fanlight window was open and the stink confirmed it.

I looked up at the roof where the aerial should be. But that was at the front. It wasn't visible round the back. The cable would loop over the roof and down the outside of the rear wall. Wouldn't it? Unless it went through a hole in the roof and down inside the building.

In which case, I was stuffed. Shirley, too. And, most of all, Rosina.

Only one way to find out. I started a fingertip search of the wall inch by inch.

I soon found that it wasn't as simple as I'd expected. I clenched my teeth in frustration. Worried about Shirley standing in the shadows with her compact at the ready. What if some local Lothario happened along unexpectedly and spotted her? It would top tagging onto a bus queue behind Sophia Loren, Virna Lisi, and Claudia Cardinale.

Italian guys are hot-blooded. The Lothario might fancy his chances. With Shirley? Italian Lotharios don't compare with Aussie girls. They're too fussy about their hair. The Lotharios, that is. The guy wouldn't stand a chase.

But a ruckus between Shirley and a Lothario would get others running.

I needed to hurry.

There were several cables fixed to the back wall of the *Garibaldi*. Some of them would carry electricity from overhead power lines.

If I sawed through a power cable with Shirley's nail file, I'd end up as a frazzled black heap on the ground. I continued my fingertip search along the wall. I found a black slightly flat cable not much further on. Then another one. As there was more than one, the flat cables must be for electrics, I figured.

There would only be one aerial cable. And it would probably enter the building near the TV set.

I found it a few seconds later. A round job which looked brown in the yellow beams of the bulkhead lights, but could've easily been black.

From within the bar, a ragged cheer was followed by a groan. Sounded like Italy had missed a shot at goal. And the first half had only a minute or two left to run. I had to get to work.

Shirl's nail file had a sharp cutting edge. (Goodness knows what she used it for.) But it proved great to cut through the plastic wrap around the cable. The cable began to buzz when I reached the metal wire inside. No electric shock. A little tingle in the ends of my fingers. But perhaps that was just my nerves.

Yet the metal wouldn't give. Even to Shirl's nail file. The wire was harder than I'd expected. I applied more pressure from my fingers to the nail file. One of my fingers started to bleed. I sawed away. A hero to the end. It made little difference.

The metal cable wasn't going to break.

Snap!

It broke.

The wire split in two. The plastic stuff ripped off. I was left with two ragged ends. Somewhere on the roof, a signal beamed through. It showed a ref in Middlesbrough blowing his whistle for half-time. The ref could blow until the pip popped out of the whistle. The fans in the *Garibaldi* would never hear it.

That TV signal was going nowhere.

Inside the *Garibaldi*, it sounded like a riot had broken out. Imagine Elvis Presley singing *Jailhouse Rock* while the inmates bang every surface with whatever comes to hand. In this case, empty beer bottles.

It took fully three minutes before wiser heads had formulated the obvious Plan B. I imagined them raising their voice. Telling the idiots to shut it. Explaining to their less astute *amici* that this wasn't the end of the world. Even if it felt like it. The *Garibaldi* didn't own the only TV in town. There was one at the *Bar Mazzini*.

Behind the windows, shadows moved. Drinks were hastily swallowed. Bar tabs settled or rolled over to the next night. The tramp of feet receded into the night. Goodbye *Garibaldi*. Here we come, *Mazzini*.

Slowly, the sound of silence crept over the place.

I sneaked back to the front. I hugged the wall at the corner.

I played a shifty type and snuck a quick glance in Shirley's direction.

Nothing.

I waited.

Something rattled. A rat rummaged around some dustbins.

And then, the double flash. Great work, Shirl!

I became a wraith again. I slid along the front of the *Garibaldi* and slipped swiftly through the door.

Inside, the first thing that hit me was the fug.

It was like I'd stepped back into one of those London smogs the city used to get when I was a kid. Consider a hundred guys watching a footie match for forty-five minutes. They'll smoke three fags each to keep their nerves under control during a tense game. The blokes at the back would have viewed the TV set through a thick mist.

I focused my eyes and peered deeply into it, but I couldn't see anyone.

I took a quick look around and found the door to the flat in the wall to my right.

Rosina's key fitted the lock first time. I turned the key and the door opened. I stepped inside and closed the door behind me.

I was on a roll. This was going to be easy.

Inside the door, there was a short passage that led to a narrow staircase to the flat. I beetled eagerly up like it was the stairway to heaven.

There was a short corridor decorated with grubby green wallpaper with a palm tree motif. There were three doors on one side of the corridor and two on the other.

Rosina had said her bedroom was on the left and the door

had bolts on the outside. The brute Brando took to locking her in when she failed to tickle his fancy.

I stepped sharply along the corridor. The first door had two bolts – one at the top and one at the foot, both undone. I glanced to the right. The next door also had bolts. I crept further along the corridor. So did the third door. The doors on the other side of the corridor didn't have bolts.

Had I misunderstood Rosina? I thought she'd meant that only her room had bolts. If three doors had bolts, she should have told me which one.

Besides, bolts on the outside of doors? What the hell went on in here? Still, no time to worry about that. At least none of the doors were actually bolted.

And no plan is perfect. If I was quick, I could look in all three rooms to find Rosina's passport.

I opened the first door and stepped inside.

The room was dominated by a large double bed.

A woman with bottle-blonde hair and a surly expression was lying on the bed. She had a bulging waistline, industrial thighs, and two huge breasts which flopped towards her armpits like they were looking for somewhere warm to snuggle up for the night.

She was wearing a black suspender belt and stockings with a hole in one so her pinkie showed through.

She glanced towards a door that led to a bathroom. At least, that's what I assumed it was as I could hear a shower running.

She gave me a surprised look as I pushed into the room and said: "*Torna tra dieci minuti. Ho un cliente.*"

With only ten minutes to take his pleasure, it sounded like her client was on the budget plan.

And at that moment, her client stepped into the room from the bathroom.

Fresh from the shower, he dripped with water.

Brando.

There were no flies on Brando. (He was naked, so I could verify that.) He'd planned for a quickie during half-time. *Forza Italia* and back to the match. And a great Italian victory. One way or another.

This thought fired through my mind faster than a shot at goal.

And faster than anything Brando could muster. Especially as he was wet and without the benefit of his usual clothes.

I reopened the door, stepped swiftly outside, and shot both of the bolts.

I hurried down the corridor to the second door as Brando started to hammer on the first. I didn't know how strong the door was, but you wouldn't bother to add bolts if the door could be bust with a couple of good punches.

Besides, I didn't think Brando would want to take me on in the all-together. He didn't look like a guy who embarrassed easily. But everyone has their private demons. Already his few brain cells would be running the odds on a slippery naked man taking on a well-prepared antagonist who would stop at nothing.

And, at the moment, I was living up to my billing.

I grabbed the handle of the second door and charged inside. There was a smaller bed and a dressing table with a cracked mirror. There was a picture frame with a photo of a younger Rosina with two older people – presumably her parents.

I charged over to the dressing table as the hammering and shouts of anger crescendoed from the adjacent room.

I yanked open the top drawer. The passport was at the back, hidden behind a sewing kit.

I raced out of the room as Brando started to shoulder charge the first door. Or perhaps it was the woman. She carried enough weight to make it count.

But as the door started to crack on the hinges, I was away down the stairs and out into the night.

Shirley saw me race across the road and came out to meet me.

"You took your time," she said.

"I met an old friend," I said. "But not one I want to see again. Let's get out of here."

Chapter 4

England. 20 July 1966

Detective inspector Ted Wilson looked me up and down and raised a critical eyebrow.

He said: "You look like that bloke with the blunt razor blade in the advert about those new electric shavers."

I ran a hand around my stubbly chin.

"And you look as though you've slept in your clothes," he added.

"I have," I said.

Ted had met us at the arrivals gate at Gatwick Airport. Shirley had taken Rosina off to one of the airport's shops. Women's stuff, apparently. My presence definitely not required.

I was pleased. It gave me a few moments to brief Ted on how we'd escaped from Sicily. It hadn't been easy.

The minute Brando saw me at the *Trattoria Garibaldi*, I knew we wouldn't be safe in Taormina. If Brando had links to the Mafia, they'd have eyes and ears everywhere. Shirley and I had rushed back to our hotel and scooped up Rosina – reunited with her British passport. We'd hurried down the steep steps to the Taormina-Giardini Naxos railway station. We'd jumped on a late train to Catania. We'd found a small *pensione* near Catania railway station and holed up for the night.

I admitted to Ted that none of us had got much sleep. We'd figured Brando wouldn't have had time to extend his overnight search as far as Catania. After all, it turned out that Italy had lost the game against North Korea. The fans would be drowning their sorrows. They'd be too drunk to organise a hunt for a wife on the run.

The following morning, we took a bus – less easy to trace than a taxi – to Catania airport. If Brando had worked out that Rosina planned to flee back to England, he'd have people watching the international departures gate. So, I went straight to the ticket desk and cashed in the return tickets to Gatwick Shirley and I had booked. I used the cash to buy three single flights to Rome. On a domestic flight, we'd be leaving from a different part of the airport – and I figured Brando wouldn't have it covered.

We made a successful getaway from Catania, but when we landed at Rome's Fiumicino airport, Rosina thought she saw a suspicious type monitoring the arrivals gate. I decided it was too risky to try and fly out from Rome, so we booked the overnight train to Paris – and flew home from there. We'd spent all the money I'd raised by selling the engagement ring.

I looked at Wilson. He gawped at me like I'd told him we'd just flown in from Mars.

I snapped my fingers in his face to bring him back to reality.

"So, you see, Ted, there's a good reason why I'm not my usual clean-shaven self."

Ted shook his head. "You can run but you can't hide."

"As Joe Louis is supposed to have said. But I'm not in a boxing ring. I'm on my home turf now and if the Mafia come calling, I'll have them in plain sight."

Ted was about to say something but Shirley and Rosina reappeared. Rosina was carrying a large carrier bag with the name of an expensive shop stencilled on the side.

"Shirley has been so kind," Rosina said. "She has bought me things to wash and clean my teeth. And she bought me some lovely ladies' underclothes."

Rosina noticed Ted giving her a queer look. She blushed. "Oh, sorry, you're not interested in ladies' underclothes, Mr Wilson."

"For Ted, it depends which lady is wearing them," I said.

I thought I saw Ted colour up. But it was probably a trick of the light.

The relief – light-headedness, even - we'd felt on arriving back in Britain had evaporated by the time we'd reached Crawley.

We were all in a more sombre mood when we pulled up outside Sergio Parisi's café. It was a small corner building not far from Crawley railway station. It didn't look like the kind of place that would win enthusiastic praise from the *Good Food Guide*. A fading menu in the window listed the bill of fare. Chips featured on most of the dishes. At least Arnold Wesker would approve. Shirley and I had seen *Chips with Everything*, his acerbic take on Britain's class system, a year earlier when it reached Brighton's Theatre Royal.

Parisi lived in a small apartment over the café, Ted told us. There was a separate outside door to the flat, but also a set of stairs to it inside the café.

Ted had arranged for a woman PC – Julie Parrott – to take Rosina inside the premises. Rosina asked if Shirley would also go with her. Shirl put her arm around Rosina's shoulder and WPC Parrott shepherded them through the door.

Ted and I strolled over to a bench next to a bus stop and sat down.

I said: "Back at the airport, I thought you were about to say something just as Rosina and Shirley reappeared. I'd just mentioned the Mafia."

I looked at Ted and raised a quizzical eyebrow.

Ted shrugged. "Probably nothing, but we've had our eye on old Sergio for some time, him being Italian and everything."

"Since when has it been a crime to come from Italy?"

"Since he supplemented the meagre earnings from his egg and chip sales by flogging dodgy booze and fags."

"You have proof of that?"

"Nothing to take before a judge yet, but we've been keeping an open mind. You see, it's been part of a pattern." Ted glared at me. "This is off the record. Right?"

I put on my hurt expression. "When have I ever abused a confidence, Ted?"

"I don't have time to draw up a list, but watch it this time. Anyway, the point is we think Parisi was part of a network of smuggled fag and booze sales throughout the south-east. Often through workers' cafés or small corner stores. The brass want to roll up the whole network in one fell swoop – and catch the big bosses at the same time."

I decided to keep mum about our own brush with the Mafia, but I wanted to know more.

"And they think those bosses may be Mafia?" I asked.

"Who can tell?"

"So you don't know?"

"Don't quote me on that."

"This is off the record."

"Let's keep it that way."

Ted relaxed back on the bench, took out a packet of Capstan Navy Cut, shook out a ciggie, and lit up. I nodded at the smoky cancer stick. "Not one of Parisi's?"

"No."

"How was he killed?"

"A blow to the back of the head. Shattered the occipital bone."

"The what?"

"The bone that rests at the top of the spine. Helps to hold up your head."

"So not good news if it breaks."

"Especially when sharp fragments of the bone cut into the spinal cord. Then it's goodnight Vienna."

"A Mafia killing?" I asked.

"Not their style. They like something more theatrical. An orchestra with the fat lady singing. Besides the body had been arranged to make it look like an accident. As though he'd fallen backwards and cracked his head on the sharp metal hob in the kitchen. The hob had traces of skin and blood but the forensic boys could tell they'd been smeared there after death. A real amateur's job."

"So someone who wanted to confuse the police."

"Don't catch us that easily," Ted said.

I said nothing.

Instead, I asked: "Any motive?"

"We're looking to see whether anyone else in the smuggled gear network may have had a grudge against Parisi."

"It would have to be something serious."

"The London gangland style is for bosses to have their own territory for crime. And woe betide anyone who crosses the boundary. The Richardsons claim south London, the Krays rule east London."

"And you think a gangland boss may have carved out a territory in Crawley and put down a public marker by killing Parisi?"

"We don't know. But someone has to be behind the killing. And it's likely that they'd have a motive for it. Still, these are early days in the case."

"Why wouldn't you explain to Rosina on the phone what had happened to her father?"

Ted sucked on his Capstan and blew out a stream of grey smoke.

"Not me. That was Tomkins. He thought the girl would go into a meltdown if we gave her too many details. I think she should've been told. Anyway, Julie Parrott's the girl to take Rosina gently through what's been going on and what we'll do next."

"And what will you do next?" I asked.

"What we always do," Ted said. "Solve the case."

I said nothing.

We were silent for a moment while Ted puffed on his fag.

Then he said: "Shame old Sergio died when he did."

"I expect he'd agree with you… if he could."

"No, seriously. He'd just had a bit of good luck."

Ted gave me a teasing look. It meant he wanted me to ask the question.

I complied with good grace. "And what was the luck?"

"He'd just won a ticket to the World Cup Final at Wembley."

"Who has the ticket now?"

"We don't know. It's vanished."

I said: "You've looked under the bed, I suppose?"

Ted slouched back on the bench like he'd said enough and planned to be tight-lipped for the rest of the day.

"Looked everywhere," he said.

"Perhaps he'd given it away before the unnamed assailant croaked him."

"Who'd give away a World Cup Final ticket? Especially a football-mad fan like Parisi."

"He played the game?"

"He was on the committee of Crawley Rovers football club. Sometimes turned out as a linesman. In home games, he ran the line."

"Better than crossing it by selling dodgy fags," I said. "How did the ticket come Parisi's way?"

Ted stubbed out his fag on the edge of the bench. "It's a long story," he said.

Actually, it turned out to be quite a short one.

Ted explained: "About a week before Parisi died, Crawley Rovers received an envelope containing the ticket. It came through the regular post."

"Who sent it?"

"There was no covering letter and no indication where the ticket came from. The envelope carried a local postmark. But thousands of letters are posted in Crawley every day. At first the club couldn't believe its good fortune. But then they realised that, in reality, they had a problem. There wasn't a man or woman in the club who didn't want that ticket to Wembley. The club's committee met to consider the matter. After two hours of heated debate, they'd made no decision about how to allocate the ticket. It seems everyone in the club could make a good case for having it."

"I can believe it."

Ted nodded. "Finally, some smart-arse with a classical education suggested that as chance had delivered the ticket into the club's hands, why not call on Tyche, the Greek goddess of chance, to see who got to use it?"

"They held a raffle?"

"With the first and only prize being the ticket."

"And that's what the club did?"

Ted grinned: "Tyche wasn't available so they called on the club chairman, Vernon Stoker, to pull the winning ticket from the hat. It had Parisi's name on it."

"When was that?" I asked.

"Two days before Parisi died. Hope that never happens to me," Ted said.

"Winning a World Cup ticket or dying?" I asked.

But Ted never had a chance to answer. Because at that moment WPC Parrott stepped out of the café.

She was followed by Shirley and Rosina. Shirley had her arm tightly around Rosina. And Rosina had been crying.

WPC Parrott drove the three of us back to Brighton.

No one said much on the journey. Rosina stared with blank eyes out of the window as though she didn't even see the countryside.

I tried to ask about what Shirley and Rosina had seen inside the café. Shirley gave an imperceptible shake of her head. Her warning: not now.

But Shirl did mention that she'd arranged for Rosina to stay with her for a few days.

It was lunchtime by the time we reached Shirley's apartment. There was no food in the place – after all, we'd expected to be in Taormina – but I rustled up some sandwiches from a nearby café. Shirley made a huge pot of coffee.

Rosina relaxed a little after she'd eaten and drunk a mug of sweet coffee.

She turned to Shirley and said: "It was the photograph that made me cry."

I looked at Shirley: "Photo?"

"Of Rosina's wedding day in Taormina," Shirley said. "The picture showed Sergio walking Rosina up the aisle. Giving her away."

"It was on the shelf where he always kept it," Rosina said. "I never liked that photo."

"Of your wedding day. The happiest day of a girl's life," I said.

"Not for me. Because I never wanted to marry Brando."

Shirley and I exchanged worried glances.

"Do you want to talk about it?" Shirley said. "Sometimes talk helps."

Rosina took out a floral handkerchief and blew her nose.

She said: "I'm sorry that my papa is dead, but at least he can't force me to go back to Brando now. Like he forced me to marry him."

Rosina shifted uncomfortably on Shirley's broken-down sofa. Shirl sat down beside her.

"No man can force a woman to marry someone she hates," Shirley said.

"Perhaps not in England. But although papa's life was in England, his spirit was always in Italy. Especially in Sicily. He originally came from Palermo."

"So how did he end up in England?" I asked.

"In the war, he was conscripted into the Italian army. He was sent to fight in North Africa. There was no choice. The government and the army were controlled by the *Fascista*. By Mussolini, a bombastic buffoon who strutted around like a peacock."

"And your father was captured by the British as a prisoner of war?" I asked.

Rosina's eyes widened in surprise. "How did you know?"

"Thousands – no tens of thousands – of Italians surrendered to the British. Like your father, they didn't want to fight in a war they didn't believe in."

Rosina nodded. "They brought my father to England as a prisoner of war. For a time, he lived in a camp. But then they needed people to help on the farms. They needed more food urgently. My father volunteered. He worked hard. The other farm workers treated him fairly. He came to like living in England. After the war, he acquired some money he had in Sicily and opened a café in Crawley. His wife joined him and I was born here two years after the war ended."

"But how did Brando come into the picture?" I asked.

"Every year, an old man – my father always called him Signor Cavaletto - came to visit my papa. Always in July. He would stay for a few hours, locked away in my father's room. I could hear their voices talking in Italian. Signor Cavaletto had dark eyes – the kind I always imagine see wickedness wherever they look. I always kept out of his way. But three years ago, Cavaletto caught me sneaking up to my own room. I had just turned sixteen. He smiled at me, but it didn't put me at ease. Then he said: '*Sei diventata una bella.* You will make a good wife for my son Brando.' I gave him a dirty look and stomped into my room. I could hear him laughing."

"You did right, kiddo," Shirley said. "The whacker sounds like a slimeball."

"My papa didn't think so. He was fixated on the wedding match. From that time onwards, there was never a day when papa didn't extoll the virtues of marrying Brando. He wore me down."

"You should never have given in," Shirley said.

"It wasn't that easy. Sometimes, my father seemed desperate

for me to marry Brando. It was almost as though his life depended on it."

"You don't mean that," Shirley said. "You're tired. Been through a lot. Too much to take in. You need a good rest. Let's get you to bed. You'll feel better when you've slept."

Gently, Shirley raised Rosina off the sofa and guided her towards the bedroom.

I watched them pass through the door. Shirl glanced back. There was a tiny wrinkle that appears on her forehead when she's worried.

I was worried, too.

I wondered whether Parisi's life really did depend on Rosina marrying Brando.

And what would happen now that she'd kicked Brando into touch?

Chapter 5

After Shirley had put Rosina to bed, we curled up together on the sofa.

Needless to say, I got the end with the broken spring.

Shirl leaned her head on my shoulder.

She said: "Guess our romantic trip didn't turn out quite as expected."

"Nope."

"You're back in Blighty without a fiancée. And without a ring."

"But I still have the best girlfriend in the world. And hope in my heart."

"Keep that hope, big boy, it may be some time before any good news heads our way."

"Already has," I said. I told Shirley what Ted had said about Parisi winning a World Cup Final ticket which had gone missing. "I'm betting that no other journos have that angle."

"You're a cynical bastard. Guy's lost his life and you think the story's that he's lost his ticket. I'll tell you what I think about that..."

But Shirl never did because her phone rang.

She sprang up from the sofa and darted into the hall. For the next few minutes, I could hear Shirl muttering down the phone.

She came back into the room grinning like she'd just won the World Cup herself.

"Guess what, buster? That was the *Daily Mirror* on the phone. It turns out the model they'd booked for a series of photoshoots has got a cold sore on her top lip. Looks like an alien species is taking over her face, apparently. They want me as replacement."

"What's the job?"

"It runs over the last stages of the World Cup – from the quarter-finals to the final. Each day, the *Mirror's* football tipster will predict the result of the match – and I'll pose in the team's strip. Means they'll need to shoot me wearing the strips of all eight quarter-finalists. Just so they're ready for a tip on any of the teams."

"*Hmmmm!*"

"What do you mean, *hmmmm!*"

"I was just thinking which strip I'd like to see you strip."

Shirl stuck out a playful tongue. "Keep your mind on the footie, buddy. Leave me to strike the pose."

"You'll be great," I said. "When do you start?"

"That's the thing. The shoot is tomorrow. I'll have to catch the early train up to London."

"That's okay. I can make sure Rosina is all right before I head to the *Chronicle*. The poor girl is exhausted. It will do her good to have a day's rest here."

Frank Figgis, my news editor, stubbed out the dog-end of an early-morning Woodbine and tossed it into his wastepaper basket.

He said: "The last person I expected to see first through the newsroom door this morning was you. I thought you were still on leave. Weren't you supposed to be proposing marriage to that girlfriend of yours?"

"That was the idea."

"And she sensibly turned you down?"

"I didn't get to propose."

I told Figgis how Shirley and I had encountered Rosina in the Taormina amphitheatre.

Figgis put aside the packet of Woodbines he'd been fiddling with. He looked at me with his hard little eyes. Pressed his thin lips together as he heard my tale. Ran a hand over his slicked-down black hair. Brushed an imaginary crumb off his jacket. Adjusted his tie, the blue and yellow one with the gravy stain.

I finished talking and leaned back in the guest chair.

Figgis said: "You mean to say, you were on the run with the daughter of the murdered man and you didn't call it in?"

"There wasn't time."

"Yeah! Well, I've had to put Phil Bailey on the story. He's done his best as a general reporter, but we're running behind the other papers on this one."

"Not any more. Now we've got a World Cup angle into the story."

I told Figgis about the missing Cup Final ticket.

"We'll run it in our midday edition."

"No, at the moment the story is just that the ticket's missing. Interesting, but unfinished. Let me see if I can trace it."

"Think you can?"

"Give me a couple of days."

"Okay. In the meantime, do an interview with this Rosina."

"No." I folded my arms in a petulant gesture to show I meant it.

"What do you mean – no?" Figgis growled.

"Rosina is in a vulnerable state at the moment – and I'm not going to make it worse for her."

Figgis curled a lip. "Very noble of you."

"I'm new to nobility, but I'll get the hang of it. Rosina will fit into the story at the right time."

"Have it your own way. But I'll need some copy – at least for today's night final."

I nodded. "You'll get it."

I stood up and headed towards the door.

Figgis cleared his throat noisily.

"It's good to have you back," he said. "I think."

If I was going to burnish my new-found reputation for nobility, I'd need to find a way to keep Rosina out of the story.

Figgis had made it clear he wanted some copy.

I thought about that as I drove my white MGB past the pylons which mark the Brighton boundary on the London Road.

I was heading for Crawley. Sergio Parisi had been a man with secrets. The cops had uncovered some of those in the search of his café and apartment. Or, at least, thought they had. Which is not the same thing.

I had a hunch I'd be able to dig out more about Parisi's life at Crawley Rovers football club.

The club's ground was near a housing estate at the Three Bridges end of town. There were neat streets of terraced and semi-detached houses. They had been put up after the war years for families bombed out of the east end of London. The streets had begun to show their age. Weeds grew between paving stones. Garden gates hung from loose hinges. Paint flaked on front doors.

But the streets had the bustle of a place where incomers have built a new community – and have made it clear they're there to stay.

A corner shop had a contents bill for the *Crawley Observer*, the local weekly rag. It read CAFÉ KILLING: NO ARREST.

And from what Ted had told me the day before, it didn't look like there would be. Could this end as one of those unsolved killings? It seemed possible. But perhaps the missing Cup Final ticket would lead to a clue.

To tell the truth, I found it difficult to believe anyone would kill for the ticket. But when passions are inflamed, murders happen for the most trivial of reasons.

The club's ground was surrounded by a six-foot wall built out of whitewashed breeze blocks. There was a small ticket office with a single turnstile. A notice in the office window informed me that if I wanted a match ticket, I'd have to stump up a bob – a shilling.

There was an exit gate next to the turnstile. It was swinging open. I pushed inside onto a cinder path that surrounded the pitch. Because this was July, the football season had ended a couple of months earlier. The goal posts had been taken down, but I could see from the worn turf in the penalty areas where they'd been.

There was a row of advertising boards down one side of the pitch. They promoted the *Crawley Observer*, Banerjee's Curry House, Stoker Motors for "deals on wheels" - and Parisi's Café. Well, they'd have to take that one down before next season.

Behind the ad boards, there was a small stand with a couple of hundred seats banked up so that each row was about a foot higher than the one in front. No doubt fans would huddle in there on those Saturday afternoons when wind-blown rain swept across the ground. The home and away team dressing rooms were located under the stand.

At the far end of the ground, there was a single-storey building that acted as a snack bar. At one end, there was a sign over a door. It read: Office (strictly no admittance).

I walked over to the door, opened it, and stepped inside.

I found myself in a square room lined with beige wallpaper that had damp blotches on it.

Anyway, nobody screamed: Strictly no admittance - get out!

I took that as a positive start.

There was a beaten-up old desk – I've seen more impressive firewood – on the far side of the room. The desk held an Olympia portable typewriter and a telephone. There were a couple of wire baskets loaded with papers.

Behind the desk, a middle-aged woman with horn-rimmed spectacles was moving a piece of paper from one wire basket to another.

She looked up as I entered the room and decided to put the paper back in the first basket.

She had shoulder-length auburn hair which was streaked with grey. She had prominent cheek bones and a pointy chin which reminded me of a puppet I once saw in a Punch and Judy show. (Not the crocodile). She was wearing a fawn blouse and had a string of fake pearls around her neck.

She said: "If you've come about the season tickets, we haven't got the new ones in yet. I was just saying to Lennox, we ought to have them by now."

A man had been sitting in a worn armchair partly hidden by a filing cabinet. He stood up and crossed the room to the desk.

He was more than six feet tall, had broad shoulders, and a muscular build. He had an ascetic face and brown hair, cut short. He walked with a kind of precision which made me think he'd seen military service and been drilled on a parade ground.

He said: "If you ask me, Betty, there's a lot of things we ought to have by now. A new mower, for a start."

"You're always moaning about something, Lennox Slattery."

Slattery gave Betty a dirty look. "Who says I don't have cause? I'm going back to my groundsman's hut."

He focused on me. "You'll always find a haven of peace in a groundsman's hut," he said. "Only place I can be alone."

He turned around and marched out of the room.

Betty stuck out her tongue at him after he'd turned his back on her.

She grinned at me. "Don't mind him. He's a grump most of the time. Lives in that groundsman's hut. Won't let anyone else near it. Dangerous machinery, he says. Dangerous, my aunt Fanny! More likely he's running some racket down there. Selling the old footballs. Or some fiddle like that. But what do I care? I've got enough troubles here. Anyway, did you tell me why you're here?"

I said: "I'm not here about a season ticket."

"What is it, then?"

I pulled out my press card, showed Betty and said: "Colin Crampton, *Evening Chronicle*."

Betty said: "You're not a sports reporter."

"How can you tell?"

"You don't have muddy splotches round your trouser turn-ups."

I looked down at my immaculate grey flannels.

I said: "With observations like that you could be a detective."

Betty lounged back in her chair. "I thought about it once, but I can't stand the sight of blood. Rather just watch *Dixon of Dock Green* on the gogglebox. Anyway, if you're not a sports reporter, what are you doing here? This room is strictly no admittance, you know."

"I've come about Sergio Parisi."

"Oh, him!"

I picked up the vibe right away. "You didn't like him?"

"I wouldn't say that. Not as much as some others might. The groundsman's hut grump for one."

"Any others, in particular?"

Betty gave a dismissive sniff. "You won't catch me telling tales out of school."

I grinned. "Let's pretend we're still in the classroom. So not out of school."

Betty gave me a hard look.

So I swiftly added: "And, by the way, didn't I see a kettle on the table in the corner? Thought I caught a glimpse of a bottle of milk and packet of digestive biscuits."

"Packet's empty. And the tea money has run out."

But she stood up and made to head for the table.

I reached into my pocket for some loose change. "Here. Buy a couple more packets next time you're down at the corner store."

Betty took the coins. "Two shillings. Very generous. Might be enough over for a packet of custard creams."

I'd willingly have shelled out for one of those big chocolate biscuit assortments you see around at Christmas time. I had a feeling Betty – who didn't tell tales out of school – was actually going to tell me a whole lot of them.

While Betty made the tea, I had a nose around her office.

Behind her desk, there was a pin-board. It was loaded with notices and memos. Press clippings of matches Rovers had won. Old team sheets. A holiday rota. A photo of the last season's team, all lined up. The captain with the ball between his legs. The goalie in a sweater and a pair of gloves.

Beside the team shot, there was another picture. This one showed a barrel-chested man sitting next to a scrawny bloke with big ears and crooked teeth. The man mountain was Vernon Stoker, the club's chairman. I thought I recognised the crooked teeth guy, but couldn't remember who he was. The pair had their arms round each other's shoulders, like they were the best of pals.

At the far end of the back wall, there was a recess that turned the whole place into an L-shaped room. I wandered over and had a look.

The short bit of the L was furnished more smartly than Betty's long bit of L. There was a faded Wilton carpet on the floor. The desk was made from wood that had a patina of age – and money. And there was one of those fancy chairs in red button-back leather behind it. No overflowing baskets of papers on this desk.

Instead, a neat pile of old copies of the *Evening Chronicle*. I took a closer look. The papers had all been folded open at the page with the crossword puzzle.

From the other side of the room, Betty saw me having a nose. "That is Mr Vernon Stoker's workspace," she said. "He's the club's chairman. And benefactor – as far as an over-sized tightwad can be."

"Seems very neat and tidy."

"That's because he's not often here. Spends most of his time at his car showroom."

"Elsewhere in Crawley?" I asked.

"No. South-east London. Place called Beulah Hill, I think. Though I've never been there. Tea's ready."

Betty crossed the office and sat in the chair Lennox Slattery had occupied.

There was another alongside and I flopped down in it.

Betty handed me a mug of tea and I took a sip.

I said: "I hear the club received a World Cup Final ticket. Could Stoker have been behind that?"

"No way. If there's ever anything going free, Stoker grabs it. If you shake hands with him, you should count your fingers afterwards."

"A slippery operator?" I asked.

"You could say that. I couldn't because I work for him. But, anyway, the Cup Final ticket arrived through the post. My eyes virtually popped out on three-foot springs when I saw it. I can remember the ticket details even now. South stand. Block 29. Third row from the front. Aisle seat."

"How did it arrive?"

"In a stamped brown envelope."

"Any covering letter?"

"No."

"Nothing written on the envelope?"

"Only our address here."

"And that was hand-written?"

"Written in block capitals. Anyone could've done it."

"That would disguise the handwriting."

Betty shrugged. "I suppose so."

"Have you told anyone else about the envelope?"

"No. Didn't think they'd be interested."

"What did you do when you realised the ticket was genuine?"

"I called Mr Stoker."

"And what did he tell you to do?"

"Keep it to myself. Fat chance of that. Lennox was in here when I'd opened the envelope. Saw the ticket like me. Even had the cheek to claim it'd been sent to him. By a friend, if you will. If Lennox has a friend who can get his hand on a Cup Final ticket, I'm the Queen of the May. Anyway, once Lennox knew, there was no question of keeping it secret. Ten minutes later, the news had reached the whole team. Half an hour later, the rest of Crawley. Old man Stoker was furious when he got here."

"When was that?"

"A couple of hours later."

"And he decided to hold the raffle to see who got the ticket?"

"No, that would be the club committee. But Stoker was pulling strings behind the scenes."

"Why would he do that?"

Betty took a sip of her tea while she thought about that.

"Because he wanted Sergio Parisi to win the ticket," she said. "And he fixed the raffle so he would."

Chapter 6

I was so surprised, I slopped some tea down my summer jacket.

Natural undyed linen, too. Savile Row tailoring. Or so they'd told me in the market.

Pulled out my handkerchief to mop up the spill. Tried my best, but I'd booked myself another dry-cleaning bill.

"Let's get this clear," I said. "You have proof that Vernon Stoker fixed the Cup Final ticket raffle so that Sergio Parisi would win it?"

I took out my notebook and flipped to a blank page. I licked the tip of my pencil. It's a useful non-verbal signal to interviewees that you're now expecting the unvarnished truth.

"Proof of my own eyes," Betty said. Had a slurp of her tea. Managed it without spilling a drop. Her riposte that I wasn't the only master of non-verbal signals around here.

"How did he do it?" I asked.

"Well, as you can imagine everybody wanted in on it. So we had to have some rules. Mr Stoker said that anyone could have a ticket in the raffle as long as they had a genuine connection to the club."

"So, all the players, presumably?"

"Of all the teams, including the reserves and the junior side. Then all the officials and stewards on match days. Match programme sellers. And the owners of the firms that advertise in it. It was getting to the point where everyone in Crawley could invent some link to the club. But Mr Stoker was strict. He said the link had to be direct. The committee finally agreed on a list of one hundred and forty-one people."

"And they each had an equal chance?" I asked.

"Yes. I distributed small squares of paper all the same size. Everyone had to write their name on the paper, then fold it twice in a particular way so they all looked the same. Then, on the day the draw took place, everyone brought along their piece of paper and dropped it into a top hat. Mr Stoker brought the hat with him. When all the papers were in the hat, Mr Stoker, thrust his hand in, wiggled it around a bit, and drew out one paper. He handed it to me and asked me to read it. The name on the paper was Sergio Parisi."

"Was Parisi there to see his triumph?"

"Of course. He was standing towards the back. Pandemonium erupted. Everyone was shouting at everyone else. I waded into the melee and tried to get some calm. Eventually, I did. I was going to suggest to Mr Stoker that he say a few words to everyone. But when I looked for him, he'd gone."

"Gone where?" I asked.

"I don't know. But he'd taken the hat that had all the papers inside with him."

"But he'd just drawn the winning name in front of more than a hundred people."

Betty leaned towards me with an enigmatic smile on her lips. "Mr Crampton, how does a magician manage to pull a rabbit from a hat?"

"He puts the rabbit there beforehand," I said.

I thought about that for a moment. Could Stoker have secreted a Parisi ticket in the hat beforehand, so he could seem to draw it by luck? I suppose it was possible, but why should he do it?

If he had, it would certainly give him a reason to scarper afterwards. The crowd could have demanded a check on the other tickets in the hat. If a second Parisi ticket had turned up, there'd have been a riot.

To accuse a football club chairman and prominent businessman of cheating people in a raffle would be a big deal for any newspaper. If he had, it would be a scoop. Especially as the raffle was for a World Cup Final ticket. Figgis would love to run the story big across the front page. But he'd also want a ton of evidence to keep the lawyers happy.

And Betty's suspicions didn't amount to evidence.

There was another point that was also preying on my mind. If Stoker had fixed the raffle, had he also fixed for the raffle ticket to be stolen from Parisi afterwards? Indeed, was that why he'd set up Parisi to win it?

It didn't make any kind of sense to me.

But the stories that make the biggest headlines often start that way.

I said: "You said there was pandemonium after Stoker drew the winning ticket. Was that because everyone else suspected a fix, too?"

"No. It was because Parisi was just about the most unpopular winner there could've been," Betty said. "There were people in that room who would cheerfully have killed him for a bus ticket let alone one for the World Cup Final."

I took a deep breath and a quiet moment to consider that.

It was a damning charge to make, and Betty seemed the kind of person who's big on opinions but small on supporting evidence.

I glanced at my watch. It was twenty past twelve.

I said: "There's a pub on the Brighton Road just outside town that does a decent steak and kidney pie. How about I buy you lunch?"

There were only a couple of other customers in the saloon bar of the White Lion.

We took a table at the far end of the bar, well out of earwigging range. I hoped what Betty planned to tell me would be explosive – and I didn't want any nosey drinkers overhearing.

I treated myself to the steak and kidney pie. Betty had an omelette *fines herbes* and salad. The healthy option.

When we'd been served, I picked up my knife and fork and cut off a juicy piece of kidney. I chewed it meditatively. (Actually, it turned out to be a bit dry.)

Then I asked Betty: "What motive could Vernon Stoker have for wanting Sergio Parisi to win the Cup Final ticket?"

Betty toyed with her omelette. "I've wondered that myself. It's not that Mr Stoker even liked Sergio. But then he didn't like most people. He's that kind of person. It's not as though Mr Stoker owed Sergio any favours. Other way round, if you ask me."

"What do you mean by that?"

Betty popped a large piece of omelette into her mouth. Gave her a reason not to talk while she chewed. Found a reason to push the salad around on her plate. Avoided my eyes.

I said: "What favour did Sergio owe Stoker?"

Betty's cheeks reddened a little. "I spoke out of turn. Forget it."

"Sergio owed Stoker money, didn't he?"

Betty's eyes flashed alarm. "How did you know that?"

"Only one reason the proprietor of a beaten-up old café would owe a big-time London car dealer. He borrowed money from him."

"It's true. I discovered it by accident. Mr Stoker left a confidential file on his desk. I picked it up by mistake thinking it was the one with the letters he wanted me to type."

"Easily done."

"I saw a letter from his bank. He'd transferred eight hundred pounds to Sergio. Apparently, the local council's health police had inspected his kitchen – Sergio's not Mr Stoker's. They were going to close him down unless he made some big improvements. He simply didn't have the money."

"From what you've said, Stoker isn't the kind of character to help out ailing café owners with large cheques."

"He is careful with money, if that's what you mean," Betty said primly. "But I must admit I was surprised when I saw the amount. Especially as each of them never had much good to say about the other."

51

"Would Stoker murder Sergio?" I asked.

"I never looked on Mr Stoker as a cold-blooded killer."

"But back at the ground, you told me there were plenty who'd kill Sergio for a bus ticket."

Betty finished her omelette and tucked her knife and fork neatly together on her plate.

She burped gently as she leaned across the table in a confidential way.

"Well, there's Judith Kershaw for a start. She's on the club's committee. Even though she's a woman she'd have the strength to take on a small bloke like Sergio. She's games mistress at St Hilda's – it's a girls' school outside of town."

"Jolly hockey sticks and all that?"

"Not for Judith. She teaches her girls to play football. Something of a player herself, she likes to make out. Wants to start a women's team at the Rovers, but the men on the committee won't wear it."

"With Sergio leader of the opposition?"

"It got quite heated at a meeting a month ago. I was taking minutes. Judith wanted to start a women's team for the new season, but the others threw up practical objections. When men want to stop women doing something, it usually comes down to a lack of lavatories."

"And that was Sergio's reason for stopping the women?"

"Not only his. But he was nasty about it. Said that football wasn't a game for sissies. Said that if God had intended women to put on football boots, he wouldn't have provided them with stiletto shoes. Can't see why he had to bring that into it."

"God?"

"Stiletto shoes."

"Did Judith make any threats against Sergio at the committee meeting?"

"Not at the meeting. But she spoke to me afterwards. Me being who I am."

"The secretary?"

"A woman. Judith was seething. I've never seen her so angry. It wasn't just that the committee had turned down her idea. It was that Sergio had then trashed even the thought of it."

"And she threatened to kill Sergio?"

"Her last words to me as she stormed off were: 'I could murder that dinosaur.'"

"Meaning Sergio?"

Betty nodded. "She certainly wasn't thinking about the one in the Natural History Museum. Besides, it's been dead for seventy million years."

She glanced at her watch.

"You need to get back?" I asked.

Betty nodded.

"I'll drive you."

In the car, Betty stared gloomily at the passing countryside.

I thought she was deciding whether to tell me something else.

As we turned off towards Crawley at Handcross, she made up her mind.

She said: "Although there are plenty who'd like to see the back of Sergio, there's only one other I've heard use the m-word."

"Murder?" I asked.

"Yes. It was Cyril Hands. He's the first team's goalkeeper."

"The custodian of the citadel as Victorian football reporters used to write."

"Trouble is, Cyril is not much of a custodian. You'd think a bloke with a name like his would be able to grab a ball when it came his way. He wears keepers' gloves, but it's as though they're slicked with oil. The ball just seems to slide through them."

"Why not get new gloves? Or a new goalie?"

"Not as easy as you think. The young guys these days all want to be goal scorers. They don't want to spend their Saturday afternoons standing in a muddy goal-mouth. More like Jimmy Greaves than Gordon Banks. So Cyril is stuck with it. He's a simple soul. Works a corporation dustcart for the council during the week. The fact is, he's not much good at anything else."

"And Sergio lets him know he isn't?"

"All too often, I'm afraid. In the last game of the season, Cyril only let in three, which is good for him. But after the match, Sergio marched into the dressing room and gave him a mouthful while all the guys were in the team bath."

I gave Betty a cheeky glance. "You weren't in there with them?"

She blushed. "Goodness, no. I heard this from three or four of the team afterwards. Fully clothed."

"You or them?"

"Mr Crampton!"

"Sorry, I couldn't resist that. What did Sergio say about Cyril?"

"By all accounts, he had a wicked turn of phrase. Said when Cyril fumbled the ball, he looked like he had vegetable marrows for fingers. Said for all the good he was doing he might as well dump himself in his own dustcart. I was told he left Cyril with a soapy face and close to tears. Two of my informants heard him say he'd see Sergio dead and in the dustcart one day."

"That sounds like a threat uttered in anger."

"Maybe, but Sergio has been winding Cyril up for years. Now Cyril is like a volcano ready to blow. Perhaps he has."

When we arrived back at Crawley Rovers' ground, there was no sign of Lennox Slattery.

But he must have been around earlier because he'd taken a telephone message and left it on Betty's desk.

Betty picked it up and read it. A worried frown wrinkled her forehead.

"This is bad news," she said. "Wayne Matthews won't be able

to make tonight's training session."

"A member of the squad?"

"Yes. He's centre forward – and the team's leading goal scorer. Often the only goal scorer, when he's playing."

"You don't play your leading goal scorer in some matches?" I asked. "Isn't that a rather eccentric tactic?"

Betty sat down heavily behind her desk. "Wayne would love to play in every match. We'd all like him to play. But he has a son – Christopher – who's badly affected by polio. Although most kids have had the Salk vaccine for the last 10 years, Christopher contracted polio before he had the injection. Now he walks with a leg brace. We feel really sorry for the kid – especially as he's football mad. Follows every game in the World Cup."

"Be great if he could've had the Cup Final ticket," I said.

Betty nodded in a resigned sort of way. "Someone suggested at the most recent committee – Judith Kershaw, I think – that Christopher should be given the ticket. But Mr Stoker said it was only fair to offer everyone in the club the chance to have it – and he wanted the raffle to go ahead. There was a big debate about it – and Judith nearly got her way."

"Why nearly?"

"It was clear that counting heads around the table the vote would be even, but Sergio wasn't there. He'd originally sent apologies for absence. But he turned up seconds before the vote was taken. And he supported Stoker. The raffle went ahead. Christopher lost out on a World Cup Final ticket. When Wayne heard about it later, he flew into a rage. Said it was wrong for someone who'd not heard the arguments on both sides to turn up and swing the debate."

"And said he'd kill Sergio?"

Betty shrugged. "He would have needed to join a lengthening queue."

Chapter 7

I left Betty hammering out a sharp memo about poor attendance at training sessions.

I had a lot to think about as I walked back to my car.

It was clear from what Betty had told me that Sergio Parisi was not a popular man. But a lot of people find themselves on the receiving end of frowns rather than smiles from their fellow men and women. That doesn't mean said fellow men and women are looking for an opportunity to croak them.

This whole story seemed to revolve around the Cup Final ticket. There were three mysteries. First, why did Vernon Stoker apparently want Sergio to win the ticket? On the face of it, there was no reason Stoker should owe Sergio any favours. After all, he ran a car sales showroom that evidently left him with enough spare cash to invest in a losing football team. The only conclusion was that Sergio must have some kind of hold over Stoker. But Betty was unable to provide any clue as to what that might be.

Secondly, why had the Cup Final ticket gone missing? There wasn't any clue about that. When he'd told me about it, Ted Wilson had suggested the missing ticket must be linked to the murder. But that was an inference, not a fact. Perhaps the explanation was innocent. Perhaps Sergio had simply lost the ticket. True, that would have made an own goal in a big match look like a minor slip-up. But accidents happen.

Which brought me to the third point. Was anyone else involved in the apparent loss of the ticket? Perhaps Sergio had passed the ticket on to someone else. A generous gesture? Or perhaps a bribe to get something he badly needed? After all, Stoker had loaned him money. Perhaps that was all gone and there was no more coming. Perhaps Sergio urgently needed another benefactor. But, if so, who could that be? Ted hadn't suggested that line of enquiry. That didn't mean it shouldn't be followed.

I reached into my pocket for the car keys. As I did so, a Crawley Urban District Council dustcart drove by. The three guys on the front bench seat looked cheerful.

I checked my watch: four o'clock.

The end of a dustman's day. They'd be heading to their depot.

Cyril Hands worked on the dustcarts, Betty had told me. And Cyril was one of the hotheads who'd threatened to kill Sergio.

No doubt all the dustcarts were checking in at the end of the day. Perhaps I could catch Cyril in a vulnerable moment when he was tired after a hard day humping bins. Maybe I should have taken Betty's suspicions about Cyril more seriously.

After all, in his job, Cyril was an expert in disposing of things.

I jumped into the MGB, fired up the engine and, like Marie Lloyd in her song, "followed the van".

The refuse disposal depot proved to be in Tilgate, on the outskirts of town.

I watched the dustcart ahead of me turn in through the entrance to the depot. I pulled into the side of the road further back. I needed to think about how to handle the matter.

I thought I would recognise Cyril from the team photo I'd seen on Betty's pinboard. In the pic, goalie Cyril was the only one wearing gloves.

I hadn't recognised Cyril as one of the men in the dustcart I'd followed. I figured he'd arrive on one of the other carts.

Another cart drove up from the other direction and turned in through the gates.

I climbed out of the MGB and headed up the road to the depot. I stepped through the gates into a yard with a long low-slung building on the other side. The place had an open front and roof made out of corrugated metal. Half a dozen dustcarts were drawn up inside the building.

The air was thick with the stink of rotting rubbish. I just knew it would hang around in my nostrils for the rest of the evening.

As I approached, a man wearing blue overalls and a rat-catcher's cap came out of the building.

He gave me an unfriendly look and shouted in a gruff voice: "No members of the public allowed. Clear off."

I strode towards him like I didn't care and when I was close enough said: "I'm from the council. Wages office."

"We got our pay packets this morning."

"I know, but we made a mistake in one of them. Cyril Hands. He'll be short for the weekend if we don't correct it."

The bloke gave a knowing smile. "Cyril short? That's a laugh."

"Is he here?"

"Clocked off ten minutes ago. He'll be in the Flag and Trumpet with Nifty and Bill by now."

I nodded. "Don't mention this. In the wages department we don't like people talking about our business." I gave him a friendly wink. "You get my drift?"

"Loud and clear, guvnor."

I turned and stalked out of the yard like a bloke who owned the place.

The Flag and Trumpet turned out to be a couple of hundred yards from the depot.

I drove into the car park wondering how I should play my encounter with Cyril. If he was having a quiet drink with Nifty and Bill, I could hardly appear on the scene and accuse the bloke of murder.

As it turned out, when I pushed into the public bar, there was no sign of Cyril.

But there were a couple of blokes over by the window dressed in the same kind of overalls I'd seen at the depot. They were sitting at a table and had pints of beer in front of them.

I walked up to the bar. The barman had sweat on his forehead and dirt under his fingernails. He was wearing the kind of green apron you see on hospital porters when they're wheeling dead bodies around.

The barman said: "I've just been in that bleeding cellar changing a barrel."

I said: "Not on my part, I hope. I'd like a gin and tonic with one ice cube and two slices of lemon."

I got two ice cubes and one slice of lemon.

I said: "I don't see Cyril tonight."

The barman said: "Neither do I."

"Are those two blokes sitting over by the window Nifty and Bill?"

"They're definitely not Laurel and Hardy."

He pulled one of the beer pumps and a grey slime poured out.

He said: "Bugger. That shouldn't happen. I've got to go down that bleeding cellar again."

"What a pity. We were having such a pleasant conversation."

I took a fortifying sip of the gin and tonic. It was too cold and not lemony enough.

I swallowed my disappointment and walked over to the window table.

One of the blokes lifted his glass and took a monster gulp of beer.

I said: "I don't see Cyril."

The beer swigger said: "That's because he's not here."

"Do you know where Cyril is?"

"Somewhere else," said the other one. He lifted his glass and took a couple of gulps. Put the glass down and burped theatrically.

I said to the burper: "Are you Nifty?"

He said: "No, I'm Bill. But I can be pretty nifty when it's needed, if you know what I mean." He waggled a thumb at Nifty. "Besides, Nifty isn't his real name."

Nifty said: "My mum christened me Nigel, but it didn't seem right for a dustman. So, I changed it to Nifty. Anyway, who are you?"

"Colin Crampton, *Evening Chronicle*. I'm doing a story on the tragedy that's affected Crawley Rovers."

Nifty said: "You mean the tragedy of them being relegated again?"

Bill said: "No, he means that café owner who was killed? Sergio something."

I said: "Parisi. I'm trying to get reactions from team members. I thought Cyril could help."

Nifty said: "Cyril couldn't stand him. He was always moaning about him when he were driving the cart. I remember a couple of weeks back he were complaining Sergio had been needling him about the number of goals he'd let in last season. Eighty-four, apparently."

Bill chimed in. "Nifty told him not to put up with it."

"I told him not to put up with it," Nifty confirmed. "I said he should confront this Parisi. I told him to go round to the café on his day off and have it out with him. Let him know where he gets off."

Bill piped up. "He said he would, too."

"And did he?" I asked.

Nifty and Bill exchanged glances.

"Don't know," Nifty said.

"Cyril wouldn't say," Bill added.

"When we got back to work on Monday morning, the news about Parisi's murder was all over the papers," Nifty said.

"On the telly, too," Bill said.

"Cyril seemed shook up about the whole thing. We didn't like to trouble him," Nifty said.

"Particularly as it was raining," Bill said. "We get covered with crap from the bins when the sun's out. But when we get covered with wet crap it's worse. I don't know why we do it."

"Because we're a team," Nifty said.

Bill's eyebrows twitched. "Are we?" he said.

I said: "I'd buy you both a pint, but the barman's down the cellar. He could be in all sorts of trouble."

"We know the feeling," Nifty said.

"Only too well," Bill added

I left the pair supping their pints.

I found a telephone box a couple of hundred yards from the Flag and Trumpet and called in some copy for the paper's night final edition. At least that would keep Figgis happy.

Then I climbed into the MGB and headed back to Brighton. I'd thought my trip to Crawley would provide some answers about Parisi's murder.

But I was returning with more questions.

"Jeez, what a girl has to do to make an honest living," Shirley said.

We were perched on bar stools in Prinny's Pleasure, a pub in the North Laines part of Brighton. The bar had fading green paint on the walls and a carpet that squelched when you walked on it. The place hung with a stink of stale beer as strong as a tarantula's cobweb. As a journo, I used it because there were never any other customers. So there was only a remote chance I'd be spotted with the dodgy characters from Brighton's *demimonde* I met there.

Jeff Purkiss, the landlord, had a stubbly chin and, usually, a piece of bacon stuck between his teeth. His dress sense peaked at a tee-shirt with a hole where the armpit should be and stained jeans.

He served our drinks – gin and tonic for me and Campari soda for Shirley.

I said: "I thought modelling only involved standing around and looking beautiful."

Shirl nudged me in the ribs.

"I was about to add – the second of which you can do without even trying."

"Jeez," Shirley said again. "That lensman today sure was trying."

"In the sense of doing his best or being a nuisance?" I asked.

"Both. I never realised I'd have to model so many different outfits."

"Eight, I guess, as you were modelling the quarter-final teams' strips."

"Yeah! England, natch, West Germany, Soviet Union, Hungary, Portugal, Uruguay, Argentina. And North Korea. They went okay, except North Korea. There was a man there, watching me, like I was some kind of threat to him. Creepy."

"Probably a spy."

"Sure. He tried to spy on me while I was putting the kit on. Didn't like it one bit. White shirt with blue collar and cuffs. It had a funny little flag in blue and red across the chest. When I moved, it looked like my tits were waving it."

"That should cheer their fans."

"Watch it, buster. These boobies were made in Australia – and don't you forget it."

I grinned. "I never do."

As usual, Jeff had earwigged our conversation.

He said: "I was asked to pose once."

"As a human being?" I asked. "You'd never have been sufficiently convincing."

Jeff said: "As a model."

"We're not interested," Shirl said.

"In the nude," Jeff said.

"Definitely not interested," I said.

"I would have done it, but I wanted to cover up just one little thing in the picture."

"Don't tell me," I said.

"Well, quite a big thing," Jeff said.

"*Ugh*," Shirley said.

"Especially when it stuck out," Jeff said.

"Double *ugh*," Shirley said.

"It was a corn on my big toe. Made the toe come out from my foot at a sharp angle. Spoilt the perfect symmetry of my feet."

"Let's take our drinks somewhere else," I said to Shirley.

"Yeah! A different pub," Shirl said.

We climbed off our bar stools and picked up our drinks.

Jeff said: "Anyway, after a long negotiation with the photographer, we decided…"

But we didn't hear what they decided because we'd reached the table at the back of the bar.

Now we were out of Jeff's earshot, I filled Shirl in on what I'd discovered during the day.

"I don't want to tell Rosina too much at this stage," I said. "Partly because I need to know much more and partly because I don't want to give her false hope."

Shirley put an arm around me and kissed my cheek.

"You're a good man, Colin Crampton," she said.

"You're not such a bad woman," I said. "Especially if you're going to wear that North Korean shirt when we go to bed tonight."

That earnt me a playful punch on the arm.

We had a shock when we arrived back at Shirley's flat.

Rosina had looked sad but calm when we'd left her in the morning. She'd promised to spend a quiet day in the flat.

But when we walked in, she rushed into Shirley's arms and burst into tears.

Shirley gave her a special hug and seated her on the sofa.

We soon discovered the cause of Rosina's distress. During the afternoon, there'd been three phone calls. She'd wisely not answered the phone, the first two times.

But she'd picked up the receiver the third time the phone

rang.

"Nobody said anything," she said in a frightened little voice. "I could just hear breathing."

"What did you do?"

"I said, 'Who are you?' but there was no answer. Then I started to cry and…"

"And what?" Shirley asked gently.

"And whoever it was started to chuckle. A low sinister chuckle, like he loved hearing me cry. I slammed down the phone and sobbed."

"You poor thing?" Shirley said.

"Do you have any idea who it was?" I asked.

"It must be Brando," Rosina said.

"The bastard couldn't have found Rosina so quickly," Shirley said. "It's just not possible."

I shook my head.

"I'm afraid it's all too possible. Remember that if Brando is Mafia, he belongs to an organisation with a long reach. He'd have discovered our names and addresses from the information we'd lodged with the reception at our hotel in Taormina. With a name and address, it's not difficult to find a phone number in the directory."

Shirley jumped up and paced the room in anger. "We'll have to go to the police."

"Not Brighton cops," I said. "Tomkins wouldn't listen. Even if he did, his blundering would lead a determined hunter to his prey."

"So what are we going to do?" wailed Rosina.

I said: "There's only one thing I can do. Find Brando – and warn him off - before he finds you."

Chapter 8

If Brando Cavaletto was hiding out in Brighton, the man who would know was Marco Fratelli.

In my book, Fratelli was a good man gone bad. He'd been a member of the small Italian resistance, fighting the Nazis, during the war. The Nazis had continued to occupy Italy after the country ceased to be Hitler's ally in 1943. I'd heard Fratelli had been fearless as an undercover agent. Risked his life several times to rescue innocent men and women from the Gestapo. Was one of the group of partisans who hung Mussolini's dead body upside down from a garage's metal girder in the *Piazzale Loreto*, Milan.

But peacetime didn't suit him. In the early nineteen-fifties he'd moved from Italy to Britain, where the risks were less and the rewards greater. He ran a little *ristorante* called *Casa Marco* in Kemptown, at the eastern end of Brighton. It occupied a run-down building in an alleyway that linked two backstreets. The joint had no fancy fascia. No neon lights. No menu in the window. The notice in the front door always read: CLOSED.

In short, the place wasn't easy to find. That was the whole point. Fratelli didn't want walk-ins.

The guys who got inside usually had fat wallets when they entered. Not so bulky on the way out. They'd have lost their cash in the card game that went on in the back room. Or in sampling the *dolce vita* upstairs with one of Fratelli's girls at five pounds a time.

It was just after nine when I stepped inside. The place was crowded but the conversation subdued. A fug of cigarette smoke hung in the air. The red wall lamps flickered through a thin mist. Candles on the tables guttered as a draught followed me in from the open door. Thoughtfully, I closed it.

At a table near the door, a bloke with greying sideburns

nuzzled close to a girl with dangly earrings and a lot of lipstick. His left hand held a smouldering Havana cigar. Possibly one of those reputedly rolled between the thighs of virgins. His right hand caressed the girl's thigh. Or perhaps he was just fumbling for another cigar.

Fratelli was leaning on the bar, a flash chrome job trimmed with plush red velvet. Gilt-edged mirrors lined the wall. All the better to let Fratelli see what was going on without turning round.

He was talking to a tall bloke with fair hair and a conspicuous bald patch. The bald bloke had a girl clinging possessively to each arm. (Ten pounds unless the pair gave him a discount for a bulk buy - or Green Shield stamps.)

As I crossed the room, the bloke nodded to Fratelli and guided the girls to the stairs which led to the rooms upstairs.

I moved alongside Fratelli and nodded towards the retreating bloke.

"Another satisfied customer, Marco?"

Fratelli grinned. "He will be."

I said: "Mine's a gin and tonic."

Fratelli gave the order to the barman. "With one ice cube and two slices of lemon."

"And in honour of Garibaldi's birthday, make it a double gin," I added.

Fratelli frowned. "You're too late. Giuseppe Garibaldi, the great Italian patriot, was born on the fourth of July."

"I was referring to the date when the biscuits were first made," I said.

The barman put my drink in front of me. I hoisted the glass and gave it the punishment it merited.

"I assume you haven't come in to waste my time with facts about biscuits?" Fratelli said.

"Of course not. Although I could mention that Garibaldis were first made by a man called Jonathan Carr in 1861. I'm surprised he didn't name them after himself. But, then, perhaps he knew they'd end up being called dead-fly biscuits."

I took another pull at my gin and tonic. "There's a man called Brando Cavaletto in town. Do you know where he is?"

Fratelli considered the point. Raised his glass. Found it was empty. Looked for the barman who'd disappeared. Put the empty glass down heavily.

"Who is this Cavaletto?" he asked.

"He's the son-in-law of Sergio Parisi."

That had Fratelli's attention.

"The Crawley café owner who was murdered?" he asked.

"The very same."

"You're not suggesting this Cavaletto did the killing?"

"No."

"Because I do not harbour murderers."

"I always knew you had standards. Does that mean you observe the Fifth Commandment?"

"Thou shalt not kill. As far as possible."

"Don't feel you have to commit yourself."

"I never do."

I said: "Sergio's daughter Rosina is married to Cavaletto. They lived in Sicily. But not happily. Cavaletto beat her."

"I do not approve of husbands beating their wives," Fratelli said.

"I'll pass the word. The point is Rosina has left Brando and now Brando is threatening to kill her."

"It is a Sicilian tradition that when a wife runs from her husband, he is shamed. He has no choice but to kill her."

"And we can't have a young woman's life getting in the way of ancient traditions. The point is that as far as Rosina is concerned, I'd like to avoid that tradition."

Fratelli nodded. "Me, too. But the fact is I do not know where this Brando Cavaletto is."

"But you'll make enquiries?"

"Possibly. I'm a busy man." He waved his arm airily around. "As you can see."

I nodded. "Yes, *la dolce vita* is hard work. Profitable, too. Especially when you can get a drink."

The barman had returned. Fratelli frowned and pointed at his empty glass.

As the barman poured a fresh drink, I said: "There's one thing I've always wondered, Marco. How do you keep this place running without interference from the cops? It's not through payoffs, is it?"

"Brighton cops are not worth the money," Fratelli said. "But as to how I keep it running... Well, a clever *signore* like you should be able to work that out. Take care."

I had been dismissed.

I gave Fratelli a friendly nod and headed for the door.

Fratelli wasn't the sort to wish his guests a safe journey home.

So instead of stepping straight out into the street, I peered through the window. To the left, a shadow moved. To the right, the dim light from a lamp flickered.

I now knew why the barman had disappeared even while his boss wanted a drink. He'd been to arrange a little committee to speed me on my way. Hopefully, with a black eye. Or perhaps a thick ear. Or even a broken arm.

The goons outside would be a couple of pieces of muscle who worked on the premises. In a place like this, Fratelli would need a pair of heavies kept out of sight in case a client got uppity.

Fratelli had nobly eschewed murder – most of the time. But that didn't mean he wouldn't smile kindly on underlings who administered a punishment beating to an intrusive reporter.

I glanced back through the haze that hung over the room. There was probably a rear exit out but I didn't know where it would lead.

Fratelli was talking to one of his girls. He had his back to me. The bloke who'd had the cigar and his hand on the girl's thigh had gone. He'd taken the girl, but left the stub of his cigar smouldering in an ashtray. I gathered together some paper napkins and bunched them into a loose ball. Then I looped the table cloth up so that it overhung the ashtray. I seized the candle from the table and added it to the combustible mix. This was arson made easy. I grabbed a brandy snifter and tipped the dregs into the ashtray.

The hot ash ignited the brandy in a blue flame. The paper napkins caught and created quite a blaze. I knocked the candle off the table so it set fire to the overhanging tablecloth.

I shouted: "Fire!"

I blundered into the table so that it tipped over. Flames spread across the carpet and set the adjacent table alight.

Girls screamed. Men shouted orders at each other.

Fratelli yelled: "Keep calm."

But nothing creates panic more than being told to keep calm.

By now, everyone in the room was on the move.

Heading for the door.

They poured into the alleyway as someone grabbed an extinguisher and the fire sputtered out.

I slipped through the door behind a couple of elderly guys who ought to have known better.

I took a quick look around. But the passageway was crowded with people jostling one another.

Fratelli's thugs would have scarpered. This was trouble. And trouble attracts cops.

In the distance, I heard a ringing bell. Those brave lads of the Brighton fire brigade had interrupted their card game and were on the way.

It was nearly midnight by the time I arrived back at my lodgings in Regency Square.

On the way, I'd called Shirl from a phone box. I'd told her that Fratelli said he didn't know where Brando was.

I'd asked her about Rosina. She'd said she'd gone to bed and was sleeping. I'd said I'd call by in the morning.

I inserted my key silently in the lock of my lodgings, opened the door, and crept inside. I stepped over the scraper mat that squeaked when you trod on it. The print of Holman Hunt's *Light of the World* on the wall had slipped to a jaunty angle. The picture of the figure in the long flowing robe reminded me of an old bloke who'd got up in the night to raid the fridge for a midnight snack.

I tiptoed across the hall towards the stairs. I was about to step on the first tread when the door to the Widow's parlour swung open and Beatrice Gribble, my landlady, appeared. She was wearing a pink Winceyette dressing gown, which travelled as far south as her mid-calf, and pom-pom slippers. She'd tied her hair in a loose bun and fixed a net arrangement over it. It looked as though she had a dead badger on her head.

She said: "I wanted to catch you, Mr Crampton."

I said: "It's too late to play hide-and-seek."

"I have no intention of wasting my time on a childish game, especially as I've made myself twenty pounds today."

"Don't spend it all at once."

"And there's every chance I can make hundreds."

I know. I shouldn't have got involved. I should've headed up the stairs. But, sometimes, it's quicker in the long run to let the Widow get it off her ample chest.

So I asked: "Where did the twenty pounds come from?"

"From my bet on the result of the North Korea versus Italy game. North Korea won one-nil."

"That was days ago."

"This is the first time I've seen you since then."

I said: "I didn't know you were interested in football."

"I have Bobby Moore in my bedroom."

"You'd better tell him to take his football boots off. You don't want mud on your clean sheets."

"Mr Crampton! I am referring to a photograph of Mr Moore. It is in a frame next to the picture of Hector."

I'd seen the snap of the Widow's late hubby. It showed a bald bloke with a furrowed brow who looked like he couldn't wait for the end of the world.

I said: "Betting on football results is a mug's game."

"Nonsense. Look at that Viv Nicholson who won one hundred and fifty-two thousand pounds on the Littlewoods' football pools a year back. She said she was going to 'spend, spend, spend'."

"She's gone bankrupt – or so I've heard." I knew I shouldn't ask the next question, but I couldn't stop myself.

"Anyway, what is this system?"

"It's been told to me strictly in confidence. I'm not to tell a soul."

"Which is why you're blurting it out to me."

"I do not blurt, Mr Crampton. Will you just listen?"

"Do I have a choice?"

"These two young men, very polite – not like you – came round to the house. Harvey and Lloyd. It turned out they'd got the wrong address, but we fell into conversation and when they heard I was a poor widow, they couldn't have been more sympathetic."

"Don't tell me. Let me guess. They said they have a secret betting system for the World Cup and, under very special circumstances, they'd let you in on it."

The Widow's eyes widened at that.

"How did you know? Have you met Harvey and Lloyd, too?"

"No, but I recognise a con-man when I see one. Or, in this case, two."

"Con-man?"

"Confidence trickster. A criminal who is often very sympathetic and polite – unlike me – and who gains the confidence of his victims and then milks them of their money."

The Widow's jaw tightened and she angrily crossed her arms. "Well, that's where you're wrong. They gave me twenty pounds

71

because I won. And I only staked five pounds. They said I would make even more money with a bigger bet."

"The twenty pounds was what con-men call a 'convincer'," I explained. "It's designed to give you the confidence to risk a much larger sum – which you'll lose."

"Well, you're wrong again. You see, they gave me written evidence of the bet they put on with my money."

"What kind of evidence?"

"When I handed over my five-pound stake money, they gave me a sealed envelope with the score of the match that would win me the bet."

"And you opened the envelope before the match?"

"No. The strict terms of the bet are that I keep the envelope sealed until Harvey and Lloyd return with my winnings. It's an honour thing, according to Harvey. But just in case I'm tempted, he signs across the envelope's seal. When they returned, they opened the envelope, while I was counting all those lovely crisp pound notes. Inside, there was a piece of paper with the match result. I'd won!"

"If you bet again, you'll lose your money."

"Nonsense, Lloyd says this was only a test for the big one – the World Cup Final. I'm taking five hundred pounds out of my building society account. Next week, they're coming round to collect the money and give me the sealed envelope with the winning bet."

"Don't do it."

"You're just jealous. If I win this money, I won't need to have so many tenants in the house. I'll be able to tell some of them to go."

"Anyone in mind?" I asked.

"All in good time," the Widow said. "Good night."

She stomped back into her parlour. I headed up the stairs with something else to think about.

Chapter 9

There was more trouble as soon as I reached the *Chronicle's* newsroom the following morning.

Cedric, the copy boy, had just brought up the morning's newspapers.

He sauntered across the newsroom while he gazed at the paper on the top of his pile. He moseyed alongside my desk with a grin on his face as wide as the Thames estuary.

He took the *Daily Mirror* off the top of the pile and flipped it onto my desk.

He said: "Now that's what I call an eyeful. That'll keep me in fantasies well into next week."

I just sat there and gawped at the *Mirror's* front page.

It was dominated by a picture of Shirley wearing the match strip of the North Korea football team. The shorts were so tight they strained at the seams. And as for the shirt, the flag motif caressed Shirl's boobs so intimately, it looked like it would never go back up a flagpole again. Shirl had a football balanced in her left hand. She gazed at the camera with her lips slightly parted and a teasing look in her eyes. Like she was about to throw the ball and expected you to catch it.

The *Mirror's* subs had put a headline over the picture: *SCORE WITH SHIRLEY. Fill in our World Cup knockout wall chart inside the paper.*

I picked up the phone and dialled Shirl's number.

She answered straight away.

I said: "Have you seen the *Daily Mirror* this morning?"

"Jeez, big boy, have I seen it? I had three marriage proposals just walking back from the newsagent."

"Don't accept any."

"Why should I when I'm still waiting for yours?"

"I'm working on it."

"Yeah! You do that."

I said: "How's Rosina this morning?"

"Wants to become a model, after she saw the paper."

"That's all we need. I'll be in touch later."

I flipped to the *Mirror's* sports pages. The tipster had picked North Korea to beat Portugal in tomorrow's quarter-final match. There were more pictures.

Shirley in the England strip kicks a ball from the penalty spot.

Shirley in the West German strip makes a throw-in from the touchline.

Shirley in the Hungarian strip jumps to head a ball towards an imaginary goalmouth.

I folded the paper and thrust it into my desk drawer.

I stood up and headed for the door. Figgis would have seen the *Daily Mirror*. I wanted to be out of the way before he aired his views to the newsroom.

There's only so much that a man with a girlfriend on the front page of a national newspaper can take.

If I'd thought the morning's police press briefing would be a haven away from front-page cheesecake, I was wrong.

As soon as I stepped through the door, Jim Houghton limped up to me.

Jim was my opposite number on the *Evening Argus*, the other paper in town. He was an old trooper, approaching retirement. But he still had a sharp news sense. His contacts book bulged with so many names it made mine look like a pauper's shopping list.

He was wearing his trademark grey suit which was frayed at the cuffs and had missed the middle jacket button for at least two years.

Jim grinned, revealing his grey teeth.

He said: "I see that girlfriend of yours is putting it about on the front page of a red-top rag."

I said: "If you mean that the popular model Shirley Goldsmith has posed for a topical shot in the country's largest-selling newspaper, I would certainly agree with you."

"Pictures like that could give you a bit of competition. There are plenty of big-money types who wouldn't mind parading around town with a girl like that on their arm."

"I hope you're not including yourself in that category?"

That got to Jim. He stood up straighter and brushed a speck of dust off his jacket.

"Just a word to the wise from someone who's seen it all before."

I said: "The trouble is Jim, it's so long ago you saw it, it's turned to monochrome in your mind."

Jim growled something I didn't hear and stomped off to his seat in the front row.

I took my customary place at the back. I kept my head down and pretended to consult my notebook. It didn't stop other journos coming up to give me a knowing nudge in the ribs.

For the first time ever, I was relieved when the door at the back of the room opened and Detective Chief Superintendent Alec Tomkins walked in. Ted Wilson trooped in behind him. He looked like he'd just had a bollocking from the chief super.

Tomkins sat down at the top table and peered around the room with a proprietorial air.

His gaze landed on me. "No representative here from the *Daily Mirror*?" he asked.

That won him a sycophantic titter from the other hacks.

"Had they sent a photographer, I could have worn my old rugby kit."

I said: "They won't be taking their Halloween pictures for weeks yet."

That got a guffaw from the press pack.

Tomkins rummaged angrily among his notes. "I want to make a statement about the successful investigation into the murder of Mr Sergio Parisi."

I flipped my notebook shut. Tomkins wouldn't tell us anything we didn't already know.

After rambling for ten minutes, Tomkins concluded: "We expect to make an arrest very soon. Now please raise your hand if you'd like to ask a question."

I ignored that. I stood up and asked: "How soon will you make the arrest?"

Tomkins flushed. "Soon means soon."

"A day soon, a week soon, or a month soon?" I asked.

"I have been quite clear. As soon as we reach the soon point."

I shrugged. "Perhaps soon could be sooner than you expect."

That raised another laugh from the hacks.

As Tomkins failed to answer more questions, I slipped out. I'd been watching Ted during Tomkins' statement. His eyebrows had shot up a couple of times. I felt that he knew something which Tomkins hadn't revealed. I wanted to find out what it was.

I met Ted half an hour later in Marcello's.

I had coffee in a glass cup and saucer.

Ted had the full English breakfast with a slice of fried bread.

I pointed at the eggs, bacon, sausages, mushrooms and tomatoes. "How can you eat all that this early in the day?"

Ted speared a sausage with his fork and cut into it. "Best time of the day to eat," he said. "Gets it out the way – at least until lunchtime."

I took a sip of coffee and said: "There was something Tomkins wasn't telling us about Parisi's murder."

Ted chewed on a piece of bacon. "A new lead. But he can't mention it."

"Because he bungled it at the outset?"

"Worse than that. A couple of uniform plods helped themselves to some of Sergio's dodgy fags and booze."

"Probably off the boats at Newhaven or Shoreham. No duty paid. No questions asked," I said.

"'Fraid so. Fact is, if Tomkins had had the place searched thoroughly at the outset, the provenance of the booze and fags would have come to light. The two cops who took the gear were too dim to notice. Or too keen to run off with their ill-gotten gains to mention it."

I drained the last of my coffee. "What does this all mean for the investigation?"

"It makes it more difficult to play our part in the broader investigation of smuggled booze and fags. The one I told you about while Julie Parrott was showing Rosina inside the café."

"Because you don't want your own light-fingered officers having their collars felt by another force?"

"Exactly. It's Tomkins' stuff of nightmares. Got to get back. Can't be missing for too long. Tomkins will have me back in uniform helping old ladies across the road."

"Tomkins' loss would be the old ladies' gain," I said.

Ted ignored that. He stood up and hurried out of the café.

I sat there and stared at the dregs in my coffee cup.

If a shadowy organisation was building a network to sell smuggled goods, it would be run on tough lines. The boss would want to keep his underlings in line. If Sergio had been one of those, could he have stepped out of line? I had no idea.

I wondered whether Rosina had known what her father was doing. I didn't think so, but I couldn't be sure. Which raised another question. What would she make of the news? She already had a violent husband whom she believed was linked to the Mafia. News that her father was also involved in crime could devastate her. But I was forgetting. There was another motive, too. That Sergio was killed for his Cup Final ticket. Several people had been heard to say they'd like to kill him. Perhaps one had.

And one of them was Cyril Hands, the Crawley Rovers' goalie

77

who let too many into the back of the net.

Cyril Hands gave a handle on his table football set a sharp twist.
The feet of a wooden player struck a small imitation football. It ricocheted off another player and flew into the goal with a thud.

He turned to me and grinned. "That's how to put them in the back of the net."

"I thought your job as goalie was to keep them out of the net," I said.

Cyril pulled a rueful grimace. "Yeah! That's the theory."

"You let in eighty-four goals last season."

"But I did save one penalty." He shrugged like a guilty man who hasn't told the whole truth. "The striker's contact lenses fell out as he took the shot. It went wide."

We were in the living room of Cyril's modest end-terraced house in the Ifield part of Crawley. There was a small sofa and an easy chair. There was a 17-inch Ekco television set in the corner. A Crawley Rovers' scarf hung over the fireplace.

The room was dominated by the table football. Two teams of wooden footballers faced one another. A red team. A blue team. They were mounted on poles with handles. You could move the poles back and forth to change the players' positions on the pitch. And you could twist the handles to make the players kick the ball.

It was a handsome item the size of a small dining room table. Designed for children from six to sixty. The sort of toy where the kids wouldn't get a look-in when dad was around. And clearly, Cyril's pride and joy.

I said: "This must've set you back a bob or two."

Cyril grinned. "Not a penny. Got left out with the bins. Don't know why. Perhaps whoever owned it had had enough. Got beat too often. Nifty and Bill helped me get it home."

"Do you often pick up useful stuff on the bins?" I asked.

Cyril shrugged again. "Sometimes. Of course, we're not supposed to – so don't mention that if you're writing about me."

Cyril was a good-looking man in his mid-thirties. He had a tanned face topped by a thatch of fair hair. He had broad shoulders and strong arms. He had quiet manners and an old-fashioned air about him. In a room full of people, he'd be the shy one standing in the corner.

Perhaps that's why on a Saturday afternoon, he was the one freezing his nuts off in the goal.

I looked around the room. There were no feminine touches. No lacy doilies on an occasional table. No ornaments on the mantlepiece. No rug in front of the fireplace. No sewing basket tucked behind the comfy chair.

All the furniture had been pushed back to the walls to make room for the football table.

I said: "I suppose you give your wife a game on the table of an evening?"

Of course, I knew what answer I'd get. That's why I'd asked the question.

Cyril twiddled one of the football table's handles. "I'm divorced. It happened about eighteen months ago. Sometimes Nifty or Bill come round to give me a game. With my job for the council and training sessions at the Rovers, I keep busy."

"Will you be playing next season?"

"If they ask me. I expect they'll stick me in goal again. Even though they do nothing but moan when I let one in. I mean to say, even Gordon Banks lets the occasional shot over the line."

I ran my hand idly along the edge of the football table.

"Do you think the absence of Sergio Parisi will make a difference?"

Cyril gave a mirthless laugh. "Absence? That's a good way of putting it."

"You didn't like him?" I asked.

"He didn't like me."

"Why was that?"

Cyril looked towards a door on the other side of the room. It led to the kitchen.

He said: "I'd offer you a cup of tea, but I'm out of milk."

I said: "You didn't answer the question. Why didn't Sergio like you?"

"I don't think he liked a lot of people. That was his way. Take the World Cup. We were all supporting England. Even though he was on the committee down at the Rovers, he insisted on supporting Italy. He was just provoking us."

"He was born Italian. He could never change that."

"Then if he didn't want to support England, why did he choose to live here? Why did he take our money day after day in that greasy spoon café of his? I laughed like a drain when North Korea knocked Italy out of the cup. I'd have laughed even more if I'd known Parisi was alive to hear of the defeat."

"You're bitter because Sergio criticised you unfairly. But that's the way football is. The guys that stand on the terraces of a Saturday afternoon aren't philosophers pondering the mysteries of the universe. They see the world in black and white. You either win or you lose."

Cyril grinned. "You're wrong about that. You can draw."

"To the guy on the terraces, that's just another way of not winning. All I'm saying is that's the way Sergio was. When he had a go at you, I don't think there'd be anything personal in it. He was just letting his frustrations rule his tongue."

Cyril shrugged. "It was his way of boasting – by running down people he didn't think were as good as him. But he was nothing special."

I let that sink in for a moment.

Cyril was silent. His gaze flicked around the room, like he wondered whether he'd shot his mouth off.

I said: "Did you ever use Sergio's café?"

"Used to. But not now. I just avoid the place."

"So you haven't been to the café recently?"

"That's what I just said."

I considered that.

I said: "I met Nifty and Bill yesterday. They told me they'd urged you to confront Sergio at his café about the way he treats you. They told me you said you'd done that."

Cyril's eyes flashed angrily. "You've been talking about me behind my back."

I gave a disarming grin. Like, what was I supposed to do? Doesn't always work. But seemed to have some effect this time.

"It's what journalists do when they're on a story," I said.

"What story?"

"Who killed Sergio?"

"That wasn't me," Cyril shouted.

I held up my hands. "Calm down. Just tell me what happened."

Cyril shrugged. Crossed the room and slumped on the sofa. I took that as an invitation to sit in the easy chair.

Cyril looked at his hands. Didn't see anything there to help.

He said: "I went to the café on Saturday afternoon. A quiet time. I thought that if there wasn't anybody there, it would be easy to talk to Sergio. You know, without either of us getting angry."

I nodded. "I understand."

"I noticed there was a girl in there, so I waited round the corner until she'd left. Then I went in. Sergio wasn't in the café but I could hear him moving around in the kitchen. Sounded like he was clearing up pots and pans. At least, I think it was him."

"And you called out?"

"No."

"Why not?"

"Because I saw something."

"Saw something. What?"

"An open envelope with the World Cup Final ticket. The one

that Parisi had won in the raffle. It was just lying on the counter. He'd been showing it to the girl."

"The one who'd been in the café while you hid around the corner?"

"Yeah. Parisi would have boasted about what a brilliant guy he was. He was like that. I just stood there and stared at it. I couldn't believe my luck. This was the perfect way to bring Sergio down a peg or two. To get my own back."

"So you took the ticket?"

Cyril looked away. Pulled a rueful grin. Part embarrassment, part apology.

"Sergio didn't know I was in the café," he said. "Nobody did. When he came back and found the ticket missing, he'd think the girl had come back and taken it. Of course, I didn't intend to keep it. Just give him a few miserable days wondering where it had gone. Then I'd sneak it through his door in the middle of the night. But the following day, we all learnt that he was dead."

"So you've got the World Cup ticket?"

Cyril's gaze travelled around the room. Alighted on the football table.

He smiled.

"Not now," he said. "I gave it away."

Chapter 10

I sat in Cyril's comfy chair and gawped at him.

He sat on the sofa and grinned. I could hardly blame him. A goalie who's picked the ball out of the back of the net eighty-four times in the last season doesn't have many moments to savour.

I said: "Let's get this clear – you've stolen one person's World Cup Final ticket and given it to a second person. What are you? The Robin Hood of the soccer field?"

Cyril said: "It's not like that at all."

"What is it like?"

"I saw an opportunity and I took it."

"Who have you given the ticket to?"

"That's a secret."

I stood up. Stepped across to the football table. Picked up the ball and tossed it casually in my hand. I rolled it down the pitch into the goal.

I turned to Cyril. "Let's get the facts straight. You have stolen property belonging to Sergio and passed it on to a person or persons unknown. You are guilty of theft as well as handling stolen goods. If you sold the ticket to this unknown person, you will also be guilty of obtaining a pecuniary advantage."

"No, I gave the ticket away. Like a gift."

"Don't get the idea you're being nominated as benefactor of the year. You're more likely to have your collar felt."

"The cops don't know."

"Yet."

"You wouldn't tell them. That would make you a grass."

"That would make me an honest member of the public reporting a crime. But let's park that thought for a moment. I'm beginning to wonder whether we shouldn't look at a more serious possibility."

Cyril bit his bottom lip. "What possibility?"

"That you killed Sergio."

Cyril leapt off the sofa. "No, no, no."

I said: "Let's try this theory. You went to Sergio's café, just as you said. You entered after the girl had left. You heard Sergio banging around in the kitchen. You saw the Cup Final ticket on the counter. But instead of pocketing it immediately, you delayed. You knew what you were about to do was wrong. But you were angry with Sergio and wanted to hurt him. So after a few seconds reflection, you took the ticket…

"No."

"…Just as Sergio walked back into the café. He saw what you were about to do. No doubt you lied that you were only taking a look. But Sergio knew what you planned. An argument started. A ferocious argument. Blows were struck and you hit Sergio on the back of the head. He collapsed and died on the floor. You immediately recognised the danger you were in. But it was now past the café's closing time. And being a Saturday afternoon, there would be no more customers until Monday morning. So you locked the café door. Dragged Sergio's body across the café into the kitchen. Made it look as though he had slipped and hit his head on the edge of the hob. Then you left the café by the back door."

Cyril clasped his head in his hands. "No, no, no. It's not true. I just took the ticket and ran."

I pointed at the sofa. "Sit down."

Defiance flashed in Cyril's eyes. His fists balled. Ready to clock me. He thought better of it. Sat down. Like the bad boy in class.

I said: "This is what I'm going to do. For the moment, I'm prepared to believe your story. But don't think that I've dismissed the murder alternative from my mind for ever. I'll keep my theory to myself. But I want the name of the person to whom you've given the Cup Final ticket."

I felt a bit of a heel. I knew my theory would have been pic apart by a rookie defence lawyer on sleeping tablets. But C. had stolen the ticket – and the price to pay was the name of the person to whom he'd given it.

Cyril was slumped on the sofa. He looked like a goalie who'd made the save of the century. And then dropped the ball over the goal line.

"I gave the ticket to Judith Kershaw," he said.

"The committee member of Crawley Rovers?"

Cyril nodded. "She's also games mistress at the St Hilda's Academy for Gentlewomen."

"Why did you give the ticket to Judith? No, let me guess. Would Cupid's dart have anything to do with it?"

"Don't know what you're rambling on about."

"You're in love with Judith."

"I thought if I gave her something she really wanted, she might be willing to meet me for a drink, or something, one evening."

"And is she?"

"She said she'd think about it."

I sighed. "Let me give you a second-hand piece of advice."

"Second hand?" Cyril queried.

"Mark Twain's advice: Never allow someone to be your priority while allowing yourself to be their option."

I don't know why but that seemed to cheer Cyril up.

He pointed at the football table. "Like a game before you go?" he said.

I shook my head. In my book, Cyril had already scored an own goal.

I stepped outside and closed the door after me.

It was the following day before I had the chance to track down Judith Kershaw.

St Hilda's Academy for Gentlewomen occupied an old

Jacobean house in one of those villages just north of Haywards Heath.

As I drove there along winding country lanes, I wondered exactly what a teacher at a top girls' school thought she was doing when she accepted the World Cup ticket. After all, she must have known it had been stolen.

The school proved to be at the end of a lengthy drive lined with rhododendron bushes. It was an imposing pad built of brown brick, mellowed by age. There were leadlight windows. Tall chimneys that reached for the sky. A dark stone archway. A heavy oak door hung from rusty cast-iron hinges. It would have made a great backdrop for a Hammer horror movie.

My MGB crunched to a halt on the gravel drive and I climbed out.

I'd been worrying about how to speak to Judith Kershaw without causing suspicion among the other staff. If a random man turned up at the school and asked to see her, they would surely want to know why.

I toyed with the idea of saying I'd called to put my daughter's name down for a place. But that would only put me on the wrong end of an interrogation. About her name. How old she was. Whether she played the violin. Whether she had her own pony. And I wanted to ask the questions.

I walked towards the oak door thinking I'd just have to wing it. Not for the first time. But it wouldn't be easy to explain why a lone man was prowling around a girls' school.

I was pondering this, when a loud blast on a whistle cut through the air.

The sound came from the side of the school. I hurried over to the corner and peered around it.

Fifty yards away, a group of girls in sweaters and shorts had just finished a game of football. They milled about. Patted each other's backs. Offered commiserations to the losers.

A woman with short blonde hair cut in a bob gave another

blast on the whistle which hung from a lanyard around her neck. She was wearing a blue track suit and football boots.

She shouted something at the girls. They hurried towards a side door that led into the school.

I stepped around the corner and strode towards the woman I hoped was Judith Kershaw. If she wasn't, I had some explaining to do.

I was half-way towards her when she saw me. She glared for a moment, then broke into a jog-trot to close the distance between us. Her lithe figure moved athletically towards me.

I'd put her at about forty. She looked good on it. She had hazel eyes, a pert nose, and a strong chin.

She jogged towards me and called out: "Stop right there."

A bossy manner, too. But I guess that came with the territory for a games mistress.

I said: "Judith Kershaw?"

"Yes. What do you want?"

"I'd like to see your World Cup Final ticket."

That put a crimp in her lithe movements. She jogged to a halt five feet from me. Her hands rested angrily on her hips. If the look from those hazel eyes could kill, I'd have called the undertaker.

"Whoever you are, you're clearly mad. I shall call the caretaker to remove you."

"What with? His mop and bucket?"

"Don't be impertinent." She raised the whistle to her lips.

"I know why Cyril Hands gave you the ticket. I want to know why you took it."

She dropped the whistle on the lanyard. Moved closer. Glanced as the last of the girls disappeared into the school.

She whispered: "Are you a blackmailer?"

"Worse than that. I'm a journalist." I flashed my press card. "Colin Crampton, *Evening Chronicle*."

"So you're going to humiliate me in your newspaper. Just

because I want to go to a football match. You wouldn't do that to a man."

"I'm not in the business of humiliating anyone. But I am in the business of writing a story about why a man was murdered – and why his World Cup Final ticket went missing."

Judith looked towards the school again. All the girls had gone inside. She took her hands off her hips. Relaxed a little. Stroked her chin while she thought.

I stood there and waited.

After a moment, she said: "We need to speak somewhere private. The sports pavilion. This way."

She turned on her heels and marched smartly across the field.

The sports pavilion turned out to be behind a stand of sycamore trees. Judith pulled a key from the pocket in her track-suit, opened the door, and we went it. The place had recently been whitewashed. The whiff of fresh paint hung in the air – cut through with the acrid tang of disinfectant.

At one end of a long room, there was a stack of folding chairs.

Judith took a couple of them and set two down facing each other.

We sat.

I said: "When you accepted the ticket from Cyril, didn't you for a moment wonder whether he'd been the person who'd killed Sergio Parisi?"

Judith shook her head. "He told me exactly what happened. He'd gone to the café to remonstrate with Sergio and found the ticket on the counter. I believed him."

I said: "Yet you now have that ticket. And the cops, who are blundering about in search of Sergio's killer, could find that suspicious. They may even wonder whether you'd visited the café and killed Sergio for it."

"That's nonsense."

"But you had a motive. You hate Sergio because he's ridiculed your dream of having a women's team at Crawley Rovers."

Judith leaned forward on her chair. "Sergio is… was… a male chauvinist pig. He thought the role of women in football is to sit in the stand and look pretty. Or perhaps we can hand round the drinks after the match. He didn't realise that we can play the game well – just as I'm teaching my girls to do."

"I've heard that Sergio was only voicing what some of the other committee members at the club were thinking. You were furious that Sergio turned up at the last moment and swung the vote against a women's team. That would give you a motive for killing Sergio."

Judith bounded off her chair. "I don't need to listen to these insults."

I said: "Calm down and sit down. As it happens, I don't think you killed Sergio, but you must be prepared that others might think so."

Judith shrugged and sat down.

"I know why Cyril gave you the ticket. He has a romantic interest in you. He thought it would make you think better of him. Even accept his invitation to a date."

"I do not go on dates… At least, not with men."

"I don't think Cyril is aware of that."

"Few are, Mr Crampton."

"What I can't understand is why you accepted the ticket when you must've known its provenance."

"At first, I thought it would be a blow for women. Especially for women in football. There will be one hundred thousand people at the World Cup Final – and only a few of them will be women. I wanted to be one of them, and to spread the gospel of women's football at the sport's supreme event."

"And that was worth overlooking the fact that Cyril had stolen something? That it made you a receiver of stolen goods?"

"How can something that belongs to the world be stolen?"

I ignored that attempt at hand-me-down philosophy. Instead, I asked: "And do you still intend to use the ticket?"

Judith's lips curled into a knowing smile.

"I no longer have the ticket," she said.

That had my attention. This was turning into a game of pass the parcel.

I said: "Who has the ticket now?"

"The chairman of Crawley Rovers, Mr Vernon Stoker."

I thought about that for a moment.

"Surely, as a football club chairman, he'd receive his own ticket?"

"The demand is so high only the chairmen of Football League clubs receive a gratis ticket. Crawley Rovers isn't a member of the Football League. I know Mr Stoker feels that keenly. He would dearly love to rub shoulders with the giants of football at the World Cup Final. That's why I gave him the ticket."

"Instead of going yourself and striking a blow for women in football?" I asked.

"I decided that giving the ticket to Mr Stoker would strike a bigger blow."

"Because you've persuaded him to set up a women's team?"

"He's promised to put the idea to the committee again – and this time support it himself."

I said: "Didn't Stoker express qualms about taking a ticket that had been stolen from a man who may have been murdered for it?"

"Mr Stoker is a used car dealer. He lives in a rough world. He is no stranger to the problems caused by the sale of stolen vehicles. And, above all, he would do anything to get a ticket to the World Cup Final."

We were silent for a moment while I thought about that.

Then Judith said: "I suppose it's pointless to ask you to keep my name out of your paper?"

I said: "I research news stories and I write what I find – the truth and nothing but the truth."

"That's what all journalists say."

"At the *Chronicle,* we mean what we say. I can't promise not to mention you. But if I do, I'll make it factual and keep the school out of it as much as I can."

Judith managed a wan little smile at that.

"In return, I'd like you to do something for me," I said.

"What's that?"

"Don't mention the fact we've had this conversation to Mr Stoker."

"Why not?"

"I'd like it to be a nice surprise when I tell him I know all about his World Cup Final ticket."

But when I reached the Crawley Rovers' ground later than afternoon, Vernon Stoker wasn't around.

I stuck my head round the door of Betty Mulligan's office. Empty. (The office, that is. I had plenty of ideas teeming in my head.)

I stepped out onto the ground and looked around. No sign of Lennox Slattery, the groundsman, either.

At the far side of the pitch, the door to the groundsman's hut was swinging open. I stepped onto the hallowed turf and made my way across the ground.

As I approached the hut, I heard a groan come from somewhere inside. I hurried on in case Slattery was in there and had just had an accident with his mower.

But when I stepped through the door, Slattery was sitting on a crate watching a small television. The TV was balanced on a pile of boxes in the corner. It was showing one of the games in the World Cup. The quarter-final match between North Korea and Portugal.

The very match for which Shirl had modelled the Asian side's kit on the front page of the *Daily Mirror.* The kit didn't look so good on the players. Just my opinion.

The TV commentator was telling viewers the match had about

ten minutes to go.

And it looked as though the *Mirror's* football tipster had given Shirl a bum steer. North Korea were taking a beating. Portugal led five goals to three.

I switched my attention from the TV to Slattery. His head swivelled round. He loosed off a nuclear-powered hate glare in my direction.

I said: "I heard a cry of pain come from the hut. I thought you might have caught something painful in your motor mower."

Slattery said: "Jose Augusto scored."

"Did it hurt that much?"

"It puts Portugal two goals in the lead."

"No doubt they deserve it."

Slattery stood up. Faced me with his shoulders hunched and his hands balled into fists.

"No, it's not all right. The biased referee awarded Portugal two unfair penalties."

"All's fair in love, war... and football," I said.

"Not these penalties. In the first one, it was obvious Torres accidentally stumbled. Probably a divot on the turf. Happens all the time in football. The ref said he'd been tripped. Didn't look like that to me."

"The ref was there to see."

Slattery gestured angrily at the TV set. "And you think I don't trust the evidence of my own eyes when I'm watching that?"

"Well, there's always room for an honest difference of opinion."

That seemed to make Slattery even angrier. "There could have been no difference over the second penalty. Eusébio clearly slipped in the penalty area. Over-watered pitch. Mad to play football in July anyway. No wonder they have to soak the pitches to keep them playable."

On the TV, the match wound into its last minutes.

I said: "Why don't you watch the end of the game?"

Slattery perched petulantly on his crate. "Why should I? It's obvious that the ref's been got at."

"All refs are biased according to all fans. That's why 'Have you lost your glasses, ref?' and similar badinage are familiar on the terraces."

"But this ref has changed the course of history."

"It's a football match. Not a world war."

"Without those two penalties, the match would have been drawn. They'd have played extra time – another thirty minutes. The match could have gone either way. I think the Koreans would have regained the form they found in the first half when they scored three goals. Yes, a ref who changed the course of history. A disgrace to a football field."

Slattery turned sullenly toward the TV as the ref blew the final whistle.

"That ref will never sleep soundly in his bed again," he muttered under his breath.

"It's good to know the Corinthian spirit lives on at Crawley Rovers," I said.

It didn't look like Slattery was about to throw a party. More likely a tantrum.

So I stepped outside and walked slowly across the pitch.

I couldn't get back to Brighton fast enough.

Chapter 11

But, as it turned out, my return to Brighton was unexpectedly delayed.

As I crossed the pitch, I noticed a young lad sitting on the steps leading up to the team dressing rooms.

I changed direction and walked towards him.

I put his age at about fourteen. The way he was sitting he could have modelled for Rodin's *Thinker* statue. He was resting his chin on his hand and he stared at the ground.

He looked like a lad with something on his mind.

But he raised his head as I approached and smiled. He had the kind of face that would make him a lot of friends throughout his life. An open face that held no dark secrets behind the blue-grey eyes. No nostrils that would ever flare in anger. No lips that would curl into a sneer. A firm chin that showed strength of purpose.

He would spend a lot of time listening patiently to other people's problems. And he would become the wiser for it.

As I got closer, I realised the lad was wearing a polio brace on his left leg. There was a strap just above the knee and another around the ankle. The two were joined by a metal rod. A broad leather strap was mounted on the rod. The strap wrapped around his leg.

I strode up and said: "You're a tad early for the first match of the season."

"September the third," he said.

"Want to get first claim on a seat in the front row of the stand?"

"I'm waiting for my dad. He's in the changing rooms checking the kit for the next training session."

"Your dad?"

"Wayne Matthews. He's the team's captain. I'm his son Christopher."

"Colin Crampton. Reporter on the *Evening Chronicle*. So you're a big football fan, too?"

"Can't get enough of it. I hate the summer when there are no matches. Of course, I can't play myself."

Not a hint of self-pity in his last words. Just a statement of fact.

I said: "I expect you've been following the World Cup."

"It's great. I think England will win it. Watched them on the telly earlier. They beat Argentina. One nil. Geoff Hurst scored in the seventy-eighth minute."

"You certainly are a fan. And a good reporter who gets his facts straight."

Christopher glanced away. A touch embarrassed by the compliment.

He ran his hands through a mop of unruly brown hair.

"There was some talk of me getting a ticket to the World Cup Final," he said shyly. "I'd have loved that. But…"

"But the club decided to raffle the ticket."

Christopher nodded. "Only fair, I suppose."

"And you'll have read in the papers that the man who won it died. Murdered in his own café."

"Yes." Christopher thought for a moment. "That ticket seemed to come with a curse."

The comment took me by surprise. I'd never looked at it in that way until now.

I said: "I guess there were plenty of people in the club who would have liked that ticket?"

"My dad says everyone wanted it. There was a big argument. They all staked their claims. And then they started to run down each other by saying they didn't deserve it. Horrible. Why do grown-ups have to behave that way?"

"Because they lack the wisdom of kids like you," I said.

The door to the changing rooms opened and a man stepped out.

Wayne Matthews, I assumed. He had the same open face that he'd bequeathed to his son. But Wayne's was set in a frown.

He focused on Christopher. Didn't notice me.

He said: "The laundry has put too much starch in the wash again. The shorts are like they've been made out of hardboard. The lads will be running round the field like their bollocks are in a box."

Christopher laughed.

Wayne noticed me. "Who are you?"

"It's Colin Crampton from the *Evening Chronicle*," Christopher said.

"We've been talking about the World Cup. I hear Christopher is a big fan," I said.

"Yeah! Not big enough, it seems," he said sourly.

"You mean about the World Cup Final ticket?"

"Yeah! Went to an Italy supporter. They're not even in the competition anymore."

"Did you know the ticket has gone missing since Sergio Parisi was killed?"

"I guess the guy who murdered him took it."

"Any idea who that might be?" I asked.

"Why should I? I just make out the match team sheets and run the training sessions."

"And score most of the goals," Christopher added.

"Not hard to see who your biggest fan is," I said.

Wayne grinned. "Chris' hero is Bobby Moore. Not that that means much, as he'll never get to see him play."

"I will on television, Dad."

"Yeah! On television!" Wayne said.

"Are you bitter about Christopher not getting the ticket?" I asked.

Wayne gave me a hard look.

He knew I wanted to ask him whether he'd killed Sergio. But that I wouldn't mention it in front of Christopher.

"Not bitter. It's like when you take a long shot at goal from thirty yards out. You've run from your own penalty area and dribbled round the other teams' defenders. The ball is on a perfect arc to carry it into the net. Then a puff of wind changes its flight. And it hits the crossbar. The goal you'd have talked about for the rest of your life has just become an empty memory."

He stopped and glanced at Christopher. Looked back at me wondering whether he'd said too much.

A moment of awkward silence hung in the air.

Then Christopher said: "We all have our dreams, Dad."

Wayne patted Christopher on the shoulder. "Yeah! And your mum will have those dreams on the fire if I don't get you home for supper in time."

Christopher struggled to his feet and took his father's arm. I watched them cross the pitch.

The father who could run the length of the field and score a goal – and the son who never would.

I had a lot to think about as I drove back to Brighton.

The ups and downs I'd had during the day made the roller-coaster on Palace Pier look as flat as an ironing board.

I'd thought that if I could trace the Cup Final ticket, I'd find Sergio's killer. Now I wasn't so sure.

I still hadn't made up my mind whether butterfingers goalkeeper Cyril Hands could have killed Sergio. With his table football set and his moon-eyes for Judith Kershaw, he came across as an amiable dope. Yet a guy who lets in eighty-four goals but still keeps going must have some backbone. And there was no doubt he'd been needled for a long time by Sergio.

Then there was Judith Kershaw. On the face of it, she was the recipient of an unexpected gift. But was she quite as innocent of Sergio's killing as she seemed? She was quite prepared to break the law by handling stolen goods – the Cup Final ticket. I'm no expert on games mistresses at posh girls' schools – Shirley can confirm that – but I guess not many conspire in serious crimes. Could that gift of the ticket have been quite as unexpected as Judith suggested? In fact, could Judith have talked head-over-heels-in-love Cyril into it?

She'd said she'd passed the ticket on to Vernon Stoker. But if she'd wanted the ticket badly enough, perhaps that had been her plan after all. She was passionate about her scheme for a women's football team. I had the impression she was not a woman to let obstacles stand in her way.

I didn't know what to make of Lennox Slattery. He seemed to lead a loner's life. And when the world offers you only an empty space, you have little to do but build obsessions in it. I know football fans are passionate about their teams. But Slattery was clearly worked up about the penalties Portugal had been awarded. Perhaps one of his obsessions was a finely tuned sense of justice. Especially as meted out by football referees.

Then there was poor Christopher Matthews and his father Wayne. Chris was a great kid, disappointed that he'd not been given the Cup Final ticket but realistic enough to understand why. After the knocks life had dealt him, he'd know how to handle disappointment.

But Wayne wasn't like that. He'd felt deeply the committee's decision to raffle the ticket rather than give it to Christopher. But could he have murdered Sergio for it? He couldn't kill Sergio and then suddenly produce the ticket without throwing suspicion on himself. On the other hand, if Sergio died at the hands of a person or persons unknown, then the committee would need to decide again what to do with the ticket. Perhaps, then, they would give it to Christopher. But that would have involved Wayne leaving the ticket intact at Sergio's café. And it had disappeared.

Which brought me back to Cyril Hands again. Perhaps his story about finding the ticket on the counter was true. And if that was the case someone unconnected with Crawley Rovers could have killed Sergio.

As I pulled the MGB into the kerb outside the *Chronicle* building, I felt I was no further forward. And Figgis would be wanting copy. I decided I'd turn out a few hundred words of speculation. A piece written from the wrists, as we'd say in the newsroom when we needed to produce copy without any hard information. Figgis would know what I'd done, but I banked on his letting it go.

But when I reached the newsroom, Figgis had left for the day. Anyway, he knew I was on the case.

I called Shirley. She sounded a bit down. Rosina had felt queasy and was now asleep in bed. Shirl put it down to a delayed reaction to the flight from Sicily. I thought she was probably right. I agreed to call at the apartment first thing the following morning.

I sat at my desk in the newsroom with an idea nagging at the back of my mind. It was like a little voice telling me I had something to do. I wished I could think of a way to get young Christopher Matthews a ticket for the World Cup Final.

And the nag at the back of my mind was turning into an idea. It would involve making a call from the newsroom when no one else was around.

I glanced around the place. Only Phil Bailey was still at his desk – head down and typing out a lengthy court report.

I pulled the telephone towards me, lifted the handset, and dialled a London number.

It was nearly ten o'clock before I arrived back at my lodgings.

I'd treated myself to a fish and chip supper at Bardsley's in Baker Street. I'd washed down the cod in crispy batter with a couple of glasses of a flowery Sancerre. So, I was in a benign mood.

But that didn't last long after I opened the door and crept into the hall.

Light leaked from under the Widow's parlour door. She had the television on with the volume turned up. I could hear Richard Baker reading the news.

The Widow had a thing about Richard Baker. I think it had something to do with his spectacles. Baker was saying something about the economy (not good). But the Widow wouldn't bother about that. She'd be drooling over the set, lost in some disgusting fantasy.

I put my ear to the door, to see if I could hear anything else.

"Mr Crampton," said an imperious voice behind me. "What are you doing with your ear to my door?"

I spun around. The Widow was coming up the passage from the kitchen. She was carrying a glass filled with a brown liquid.

I said: "I thought I heard voices. Could have been burglars."

She said: "You can hear Mr Richard Baker reading the news. I have just been to the kitchen to pour myself a refreshing glass of milk stout. I wouldn't normally drink at this time of night, but I have a problem on my mind."

I said: "Sorry, I can't be of assistance," as I scooted towards the stairs.

Too slow. The Widow got there first and barred my escape.

She took a draught of her stout. It left a moustache of white foam on her upper lip.

She said: "I have been to the building society today and taken out five hundred pounds in cash. But now I realise I have nowhere safe to keep it."

"You could always put it back in the building society."

"I need the money for Wednesday morning."

"What's happening then?"

"Those two charming young men, Harvey and Lloyd, have promised to call and set me on the road to riches beyond my wildest dreams."

"I thought your wildest dreams usually involved Richard Baker."

"Mr Crampton, don't be disgusting."

But the Widow blushed.

"I thought I warned you about Harvey and Lloyd," I said. "They're con-men. They'll have the five hundred pounds and be away on their toes. Trust me, I'm a crime reporter."

"In my book, that is not a recommendation. But you still haven't answered my question. Where can I safely put my five hundred pounds until Harvey and Lloyd call?"

"What about your bureau? You can lock that."

"I've lost the key."

"You could put the wad at the back of the knife drawer in the kitchen."

"Too risky. If a burglar finds it, he'll then use one of the knives to cut my throat."

"You could take the backing plate off the Holman Hunt *Light of the World* picture and stuff the notes in. Replace the plate and the wad will make the front bulge out a bit. But it'll just make it look like the old bloke in the picture has put on a bit of weight."

"I could never abuse a valued artwork in that manner."

"Then I don't know what to suggest."

"You've been no help."

"Unless…" I began.

"Unless what?"

"Many ladies, I've been told in confidence, hide valuables at the back of a drawer holding their intimate underclothes."

The Widow had a hearty gulp of her milk stout.

"Mr Crampton, I think you've hit on the answer. I shall stuff the money in one of my surgical stockings and hide it in the drawer behind my Patti Page bullet brassiere with foam padding and reinforced steel frame."

She swept across the hall, opened her parlour door, and marched inside.

I headed upstairs wondering how I was going to stop the Widow handing her life savings to two con-men.

Chapter 12

When I arrived at Shirley's flat the following morning, Rosina was in the bathroom throwing up.

A horrible retching sound, like water trying to bubble down a blocked drain, came from behind the bathroom door.

Shirley paced the living room. "That's the third time since seven o'clock this morning," she said.

"Not last night's chicken vindaloo from the take-away round the corner?" I asked.

Shirl flashed me a warning look. "That's not funny."

"Agreed. Nothing is amusing about Naveen's vindaloo. Especially at seven o'clock in the morning."

"It's nothing to do with curry."

"What then?"

Shirley turned to face me. She had a resigned look on her face. "Rosina is expecting."

"Expecting what?"

Shirl clapped her hands to her head. "Jeez! Why did God even bother to invent men?" She moved closer so she could spell it out. "Rosina is expecting a baby."

I sat down so suddenly on the sofa the broken spring twanged a note. F sharp, I think.

"Rosina is pregnant?" I said in a dull voice.

"Finally, he gets it," Shirl said.

"So, this…" I began

"…is a bout of early morning sickness." Shirley finished my sentence.

"How did that happen?" I held up a hand. "Ignore that. Obviously, I know in general terms how it happened. I was thinking specifics."

"And there we have another problem," Shirl said. "Rosina hasn't admitted she's up the duff. At least, not to me. She's blaming this performance on a sudden change in temperature and the English food." This time, Shirl held up a warning hand. "No, not chicken vindaloo."

I sat there trying to take it in.

The sound of another technicolour yawn echoed from the bathroom.

I said: "The first thing we must do is to get her to admit she has a bun in the oven. This throws a new light on Brando's attempts to track her down."

"Do you think he knows?" Shirley asked.

"I don't know. But I guess Rosina must have admitted the truth to herself by now."

"Poor kid may only have been sure for a few days."

From the bathroom came the sound of a lavatory flushing. A door opened and closed and Rosina stepped into the living room.

Her face was pasty white. Her hair straggled untidily around her head. She was wearing a long nightshirt. She had one of Shirl's cardigans draped around her shoulders.

Her gaze travelled from me to Shirl and back again. Her head tilted forward a little, like it does when folk get embarrassed. They just can't help it.

She said: "I guess whatever that was I won't eat it again."

Shirl moved across the room and put her arm around Rosina's shoulders.

"We know it wasn't the food," Shirl said. "Best to admit it to yourself when you're with friends."

Rosina threw her arms around Shirl's neck, rested her head on her shoulders, and sobbed like she'd just been invited to her own funeral.

It was half an hour before Rosina had calmed enough to speak.

She sat in the easy chair clutching a mug of sweet tea in both hands. Seeking its warmth. It wasn't cold but the retching of the early morning sickness had knocked the stuffing out of the poor girl.

I leaned forward and said: "If we're to help you, we need to know the truth."

Shirley rested a restraining hand upon my arm. "What Colin means is... tell us what happened in your own words."

Rosina sipped her tea for a few moments. We sat in silence. Watched as her eyes darted back and forth. She was trying to work out what it all meant in her own mind.

She put down the tea mug and said: "If only my papa had never met Brando's family."

"What does that mean?" I asked.

"I've told you that papa wanted me to marry Brando. It suited his business with Brando's powerful family. I knew I would never love Brando, but I thought I might have a tolerable life with him if he looked after me."

"But that never happened?" Shirley asked.

"He was never often at home. In the evenings, more often he'd hang out at the *Trattoria Garibaldi* or the *Bar Mazzini*. I heard he saw other women. I could have put up with that. After all, ours was not a love match. I was part of a transaction. But it was worse."

"Because Brando had a temper?" I asked.

"And powerful fists." Rosina had another sip of tea. "One day after a particularly bad beating – but with no bruises to show for it – I was in the market at Naxos when I saw a new stall. There was a huge bowl of delicious *Nocellara* olives. They come from the *Valle de Belice* in south-west Sicily. They are big and juicy and delicious. I knew that they were Brando's favourites. And I thought I would buy some for him. I thought it would please him. Perhaps he would be kinder to me."

"I'd have laced them with cyanide," Shirley said.

This time, I placed a restraining hand on Shirl's arm.

Rosina said: "The stall was run by a young man I'd not seen

at the market before. He was called Ricardo. He had brown hair that was wild and eyes that were always looking for fun."

"And you began an affair with Ricardo?"

Anger flashed in Rosina's eyes. "You think I don't deserve love. I had no love from Brando and I wanted some. When I looked at the fun in Ricardo's eyes, I knew he could give me love."

"And a baby," I said.

"Colin!" Shirley spoke sharply.

"Yes," Rosina said. "The baby is Ricardo's. I was sure about a week ago. And I knew I had to get away from Brando. He would kill me if he discovered I was having another man's child. So I called my papa. I thought he would help me. But when I spoke to him on the telephone, I knew that he would not be able to help me as much as I'd hoped."

"Why not?" Shirley asked.

"He had troubles of his own. I tried to get him to tell me about them. Even though I wanted help from him so badly. But he just told me that he might have to go away for a few days. I told him I had to come to England as I would not be safe in Sicily. Not after Brando found I was pregnant. Papa said I could stay in his apartment. He said he would leave some money for me. He said he would get in touch with me as soon as he could."

"Did he?" I asked.

Rosina shook her head. "The next call I got was from the police. They told me my papa was dead."

"And that was the day we found you in the amphitheatre?" I asked.

Rosina nodded.

I said: "Your father told you that he would leave you some money. But when the police searched Sergio's café and apartment, they found none – except a couple of pounds in the café's cash register."

"My father was too clever for the police," Rosina said. "He

would not leave money lying around the flat. It would be in his secret hiding place."

Shirley and I exchanged surprised glances.

"Do you know where this secret hiding place is?" I asked.

"Of course," Rosina said.

She stood up and stretched her arms. "I am feeling a little better," she said.

Funnily enough, after the news of the secret hiding place, so was I.

I shifted uncomfortably on the sofa to avoid the broken spring. I said: "How did you know about this secret hiding place?"

Rosina sat down again. Picked up her mug. Saw it was empty. Put it back on the table.

"Because my papa made it while I was still living with him."

"But why did he need one?"

Rosina shrugged. "My father was a traditional Sicilian. Secrecy is part of their way of life. For hundreds of years, the island had been a lawless place. Invaders came and took what they wanted. Why shouldn't people realise they had to hide what was valuable to them? True, papa had come to live in England. But old habits die hard."

"Sergio wasn't living in Sicily now. You haven't explained why he needed a secret hiding place," I said.

"Or why you needed to know about it," Shirley added.

Rosina pursed her lips in a little angry moue. She didn't like our cross-examination. But we had rescued her from an abusive husband and brought her to England. At our expense. I felt we deserved some answers.

I leant forward. "What you tell us could help the police catch your papa's killer."

Rosina relaxed a little. "I understand. Sorry. It was shortly after Brando's father had appeared on the scene. My father had agreed to do some business with him. He was looking for new ways to make money. The health inspectors had been to the café

106

and he needed to spend a lot of money on new equipment for the kitchen."

I nodded. Betty Mulligan had discovered Sergio had borrowed money from Vernon Stoker. No doubt he was anxious to pay it back.

Rosina said: "At the time, I was not sure what business papa had agreed to do with Brando's father. But I later learnt it was illegal. That papa was selling cigarettes and drink which had been brought into the country illegally."

"Smuggled," I said. "An ancient tradition in Sussex. All the ports along the coast were a haven for smugglers."

"Brando's father wanted papa's help because he had found a new and better way to smuggle goods. By air, through Gatwick Airport, just a few miles from Crawley."

I nodded. "Yes, the airport has grown fast in recent years. That doesn't surprise me."

Rosina continued: "Anyway, it turned out that papa had agreed to be a distributor of the goods. I remember soon after Brando's father had left, it started. Visitors at night to the back door of the café. Sometimes bringing boxes from the airport. Sometimes to collect. And always payments in cash. That's why papa needed the secret hiding place. Somewhere to keep the money in case there was a problem. Papa told me that if the police came, they would find it suspicious if there were large amounts of cash around. It was only a small café and didn't do much business. Papa spent too much time at the football club."

"Crawley Rovers," I said.

"Yes. If he'd spent more time at the café, he would have made more money and not needed to be a smuggler."

I asked: "Didn't you warn your papa about the dangers of becoming involved in smuggling?"

Rosina lowered her eyelids. Looked down at her hands. "I tried. But in Sicily a daughter doesn't tell her father what to do. It is the culture. And although papa had lived in England for many years, his heart was still on the island."

I said: "When your papa told you on the phone that he might have to go away for a few days, did he say why?"

"No."

"Was it to do with his smuggling side-line?"

"I don't think so. He didn't believe the police knew about that."

"He was wrong. They were just waiting for the right time to pounce."

Rosina scratched her head. "I think it was something else he'd got mixed up in. He sounded more worried than I've ever heard before. More worried than about the smuggling."

And he was right, I thought. Days later he was dead.

It didn't surprise me that the cops hadn't found the secret hiding place after Parisi was killed. Ted Wilson had told me Tomkins had never ordered a thorough search.

I looked at Shirley. She knew what I was going to say next. She knew she wouldn't like it, but that we had no choice.

I turned back to Rosina: "Where is this secret place?"

Rosina said: "Behind the counter in the café there are two doors. One leads into the kitchen and the other into a large pantry. Papa stores the café's supplies in there. One of the walls has shelves. Behind the bottom shelf, there is a wooden backing panel. It looks just like part of the shelving, but it has hidden hinges so it can fold down. Behind the panel, some of the bricks have been taken out and a wall safe has been put in. There is no way of knowing it is there."

"Cunning," I said.

"And you know how to crack the safe, kiddo?" Shirley asked.

"There are two keys. Papa had one and I had the other. He gave it to me before I left to live with Brando. I think he was uneasy about my future. I could tell from his eyes. He knew he had let me down. The key was my compensation."

"Where is the key?"

"I keep it sewn into the lining of my purse so no one can find it. I always have my purse with me."

"And the key opens the safe?" I asked.

"Not by itself. Despite all my precautions, papa was always worried that one of the keys would be found. So, there is also a combination lock worked by a dial on the front of the safe. You enter a four-digit number and then turn the key."

"What number?"

Rosina shrugged. "I don't know."

"So, we're stuffed, kiddo," Shirley said.

Rosina leaned forward eagerly. "No, no. Papa said he would need to change the code from time to time. But he would leave the latest version nearby. It is on the underneath of the tray which he puts the café kettle on."

"So, we can crack the code and open the safe," I said. "What are we waiting for?"

Chapter 13

There were no sightings of the cops when we arrived at Sergio's café.

No sign that they'd ever been. No police tape – do not cross. No evidence the place had been the scene of a brutal murder.

The front door displayed a single gravy-stained sign: CLOSED.

Rosina had been reluctant at first to make another journey to Crawley. I couldn't blame her. It's never easy to confront a difficult past. In this case, a past that had ended in violence.

But Shirley had sat close and talked softly to her. Made her realise that she'd have to face this at some time. And that the sooner she did, the higher the chance it would help the cops catch Sergio's killer.

Because of Rosina's "interesting condition" (copyright Victorian newspapers), Rosina had sat in the MGB's passenger seat. Shirley squeezed into the jump seat at the back.

I drove up the lane at the side of the café and parked out of sight of the road.

The police had given Rosina a set of keys to the café on our earlier visit. We used them to let ourselves in by the staff door.

I closed the door behind us and we stood silently in the passage leading to the café. A tap dripped. A floorboard creaked. The stale stench of food fried long ago hung in the air.

Rosina was the first to speak. "The pantry is this way."

We walked down the corridor into the café and skirted around the counter. Rosina opened the door to the pantry and switched on the light.

We crowded inside.

The shelves Rosina had described lined one wall. They were sparsely stacked. A few tins of baked beans. A large packet of cornflakes. A bag of rice. A bottle of HP sauce. If a cook suddenly appeared, they weren't going to rustle up a feast any time soon.

Across the room, a box contained a bottle of bleach and a tube of Vim scouring powder. A couple of mops and a bucket with a broken handle stood in the corner.

Rosina pointed at the bottom shelf. "This is where the backing board hinges down."

I knelt down and peered under the shelf above. The hinged board was a melamine contraption. It looked as though it was a backing plate to the shelves. The hinges had been cleverly concealed.

I reached in and got a couple of fingers in the tiny gap between the top of the board and the shelf above. It took a fair bit of pressure but eventually something clicked. The board hinged down.

Behind the board, a brick wall had been whitewashed. Several bricks had been taken out to create a cavity. Within the cavity, I could make out the black outline of the safe.

Rosina crouched down and said: "Here's a torch."

I took it and switched on. Now I could see the safe more clearly and read the figures on a dial in the middle of the door.

I stood up and said: "We need the code number."

"That's under the kettle's tray," Rosina said.

We hustled back into the café. Shirley grabbed the kettle and moved it to one side.

Rosina picked up the tray and turned it over.

"What's the number?" I asked.

A frown wrinkled Rosina's brow. She turned the tray back and looked at the top. Switched it over again and stared at the underneath.

"There's no number," she said.

"Are you sure this is the right tray? Could there be another kettle with a tray underneath it?"

Rosina twisted back and forth as she looked around the café. "No. This has always been the only kettle. This must be the right tray."

"Let me look," I said.

Rosina handed me the tray. I turned it over and gawped.

There were no numbers. But someone – presumably Sergio – had written some words. In Italian. On a slip of paper taped to the underside of the tray.

Six words. *Vinto. Troppo. Mangiato. Prefazione senza parola.*

Shirl said: "What is it?"

I handed her the tray. Her eyes widened in surprise.

"We're right royally stuffed," she said.

"But maybe not right royally," I said.

I turned to Rosina. "Did your papa say he would be leaving a list of words?"

Rosina shook her head. "He definitely said four numbers."

"And yet we have six words," I said. "But they must represent numbers. Rosina, you speak good Italian. Mine's fair to middling. Perhaps we can crack the code."

Shirley pouted in a moue. (I don't know why she thought that displeased me. Every time she did it, I wanted to kiss her. But we had more pressing business.)

Shirl said: "If this was in Kaurna, I'd piss it."

"What's that?" I asked.

"Kaurna or piss?"

"Kaurna," I said.

"The aboriginal language around the Adelaide Plains."

"The trouble is there's never an aboriginal code around when you need one."

"Just saying," Shirl said. She pulled up a chair and sat down.

I said: "Let's look at the Italian. The first word is *vinto*. I'm guessing that means conquering."

"Past tense," said Rosina. "Could be conquered."

"Don't see how that gets us anywhere. Let's try the second word, *troppo*. Means too much."

Rosina nodded: "And *mangiato* comes from the verb *mangiare* which means to eat."

"It's this last group of words – *prefazione senza parola* ı ʮ﹍ figure out. I understand the last two words mean 'without a word', but what's *prefazione*?"

"It's that bit at the front of a book, before you get to the first proper chapter," Rosina said. "I never bother to read it."

"You mean the 'foreword'?"

"Yes, but a foreword without words would just be a blank page."

Shirley jumped up. "You're a couple of plonkers. You're yammering away like a pair of puzzled professors. That last one – the answer is obvious. It's got nothing to do with blank pages."

Rosina and I looked at Shirl expectantly.

"What have you got if you have a foreword without the word bit?" Shirl paused. All the more to emphasise her triumph.

"Fore," she declared.

"And fore and four are homonyms, words that sound alike," I said. "So how could this work on *vinto*?"

"Apart from to conquer, the verb *vincere* could also mean to win," Rosina said.

"Which makes *vinto*, won – homonym for one."

"And *troppo* means too much," Rosina said.

"Drop the much and you have too, which is two," Shirl said.

"And *mangiato* the past participle of *mangiare*, to eat, gives ate or eight," Rosina said.

I breathed out deeply. "So, there is our number: one, two, eight, four."

We stood in a circle, shoulders slumped, after the excitement of the moment. Our faces were flushed. Our hearts were beating faster.

I said: "You should open the safe, Rosina."

We trooped back into the pantry.

Rosina first. Then Shirley and me. Shirl had looped her arm through mine. She foraged for my hand. Found it and gave it a little squeeze.

I whispered in her ear: "Kaurna girl, wait 'til I get you home."

Shirl gave a girlish squeal. "*Ooooh!*"

Rosina looked round sharply. "Concentrate, you two lovebirds."

I said: "We are."

Rosina knelt down by the bottom shelf with the key at the ready. She reached in to turn the safe's dial.

Her arm moved back and forth as she called out the numbers. "One. Two. Eight. Four. I'm inserting the key now. Turning it."

Click!

We all heard it.

Pouf!

Heard the sound as pent-up air in the safe was released when the door opened.

Rosina crawled back out from under the shelf. Looked up at me. "I don't want to do it."

"You've already done it," I said. "You've opened the safe."

"I don't want to put my hand inside."

"Nothing's going to bite it off."

"If you're sure about that, you do it."

She scrambled to her feet.

I said: "Give me your torch."

Rosina handed it to me. I stooped down and shone it inside the safe.

I could see a thick brown envelope. Nothing else.

I reached inside and pulled it out.

I stood up and opened the envelope's flap. I reached inside and pulled out a thick wad of five-pound notes. Must have been a hundred of them. I handed the money to Rosina.

She took it. "So, papa meant it when he said there'd be money," she said.

I took a closer look at the envelope. Standard office issue. No address on the outside. No special marks. Just an ordinary brown envelope.

But wait a minute. I opened the flap again. At the bottom of the envelope, there was a crumpled piece of paper. Must have been crushed down by the fivers when the wad was shoved in. I reached inside and took it out. It was a single sheet of notepaper. I handed it to Rosina.

She shook her head. "You read it," she said.

"It may be personal," I said.

"You know enough about me already."

I unfolded the paper. There was a typewritten message. No heading. No salutation. No signature.

Just these words: "This is the last money you'll get for throwing the parcel under the hedge. The parcel ended up in the wrong hands. So, don't ask for more. I make a good friend. A bad enemy."

Rosina's brow had furrowed. "What on earth does it mean?"

I stood there and felt my heart pounding harder. My pores were pricked with sweat. And a troop of can-can dancers were kicking up their legs to Offenbach's *La Vie Parisienne* music inside my stomach.

I knew exactly what it meant.

I said: "It means your papa was involved in the most audacious theft since 1911 when Vincenzo Peruggia walked into the Louvre in Paris, lifted the *Mona Lisa* off four pegs which held it, and left through the service entrance."

We hustled back into the café.

Me excited. Rosina puzzled. Shirley curious.

Shirley used the kettle to boil some water and make us a cup of coffee.

We hunkered down around one of the tables and sipped our drinks.

Rosina grasped her cup with both hands. She was shaking slightly. She'd turned very pale.

Shirley put her arm around Rosina's shoulders and hugged her.

I said: "This must be very difficult for you, but it might help to know what I think has happened. Let's start with the facts and move on to the speculation later."

Rosina looked worried, but nodded.

"It's like this," I said. "Five months ago, the Jules Rimet trophy, the World Cup, went on display at an exhibition. The exhibition was held in an unusual location, Westminster Central Hall, which is owned by the Methodist Church. The cup was the star attraction in an exhibition for philatelists."

"Philly who?" Rosina asked.

"Stamp collectors. Lots of post offices around the world had issued special stamps to commemorate the World Cup. The stamp exhibition had them on show – and the Jules Rimet trophy was a bonus exhibit. The exhibition opened on a Saturday, but the next day – Sunday – it closed so that the Methodists could hold their church services in other parts of the Central Hall."

"And that's when it was stolen?" Shirley said.

"Yes. When the exhibition was open, there were always two guards standing by the display case. But because the exhibition was closed, the guards were elsewhere patrolling the building. The thieves broke in by opening a back door into the exhibition room. The door was held closed by a wooden bar on the inside. But the screws which held the bar in place could be removed from the outside. Simple. And incredible that nobody had spotted that security weakness before. I guess they weren't expecting anyone to break into a place where a burglar's haul would normally amount to a few postage stamps."

Shirley chimed in. "Yeah! It's always the obvious that shafts you,"

I ignored that. "Anyway, when the patrolling guards got to

the exhibition room that Sunday, they found the padlock had been removed by bolt cutters from the display case…"

"And the trophy was gone?" Rosina asked.

"Yes. The guards claimed they hadn't seen anyone suspicious. But they wouldn't have. The thieves had left the way they entered. Didn't have to go into the rest of the building. Well, the cops – Scotland Yard – brought in the Flying Squad to solve the case. But there were no clues. One woman claimed she'd seen someone suspicious. He was hanging around the public telephone in the Central Hall's foyer. But it didn't amount to much."

"So, at the end of the day, the soccer fans had lost their trophy. And it didn't look like football was coming home," Shirley said.

"That was about the size of it," I said. "But the next day, Monday, something unexpected happened. Joe Mears, chairman of the Football Association, had been responsible for looking after the trophy. He received a phone call from someone calling himself Jackson."

"A false name," Shirley said.

"Yes. Jackson said Mears would receive a package the next day, the Tuesday. And, sure enough, a package turned up at Mears' home. Inside was the removable lining from the inside of the Jules Rimet trophy and a ransom note demanding fifteen thousand pounds. The note said Mears should put a coded advert in the personal column of the London *Evening News* if they wanted the trophy back."

"Not the *Chronicle*?" Shirley asked.

"No, it was natural the thieves would choose a London paper for that. The ransom note said that after the advert appeared, Mears would receive further instructions on how to retrieve the trophy. But if he informed the police, the deal would be off."

"I bet he ran to the cops," Shirl said.

"He did. He got in touch with Detective Inspector Charles Buggy of the Flying Squad. Buggy told Mears to place the advert and it appeared in the paper on Thursday. Meanwhile, Buggy got in touch with a bank and they put together bundles of five-pound notes that looked like the real thing. In fact, they were sheets of blank paper with real notes on the top and bottom."

"No self-respecting blackmailer would fall for that old trick," Shirley said.

"That's where you're wrong," I said. "When Jackson got in touch again, Buggy answered the phone calling himself McPhee and pretending to be Joe Mears' assistant. Buggy could tell Jackson was nervous. But he finally persuaded the crook to meet him outside Battersea Park in London to hand over the cash in return for the trophy. So, when Buggy met Jackson, he showed the man the case with the ransom. Jackson didn't notice that it was mostly blank paper. Instead, he stepped into Buggy's car and agreed to direct him to where he could find the trophy."

"That could've been dangerous for Buggy, if Jackson had had a gun," Shirley said.

"Buggy had thought of that. He was shadowed by a team of Flying Squad detectives in unmarked vans and cars. Anyway, Buggy followed Jackson's directions towards Kennington Park Road in south London. Soon after they'd reached that area, Jackson jumped out of the car as it slowed for traffic lights and ran off. Buggy chased him. Jackson was finally caught and arrested. Buggy took him to the police station where a quick dip into the cops' mug shots of crooks revealed that Jackson was really a man called Edward Betchley. He was a used car dealer who'd been convicted in the past for theft and receiving stolen goods."

"So, the cops had him banged to rights," Shirl said.

"Not quite. Betchley denied he'd had anything to do with the theft of the trophy. He said he'd been paid five hundred pounds to act as the middle man between the real crook and the Football Association. He said he didn't know the real name of the man who'd recruited him. He just called him the Pole. So that was that. Betchley eventually got a two-year stretch for demanding money with menaces and theft. But the Football Association still didn't have the Jules Rimet trophy."

While I'd been recounting this saga, Rosina had sipped her coffee.

She'd seemed ill at ease. She shifted awkwardly on her chair as though she couldn't get comfortable. Her eyes looked duller than they had earlier. Her skin was pasty white.

She said: "I can't see what any of this has to do with my papa."

I said: "Neither could I until we pulled that note out of the safe. It's what happened next that makes the link with your papa. On the Sunday after the trophy was stolen, it was discovered, wrapped in newspaper, under a hedge. A man called David Corbett was taking his dog Pickles out for a walk. Pickles snuffled under the hedge. Corbett stopped to see what Pickles had found – and pulled out the package. He was astonished when he discovered the Jules Rimet trophy inside. He took it to the police. But, until now, nobody has ever been able to find out how it came to be under that hedge. The note in the safe suggests your papa put it there."

I looked at Rosina. She screwed up her eyes and moaned with pain. Her hands gripped her stomach and held it tight.

"This must be very difficult for you…" I began.

But Rosina wasn't listening.

Her eyes had glazed over. They disappeared into her head. She cried out in pain. Then her body went limp and she toppled from her chair.

Shirl leapt up and rushed to her. She lifted her head from the floor and cushioned it under her arm.

Rosina's eyes were closed and a thin mucus dribbled from the side of her mouth.

Shirl screamed: "Colin, call an ambulance. Tell them this is an emergency."

I rushed behind the counter and grabbed the phone.

Chapter 14

Frank Figgis shook the last Woodbine out of his packet.

He stuffed it between his lips and lit up. He blew a plume of white smoke across his desk towards me.

He said: "This smells like trouble."

I said: "To me, it stinks like a cheap gasper."

Figgis removed the fag from his lips and balanced it in his overflowing ashtray.

He said: "I was referring to this girl in hospital."

"This girl is Rosina Cavaletto," I said. "She is the daughter of Sergio Parisi, the murdered café owner. She is also fleeing an abusive husband among her many other problems. So I think she deserves some respect."

Figgis looked down and studied the liver spots on the back of his hand. It was the first time I'd seen him look genuinely embarrassed.

We were in his office at the *Chronicle*. It was two hours after I'd called for the ambulance.

Rosina had been rushed to the Royal Sussex County Hospital. Shirley had travelled in the ambulance with her.

Figgis said: "I'd just finished Sunday lunch when I got your call at home. Anyone who's waded through Mrs Figgis' Yorkshire pudding deserves a bit of sympathy."

"As does Rosina," I said. "I called the hospital just before you arrived. They say the abdominal pains have subsided and she's resting. The doctors say she's suffering from stress and exhaustion. Not surprising after what she's been through. She needs some bed rest. The doctors will be running some tests later today to make sure the baby hasn't been harmed. Shirley's staying at the hospital to keep Rosina company. She has no one else in England," I said.

That last statement wasn't quite true. The phone calls Rosina had received at Shirley's flat suggested that Brando may have followed her. But I'd not been able to find a trace of him at *Casa Marco* – or anywhere else.

Figgis clapped his hands together like a guy who's eaten a large lunch and looks forward to pudding. But not Mrs Figgis' apple pie.

He said: "Trust this story to break on a Sunday when we don't produce a paper. We'll need to keep quiet about this until we hit the streets tomorrow morning."

I nodded. "Yes, we don't want the *Evening Argus* or the nationals scooping us. But I think we have a bigger problem."

Figgis' brow furrowed like a freshly ploughed field. "What's that?" he growled.

"We don't know exactly what our story is."

"We know the name of the man who tossed the stolen Jules Rimet trophy under the hedge. Sergio Parisi. Might even have been the bloke who half-inched it. Why do you suppose he left that incriminating note hanging around?"

"It was at the bottom of the envelope, under the money. My guess is that Sergio didn't even realise it was there."

"So we've nailed him," Figgis said.

I shook my head. "The note that came with the five hundred pounds didn't mention the trophy. It could have been anything. And it didn't mention which hedge either. It could have referred to anywhere."

"People don't pay a monkey to throw any old piece of rubbish under a random garden hedge."

"True. But even if we accept that it was probably the trophy, we're still left with two questions," I said. "And a serious problem. Question one, why was it being chucked under the hedge? This was a valuable item. Admittedly, hot property. But it could have been melted down for its gold value. Three thousand pounds, I'm told."

"We could mention that in the piece."

"Maybe, but there's the second question. Who paid Parisi to do the chucking? If we accept that the package mentioned was the trophy, was the writer of the note the thief who stole it?"

Figgis took a long meditative draw on his Woodbine. The smoke seeped down his nose like his brain had just caught fire. He stubbed out the dog-end.

He said: "Very well. I accept there are questions we need to answer. But what's the serious problem?"

"We'll have to reveal how we came by this information. The cops will moan a bit because we opened the hidden safe without telling them. But that's the least of our problems. We'll need to reveal that Rosina knew about the money. At least, she didn't know the cash came with an incriminating note – until we found it. But she's in a fragile state at the moment. And in hospital. The last thing she needs is Tomkins bellowing questions at her in one of the less than comfortable interview rooms at the cop shop."

"We could say the information comes from a confidential source. Or we've interviewed Miss X."

"No-one's going to buy that. Not rival journos. Not the cops. Not even the readers. Besides, we'll have to tell the cops sooner or later – or we could be charged with withholding information from a murder enquiry."

"Looks like we're stuffed," Figgis said. He patted his jacket to search for another packet of fags.

I said: "There might be a way to get round the worst of these difficulties. But it involves risk."

"When doesn't it with you?"

"And not just for me," I said. "We have to consider the possibility that whoever sent Parisi the note, was also the person who murdered him."

"Why should he do that – after sending the man a monkey?"

"Perhaps he thought about it more. Perhaps he feared Parisi knew too much – or was going to blab about it. Perhaps he worried that, like all blackmailers, Parisi would want more cash. When this story breaks, Rosina could also be in danger."

"From whoever killed Parisi?"

"Yes."

I didn't mention that Rosina was already pursued by Brando. There's only so much truth Figgis can take in one day.

I said: "Here's what I think we should do. Let's sit on the story until Tuesday."

"What! And miss the chance of a great headline in Monday's paper?"

"Tuesday's headline will be even bigger, if I'm right. I'll have a word with my tame cop."

"Ted Wilson, I presume."

"I'll tell Ted I'm doing a cold case story on the Jules Rimet theft. I'll ask him whether he's got any contacts in the Met, the London cops, who might know more. Ted's always been popular with fellow cops because he's always first to the bar to get a round in. I'll follow up tomorrow on any leads Ted gives me. I'll see if we can make the theory that the package was the trophy stand up. That way, we're likely to have a story that can't be rubbished by the opposition."

Figgis shrugged reluctantly.

"If you put it like that, I've got no choice. We'll do it your way," Figgis grumbled.

I stood up and headed for the door.

"You're a real leader, Frank," I said. "Right up there with Alexandre Ledru-Rollin."

I closed the door.

But not before Figgis had yelled: "Who the hell's he?"

In Prinny's Pleasure I handed Shirley her Campari soda and said: "Ledru-Rollin was one of the guys behind the French Revolution.

"Not the one that got rid of Louis the Sixteenth with the

guillotine, tumbrils and storming the Bastille. The one that shifted Louis Phillipe in 1848. Ledru-Rollin is supposed to have said, 'There go the people. I must follow them, for I am their leader.'"

I'd been telling Shirley about my meeting with Figgis. It was early evening, and we were relaxing with a drink after the excitement of the day.

Shirl said: "One of these days, you'll regret winding up poor old Frank."

"In the meantime, I'm having a lot of fun." I hoisted my gin and tonic and said: "Here's to more of it."

Shirley frowned but she drank anyway.

She said: "I left Rosina sleeping. The poor kid was all-in. I think the last few days have been too much for her. The escape to Britain, the death of her papa…"

"And the worry that Brando may be on her trail," I said.

"At least she should be safe in hospital," Shirley said. "Apart from us, no one knows she's there."

I took another pull at my drink. "I'm not so sure," I said. "When the ambulance arrived outside Sergio's café, there were a lot of rubberneckers in nearby buildings goggling the incident. They saw Rosina brought out on a stretcher and rushed to hospital. Some of them may have recognised her. After all, she'd lived there. The question is would any of them blab about it to a strange face that came round asking questions?"

"You think Brando would go to those lengths?"

"We know what he's done in the past – so, yes."

"At least Rosina has had great care from the medics and nurses. They seem to think she'll recover fine."

I winked at Shirley. "Which means we've got a night off from Rosina."

"Keep your trousers on, big boy. I'm bushed, too, after the last few days we've had. I'm hitting the sack for an early night. Alone."

She drained her Campari soda.

She ran her tongue lightly over her top lip. "But there might be something in it for you," she said.

"Something?" I asked.

"If you run me home in the MGB, I might give you a goodnight kiss."

The following morning, I met Ted Wilson in Marcello's.

He had the Full English breakfast. Two eggs. Rashers of bacon. Sausages. Mushrooms. Tomatoes. Baked beans. Bubble and squeak. And a stack of toast.

I had a croissant.

On the basis of our breakfasts, I calculated I'd outlive Ted by at least ten years.

Or perhaps I'd be knocked down by a bus. Perhaps I should've had the Full English. The meaty aroma of the fried bacon was getting to me.

Some egg yolk had dribbled into Ted's beard and stained it yellow. It made him look like he was going down with an oriental disease.

He sliced off a large piece of sausage, stuffed it in his mouth, and said: "You must want something big if you're willing to pick up the tab for this snack."

I said: "I'm revisiting an old story – the theft of the Jules Rimet trophy. It's kind of a review of a cold case."

"Can't see the point of it. They got the trophy back."

"But they still don't know who nicked it."

"The judge put that Edward Betchley behind bars for two years. That's good enough for us. A result." He burped loudly. "I think next time, I'll have fried bread instead of the bubble and squeak. Fried potato and cabbage give me gyp first thing in the morning."

"Just wondered whether you knew of any angles that didn't get fully investigated at the time?"

"Not our case down here. All the action took place in London. You need to ask the Met."

I broke a piece off my croissant and it fell apart. The flaky pastry dropped as crumbs on my plate. The perfect low-calorie breakfast. You don't get to eat it.

I said: "Trouble is, if I speak to anyone at the Met, I'd need to get a contact who'd worked on the case. Not easy."

Ted scooped up a mushroom and said: "As it happens, I might be able to help. Few years back, we had that team of bank blaggers from south London run a couple of heists in Brighton. The Met seconded a Detective Sergeant called Dougal Turnbull down here. We made a good team. We had something in common. He liked a drop of scotch. Heard he'd had something to do with the trophy case. Believe he's made inspector now. I'll put in a call later this morning and let you know."

"Thanks, Ted. Now, how about some fried bread?"

Ted grinned. "Bring it on."

Detective Inspector Dougal Turnbull turned out to look a bit like Dougal the dog in the TV show *Magic Roundabout*.

He had a mournful oval face, brown eyes too close together, and a big nose. His mouth permanently turned down in a manner that suggested whatever happened next would be a big disappointment.

We were sitting in his office at Gipsy Hill police station in south-east London. It wasn't far from the house where the trophy had been found under the hedge.

Ted had been as good as his word. He'd scoffed his fried bread and then called Turnbull. He'd agreed to see me, and - a couple of hours later - there I was. Sitting on a wooden upright chair on the opposite side of his desk.

I guessed Turnbull must be a football fan. A cork noticeboard that hung behind his desk was pinned with the usual memos and hastily scribbled notes.

But pride of place was occupied by a picture cut from a copy of the *Daily Mirror*. Shirley's teasing eyes mocked me as she posed provocatively in her North Korean kit.

I nodded at the picture and said: "You a North Korea supporter then?"

Turnbull glanced behind him. "I'm Scottish so I'll be supporting whoever's playing England." He thumbed towards the picture. "But if they've got girls like that in North Korea, I'll move to Pong Yong."

"Pyongyang."

"If you insist."

I didn't mention that Shirley could be reached closer to home. Instead, I briefed Turnbull on my cover story. That I was writing a retrospective on the recovery of the Jules Rimet trophy.

I said: "I believe when the theft was first discovered, you suspected an inside job?"

Turnbull dragged his gaze away from Shirley and said: "Seemed a reasonable conclusion. The rascals knew how to enter Westminster Central Hall when they knew they wouldn't be noticed. Knew exactly how to take the padlock off the back of the display case without making a noise. Stood to reason, they had to have someone on the inside with knowledge of how to do that. We interviewed the guards. And the maintenance workers."

"But you never identified anyone?"

"No, we ruled them out. Decided the blaggers must have had someone on the outside to case the joint."

Case the joint! Did 'tecs really say that?

I said: "You had some descriptions for people who'd seen a bloke hanging around suspiciously."

"We did, but on that day, there were a lot of people hanging around. There was a church service going on in the main hall. A bunch of Methodists. Didn't see that line of enquiry would get us anywhere."

"The big mystery is why the trophy was wrapped in newspaper and thrown under a hedge. Any thoughts about that?"

Turnbull scratched his head. "Thought about that a lot. We reckon that when we'd picked up Betchley – who acted as the middleman in the blackmail – the master criminal behind it all must have got the frights. He'd be worried that Betchley would talk to save himself. We'd be closing in and the trophy was too hot to handle. He just had to get rid of it any way he could."

"Of course, Betchley may not have been linked to the theft. He may just have been a chancer trying to make a few quid on the side," I said.

"We considered that. We dismissed it. It would've been too risky. Even though he had told Joe Mears 'no cops', he must have wondered whether Mears had contacted us."

I asked: "The bloke who found the package under the hedge – David Corbett – you suspected him?"

Turnbull nodded: "At first, it seemed likely. After all, the idea of finding the trophy under a random hedge sounds too outlandish. But Corbett had a cast-iron alibi. We eliminated him from our enquiries."

"So, the real culprit is still at large?"

Turnbull frowned. "The bastard! We'll get him."

"You have new leads?" I asked.

Turnbull shook his head. "But something will turn up."

He swivelled in his chair and stared at Shirley's picture.

I decided not to tell her she had a new fan. Turnbull wasn't her type.

Chapter 15

As I was in south-east London, I thought I'd take a chance.

And it paid off.

After I'd left Turnbull, lost in whatever fantasy for Shirley he had in mind, I decided to pay a call on David Corbett, the man who found the package under the hedge.

A dog barked when I rang the bell of a flat in a converted house in Beulah Hill. Back in the Roaring Twenties, the fancy place would have hosted Charleston parties for the smart set. But those days were long gone. The house had been converted into modest apartments.

The door opened and a middle-aged man with a strong chin glared at me. He had quiffs of brown hair combed forward on his forehead.

The dog, a black and white collie, worried around my feet.

I said: "Pickles won't find another World Cup down there."

The man snapped: "Pickles! Come away!"

Pickles looked up at the man, then slunk back into the house.

"David Corbett?" I asked.

The man nodded. And frowned. "You're not one of those autograph hunters, are you?"

I handed Corbett my card. "I'm one of those headline hunters," I said.

Corbett studied the address on the card. "Brighton *Evening Chronicle*. Oh, yes. I know the paper. But you're a bit out of your circulation area up here, aren't you?"

"There are no boundaries on strong stories. Especially those that bring good fortune to people mentioned in them," I said. "Human and canine," I added with a grin.

Corbett smiled. "I agree I've done pretty well out of the press coverage. A bit more should do me no harm."

"I'd heard you'd picked up six thousand pounds in reward

money and been invited to the official dinner after the World Cup Final."

Corbett grinned shyly. "You should know better than anyone not to believe everything you read in the press."

I took the friendly rebuke in good grace.

Corbett stood back and ushered me in. We walked down a narrow hall and stepped into his sitting room. There was a window out on to a small garden. There was one of those old-fashioned cast-iron fireplaces. A toasting fork was propped against it. A faded Axminster carpet had a sofa and a couple of comfy chairs grouped around it. A small table by one of the chairs held a couple of mugs with the dregs of tea and a plate with a half-eaten digestive biscuit.

It was a cosy enough pad for man and dog.

Pickles had already curled up on a comfy chair.

Corbett said: "I suppose you've heard that Pickles is going to be a film star." He ushered me to the sofa and took a seat opposite.

"I've heard Pickles has been on TV."

"This is something bigger. A feature film for the cinema. *The Spy with the Cold Nose*. It's coming out in December. Stars Eric Sykes and June Whitfield."

"Presumably they're not the ones with the cold nose?"

Corbett grinned. "No."

"Must be a lucrative business having a star dog," I said.

"I won't deny it. What with the reward money, the fees for photoshoots, and the film money, we're moving to a new house at Lingfield in Surrey."

"Good luck with that," I said. "I'm writing a look-back on the theft and recovery of the Jules Rimet trophy. I wondered whether you could tell me a bit more about what it was like?"

"Just an ordinary afternoon, really. I had to make a phone call from the box down the road. So, I decided to take Pickles for a walk."

At the sound of his name and the word "walk" Pickles raised himself and snuffled around hopefully.

"Later, boy," Corbett commanded.

Pickles returned to his place on the comfy chair.

"Anyway, we went outside and Pickles rummaged under the hedge. The long and the short of it is that I pulled out this package wrapped in a newspaper. I unwrapped the newspaper, and there was the trophy. I just stared at it. Then I called Pickles and went back into the house. I needed a stiff drink."

"You recognised the trophy straightaway?" I asked.

"I was in shock after I'd opened the package. But then I noticed the names of countries that had won it in previous years were engraved around the base. I knew for certain then."

"Was there anything else in the package?"

"No, but there was something that you'll be interested in. The newspaper wrapped around the trophy was the Brighton *Evening Chronicle*."

It was one of those jaw-dropping moments that happen from time to time in my game.

But my jaw didn't drop. Instead, I just gawped at Corbett.

He gave a triumphant little grin. He knew he'd caught me by surprise.

He said: "Yeah! Later, when I thought about it, that was a bit strange. You'd have expected the paper to be one of the London rags – like the *Evening News* or the *Evening Standard*."

"Or one of the morning national papers," I added.

"Funny, I never mentioned that before. It didn't seem important when I had a gold trophy worth thousands of pounds in my hands."

I said: "Was it the whole newspaper or just some pages?"

"Just a few pages. I'm pretty sure it was the previous day's paper. Whoever had owned the paper had started the crossword puzzle. I thought that was strange, too. He, or she, hadn't finished it."

"What happened to the newspaper?"

"I handed it to the cops with the trophy. I don't know what they did with it."

I thought about that for a moment. I should have asked Turnbull. But the chances are the cops would have ignored it. They wouldn't expect to get many clues from a scruffy newspaper that had been lying under a hedge.

I said: "Do you remember anything else about the newspaper – about the crossword for example?"

Corbett fidgeted in his chair while he thought about that.

Pickles stirred. Might be time for walkies. Not yet. Settled down again.

Corbett said: "After the initial shock I just couldn't help looking at all of it. I remember the crossword had been started in red ink. Stood out against the black. Whoever was doing it had only completed three clues. I wondered whether they'd only done three clues because they needed the newspaper to wrap the trophy. Or perhaps those were the only three they could get. Those clues were pretty tricky."

"You remember the clues?"

"Sounds daft, I know, when I had a gold trophy there. But random things were just jumping out at me. I remember that one clue was quite appropriate as it was in a paper wrapping the trophy. *Place where bad behaviour gets a good kicking.*"

"Penalty spot," I said.

Corbett looked at me in surprise. "You do crossword puzzles?"

"Only when they're linked to crime. Do you remember the other clues?"

"You won't get this one. *South American animal is an E-type.*"

"Jaguar."

"Right again. This last one will fox you. *Four walls and a roof with a flair for self-promotion.*"

"Showroom."

"Amazing," Corbett said.

132

"Let's just say that Bart Mann, who sets the *Chronicle's* crossword, and I have the same kind of mind."

"What's that?"

"Devious. But back to the day you walked into the history books. What did you do after you'd realised what you'd found?"

"I decided I had to take it to the cops. So I put the trophy and the newspaper in a shopping bag and set off for Gipsy Hill police station. My mind was in a whirl. But there was a strange thing when I stepped out of the flat."

"Strange?"

"Well, perhaps not. Normally I wouldn't have taken any notice. But a man – rather a large man – was walking past the house. I say walking past, but I think he may have stopped. I didn't notice him at first, but I think he'd bent down behind the hedge and was peering into it. Of course, he may just have stooped to tie a loose shoelace."

"What did this man look like?"

"Didn't really get a good look at him. As soon as I appeared, he walked off smartly down the road. But he was a big man."

"How big?"

"Put it this way. You wouldn't want to sit next to him on the bus."

"Did you mention him to the police?"

"No. Didn't think it was relevant. Besides they narked me at first. Even hinted they thought I'd nicked the thing. As if I'd be so thick as to take it to the police if I'd stolen it in the first place." Corbett grinned. "But it all turned out right in the end. In fact, the best thing that ever happened to me."

Corbett glanced at the dirty mugs on the side table and the half-eaten biscuit. "Now, how about a cup of tea?"

I had much to think about after I'd supped Corbett's tea and eaten a digestive biscuit.

Not least that the trophy had been wrapped in a copy of

the *Chronicle*. Our circulation area was large – most of Sussex. You could even buy the paper at some of London's major train termini, including Victoria and London Bridge. But most Londoners wouldn't read it. So, the odds-on favourite was that whoever had wrapped the trophy in the paper had come from somewhere in Sussex.

The fact the story now had a strong Sussex angle warmed me more than Corbett's tea.

But there was also the question of the crossword clues. Had the person who wrapped the trophy completed the clues? Or had they merely used a paper that had belonged to someone else? It was impossible to know.

Yet I could get a glimpse of the person through the clues they'd managed to complete. Most people who do crosswords fill in the easiest clues first. It means there are some letters in the grid which help them solve the trickier clues. So, in building my picture of the crossword solver, I considered the clues.

Place where bad behaviour gets a good kicking. Well, a football fan would be more likely to think of the penalty spot, I reasoned.

South American animal is an E-type. Perhaps someone with a love of animals. But a petrolhead with a passion for cars would know that an E-type was a model in Jaguar Cars' range.

Four walls and a roof with a flair for self-promotion. Maybe showroom would click with someone in the sales business more than your ordinary clue-solver.

Football. Cars. Salesmanship.

There must be thousands – no, millions – of people in Britain who fitted at least one of those categories. Some who covered two. Fewer who racked up all three.

And I could only think of one.

Vernon Stoker.

And all this had jogged my memory about something else. The picture of Stoker with the crooked teeth man in Betty's office. He was Edward Betchley. I'd seen Betchley's twisted dentures in pictures of him when he was tried for his part in the Jules Rimet trophy ransom. And Betchley was Stoker's pal.

Could the chairman of Crawley Rovers football club really be behind such an audacious crime? Betty Mulligan had hinted Stoker was a "slippery operator". Looking for the main chance doesn't necessarily mark you out as a thief.

But Stoker also knew Sergio Parisi. Stoker had even lent Parisi money. Parisi owed Stoker a favour. A big one. Could that have been throwing the trophy under the hedge? As we'd discovered, if Parisi had done the deed, it had come with a healthy bonus.

But most thieves don't abandon what they've stolen.

Stoker's car showroom was in Beulah Hill, not more than a couple of miles from Corbett's flat.

I sat in my MGB and put together a theory in my mind.

Could slippery Stoker have organised the theft of the Jules Rimet trophy? He would have needed a buyer already lined up. It would be someone like those weird types who steal famous paintings. Not to sell, because they're too well known. But to drool over in the privacy of their own secret art gallery.

So, Stoker thinks he has a buyer who's obsessed with owning the Jules Rimet trophy. But at the last minute, the buyer drops out. Perhaps he's seen the huge press coverage and is worried the trophy is too hot to handle. Now Stoker has a big problem. He's incurred expenses in stealing the trophy and he'll be out of pocket. And one thing that people like Stoker never like is being out of pocket.

So, he tries the ransom route to get some payback. But Edward Betchley, the sap he hires to collect the ransom pay-off, bungles the handover. Worse, he gets himself arrested. Stoker squares Betchley with the promise of a big payoff to keep quiet about his part in the theft. Betchley will do time, but have cash in the bank when he comes out.

As a result, Stoker is now seriously out of pocket. To get some payback, he comes up with an outrageous scam. He'll pretend to find the trophy – in the presence of a couple of witnesses - and claim the reward. Enough to pay off his expenses and leave some spending money. All Stoker needs is someone to hide the trophy where only he can find it. Near to his showroom would make it seem natural. And Parisi owes him a big favour.

But Stoker hadn't bargained for Pickles getting to the package under the hedge first.

I know… the theory had more holes than a stripper's fishnets.

There was only one way to test it. And that was to confront Stoker.

When I arrived at Stoker's showrooms, he was "away on business".

Marlene, the receptionist, greeted me in a sing-song voice that grated, like Chinese opera. "Are you a potential purchaser of one of our perfectly presented used vehicles?"

I gave a casual wave at the MGB I'd left on the forecourt.

"I'm thinking of trading it in for something that makes more of a statement about who I am."

Marlene looked me up and down. Took in the checked jacket. The grey flannel trousers. The Hush Puppies. "We don't have a Hillman Minx in stock at the moment," Marlene said down her nose. "I could get one of our salesmen, Roland or Sergei, to assist you. That is, unless you're just another tyre-kicker. With so many prestige cars, we're pestered by them."

"I think I'll just take a look around the lot," I said.

As I headed for the door, I enjoyed the mental image of Marlene falling through a trapdoor into a pool filled with hungry alligators.

Outside, the place was free of tyre-kickers, the customers who always seem interested – but never enough to buy.

But there were plenty of motors that put my MGB in the shade. There was an Aston Martin DB5, with acceleration from nought to sixty in less than ten seconds. Ideal for the bank-robber who needs a quick getaway. Next to it, a Lamborghini Miura, so low to the ground it probably came with its own physiotherapist to get you in and out. Further on, a Porsche 911, just the motor for the parvenu millionaire to run his old mum down to the Co-op to pick up her groceries.

I spent five minutes looking around the cars, thinking more about Vernon Stoker, than these dream machines on four wheels.

I drifted round to the back of the car lot.

There was no sign of Roland or Sergei. But there was a workshop.

I sauntered over, like I had nothing better to do with my time.

The place had a pair of those huge sliding doors you see on aircraft hangers. One of the doors had been pushed back a couple of yards.

There were lights on inside.

I stuck my head around the door and called out. "Hello. Can anyone tell me how many horsepower that Porsche 911 has?"

My voice echoed off the metal ceiling. But answer came there none.

Looked like the grease monkeys who worked here had sloped off for their lunch.

I stepped inside and took a quick look around.

There were work benches around the walls loaded with tools, lathes, presses, power drills, iron files and a fearsome industrial guillotine.

Next to the guillotine, one of the grease monkeys had pasted a selection of his favourite cheesecake pictures on the wall. There were pin-ups of Sabrina, Jayne Mansfield and Brigitte Bardot. But the one that grabbed my attention had been cut from the *Daily Mirror*.

Shirley in her North Korean football kit certainly gave the other girls a run for their money.

I turned my attention back to the workshop.

There were chains with large hooks hanging from the ceiling.

There was an inspection pit, with a hoist above it.

A Chevrolet Corvette had been jacked up over the pit. It had had dove grey bodywork but was now being painted royal blue. The bonnet and doors were already blue but the back end was still grey. Some of the engine had been removed and was standing on a bench next to the pit. There were two sets of number plates on the bench. One set was scratched and rusted. The other – with a new registration number – was as shiny as a drunkard's nose.

So, this was Stoker's scam. He was a car ringer. He bought stolen cars, gave them a new identity, and shipped them out to buyers, probably in Europe.

Could it also be the place where famous football trophies were wrapped in old newspaper?

I was considering this point when a voice behind me, straight out of London's east end, said: "This gentleman don't look like one of our regular punters."

A second voice, with a nasal twang, said: "If it weren't for his shoes, I'd say he was a copper's nark."

I spun around.

The first voice had come from a tall sort with a quiff of fair hair and a face like a thunderstorm. He wore a blue pin-striped suit. A costly piece of bespoke tailoring. He wore an army-style tie. Possibly the Queen's Own Royal Regiment of Bovver Boys.

The second voice had come from a chubbier type with a bald patch like a monk's tonsure and a face set in a permanent sneer. He wore a double-breasted navy jacket with gold buttons, just the naval gear for Cowes Week. He'd shot the cuffs of his Van Heusen shirt to reveal cufflinks as sharp as razor blades.

Both of them were wearing Italian winklepicker shoes.

I glanced down at my Hush Puppies and said: "In ten years' time I'll be skipping around like a spring lamb. You two will be hobbling down to the pub with feet like squashed parsnips."

The pair looked at each other and then at their feet.

I pointed at pin-striped and said: "I'm guessing you're Roland."

"That must make me Sergei," the cufflink man said.

"You're sharp," I said. "A salesman who can remember his own name."

"What are you doing?" Roland said. "We don't normally invite people in here."

"Quite right. Anyone staring at the pictures on the wall could easily fall into the pit."

"I never fell into the pit," Sergei said.

"You stare at the pictures on the wall, though." Roland said.

"Hey, there's a new one," Sergei said.

"Don't let me stop you from having a look," I said.

Sergei crossed the workshop towards the pictures. "Hey, Roland, this girl you've got to see."

I said: "There's another picture of the same girl in this morning's *Daily Mirror*."

"You called in here to tell us that?"

"I thought Sergei would like to know."

Sergei said: "We ain't got today's *Mirror*."

"Too bad. They're selling fast."

Sergei turned to Roland. "We'd better get down to the paper shop."

Roland said: "We haven't dealt with this bloke yet."

Sergei said: "He can wait."

I said: "As it happens, I have to go."

Roland said: "You haven't told us yet why you're here."

I strode towards the exit. Said over my shoulder: "That is very true. I couldn't have put it better myself."

I stepped smartly through the door and hurried back to my MGB.

Chapter 16

I met Shirley a couple of hours later in Prinny's Pleasure.

Jeff had pinned up the picture of Shirley in her North Korean gear behind the bar.

He said: "When people realise a famous model drinks here, I'll be flooded with customers just longing to get a snap of you on their Kodak Brownies."

Shirley and I looked around the bar.

"There's no one else in here," I said.

"Give it time," Jeff said. He turned to Shirley. "What'll you have? It's on the house."

Shirley said: "I'll have a sidecar."

Jeff's forehead wrinkled with confusion. "I haven't even got a motorbike."

"It's a cocktail made from cognac, orange liqueur and lemon juice," Shirley said.

Jeff scratched his left armpit. "I was thinking more along the lines of a half-pint of lager."

Shirley gave a derisive laugh. "Make it a Campari soda, Gatsby."

Another frown creased Jeff's forehead. "The name's Purkiss. So, a half of lager it is, then."

I looked at Shirley and shrugged.

We took our drinks to the corner table at the back of the bar.

I told Shirley about my day. About how I now had Vernon Stoker in the frame as the mastermind behind the theft of the Jules Rimet trophy.

I told her how I'd met Roland and Sergei. And how her picture on the wall had saved me from a rumble with the pair in the workshop.

Shirl sipped her half of lager. "You be careful around guys like that."

"Around guys that drool over your pin-up pictures?"

"Guys that look for trouble."

I took a pull at my gin and tonic. (Paid for with hard cash. Jeff's offer of free drinks only extended to famous models.)

I said: "Have you heard from Rosina today?"

"I telephoned the hospital this morning and the ward sister said she'd had a quiet night."

"Rosina or the ward sister?"

"Rosina, smart-arse. But the doctor was keeping her under observation, whatever that means."

"We'll go and see her this evening."

"They only let you in at visiting time. And that doesn't start until seven."

I glanced at my watch. "Quarter past six. There might be time for another free half of lager," I said.

I parked the MGB in Bristol Gate, just around the corner from the Royal Sussex County Hospital.

Shirley bought a bunch of carnations from a flower-seller outside the hospital's main entrance.

We tramped through the gloomy corridors to Rosina's ward. A crowd of friends and relatives had gathered outside the doors. They murmured sad little words to one another in low voices. Showed each other the gifts they'd brought. Black Magic chocolates. Lucozade in bright yellow bottles. Back issues of *Woman's Own* with knitting patterns for cardigans.

We hung around waiting for the ward's doors to open.

I said: "At least, Rosina has been somewhere safe for the last couple of days. When she comes out, we'll need to think about where she can live."

"Need to keep that brute of a husband out of the picture," Shirley said.

The doors to the ward opened.

A nurse in a starched blue uniform and white cap stepped

out. Her name badge read: Sister Agnes Brake. She clapped her hands for attention.

"You may enter quietly," she said in the kind of voice teacher once used in the playground to boss us around.

The crowd obediently shuffled through the doors. We held back to let everyone else get in first.

Then we walked into the ward and headed for Rosina's bed. Curtains were drawn around it.

"Is she asleep?" Shirley asked.

I didn't mention there was another reason nurses drew curtains around patients' beds.

I walked up to the bed and pulled the curtain aside.

The bed was empty.

Shirley stepped alongside me. "This is the wrong bed," she said.

"No. It can't be."

"Perhaps she's gone to the khazi."

"They give you bedpans."

"Then they must have changed her bed," Shirley said.

Across the ward, Sister Brake was sitting at a desk. She shuffled some files into a neat pile. Opened one and started writing in it.

We crossed to the desk.

"*Harumph!*" I coughed politely.

Brake looked up from her writing. "If you have a cold, you must leave the ward. I don't want any naughty bugs infecting my patients."

"I haven't got a cold. Or a bug. Especially a naughty one. I coughed to get your attention."

"Had you considered saying 'good evening'?"

I ignored that and said: "We've come to see Rosina Cavaletto. She's not in her bed."

"I should hope not."

"Has she moved beds?"

"No."

"Where is she?"

"I really couldn't say."

Sister Brake picked up her pen.

Shirley leaned across the desk. "Listen, Sister, Rosina is a vulnerable woman who needs our help. And if you won't tell us what's happened to her, I'm going to take these carnations and stuff them right up your... Well, let's just say where they definitely won't need a vase of water."

Sister Brake gulped. She put down the pen and snapped: "Follow me."

She stood up and marched across the ward. We followed her into the corridor. She turned right, stepped smartly round the corner, and opened the door into a room.

We hustled inside. The place was furnished like an office. The room was painted the kind of green that's supposed to make you feel relaxed. Just makes you feel bilious. There was a desk with a chair behind it. There were a couple of guest chairs. There was a box of tissues on the desk. Most of them had been used.

There were half a dozen notices on the walls. About what to do if you wanted to complain about the doctor. About how to register a death. About where to find an undertaker. About how to get to Heaven. (Turns out it meant calling the hospital padre.)

So, this was the room where they brought grieving relatives when they had to give them the hard word.

We all sat down.

I said: "Is Rosina dead?"

Sister Brake shook her head. "No. At least, she wasn't when she left here."

"She's scarpered!" Shirley exclaimed.

"She discharged herself," Sister Brake said in a pompous voice.

"What for? The doctor said she was still under observation," I said.

"Any patient is entitled to discharge themselves from the

hospital unless there is a legal reason they should be detained."

"And there was no reason in this case?" I asked.

"No."

"Then why?" Shirl chimed in.

"Her husband arrived to collect her," Sister Brake said.

Shirley and I exchanged a sharp look.

There was a moment's silence while we digested that shock.

"Her husband Brando Cavaletto called to collect her?" I asked.

Brake's lips twisted into a mean little smile. "I presume Rosina had only one husband called Brando Cavaletto," she said. "Or anything else."

"How did you know he was who he said he was?" I asked.

"Because Rosina confirmed he was her husband."

"And you took her word for it?"

"Why should I not? But, no, I didn't take her word for it. Mr Cavaletto showed me his Italian passport. It had his picture. It was him."

"Did Rosina seem reluctant to leave?" I asked.

"No."

"He didn't force her?" Shirley asked.

"Certainly not. I would not have allowed it. Rosina signed the required forms and left."

"Did she say where she was going?" I asked.

"No. And it was not my business to ask."

Shirl and I looked at one another again. I didn't know what to say.

Shirley leaned forward.

"Say, Agnes, I'm sorry about that crack about the carnations. What I said was crude and physically impossible. Especially as I had a wreath in mind."

Brake's lips twitched. Not enough to make a smile. "You sound Australian," she said.

"Right on, cobber. Call me a jillaroo and I'll pick the goolies off a wallaby with my boomerang at fifty paces."

Now Brake did smile.

But Shirley became serious. "There's something you need to know about Rosina."

Over the next five minutes, Shirley gave Brake an edited version of how we'd met Rosina and brought her to Britain.

"So you see," Shirley said, "we have a special need to make sure Rosina is safe."

Sister Brake nodded thoughtfully. "This changes matters," she said. "There is something you ought to know. When Mr Cavaletto arrived, I showed him to Rosina's bed and drew the curtains around it. I thought they'd like to talk in private. But I could see that Rosina was shocked by her husband's arrival. So I found something to do at the next bed."

"And couldn't help over-hearing some of the conversation," Shirley said.

Brake blushed. "It appears that Rosina may come into some money. I'm not sure what the details are. Some of the time the two were speaking in Italian."

"And the promise of the money persuaded her to leave?" I asked.

"Not at first. But they spoke for some time. Mr Cavaletto seemed very subdued. It seems the pair could receive some money if they agreed to live together. He sounded very contrite. Pleading, almost. I think, in the end, Rosina felt sorry for him."

"Even after all he'd done to her," Shirley said.

"He promised never to do it again. I heard him say that twice. And that's when she agreed to leave. There was nothing I could do to stop her."

Sister Brake stood up. The meeting was finished. "And now, if you'll excuse me, I have patients still here that I have to attend to."

She ushered us out of the room and hurried down the corridor.

"What's this money all about?" Shirley said.

"I don't know," I said.

145

We looked at each other. But neither of us had any answers.

At Brighton Police Station, a uniformed plod knocked lightly on Detective Chief Superintendent Alec Tomkins' office door.

A muffled voice from within could have said "Come in" or "Clear off".

The plod opened the door and said: "From here on, it's at your own risk."

It was barely an hour after we'd left the hospital. Shirley and I decided the cops needed to know about Rosina's disappearance. So, we were about to land another problem on Tomkins.

We nodded thanks at the plod and hustled through the door.

Tomkins was over by the noticeboard that covered most of one wall of his office. He was rearranging some of the Most Wanted notices that filled the board. But not completely. Nestled between a Most Wanted bank robber who'd made off with ten thousand pounds and a Most Wanted smuggler of French wines, was a cutting from the *Daily Mirror*.

Shirley's North Korean photo.

Tomkins had a piece of paper in one hand and a drawing pin in the other. He held a couple more pins between his teeth. When the front desk had called to tell him we were on our way up, he'd hastened to cover up the photo. But not quickly enough.

I said: "If you're planning to eat those pins, you better get a strong drink to wash them down."

He spat out the pins and dropped the paper. "Just... operational matters... er..."

He stood up straighter and buttoned his jacket. "Anyway, what the hell do you want?"

He moved behind his desk and sat down.

Without being invited, we sat in the guest chairs.

I said: "Rosina Cavaletto has left the hospital with her husband. Did you know about this?"

Tomkins rummaged among a pile of memos in his in-tray. "I

don't seem to have been informed yet. But I thought she'd run away from this Cavaletto?"

"She had," Shirley said. "We'd helped her escape from the brute. Now she's back with him."

"So what? Who do you think I am?" Tomkins snapped. "A marriage counsellor?"

I leaned across the desk. "You're a senior police officer investigating a brutal murder. The daughter of the murdered man was beaten by her husband. So, a violent man. She fled from him and found safety in this country. And now she's disappeared with the husband who abused her. If I were leading the investigation, I'd want to know whether those events were somehow linked to the killing."

"But we know Cavaletto was in Sicily at the time Sergio Parisi was murdered," Tomkins said.

"Yes. But Rosina believes Brando is a member of the Mafia," Shirley said.

"And the Mafia has a long arm," I added.

Tomkins smirked. "Not as long as the long arm of the law."

"At the moment that arm can't even reach far enough to cover up a girl's picture." Shirley pointed at her photo on Tomkins' board.

Tomkins' cheeks reddened. "Be that as it may... If Rosina was in hospital, I can't work out how Brando knew that."

I leaned back in my chair. I told Tomkins about my theory that Brando had got information from a local who saw Rosina carted off to hospital. "It wouldn't have been difficult to call around the local hospitals until he found the one with Rosina."

"You've got it all worked out, haven't you?" Tomkins sneered.

"No, that's why we're here looking for some help from the police," I said.

Tomkins folded his arms. "Well, you've come to the wrong man. Police investigations are confidential – despite what you write in that rag of a newspaper. Can't help you. Now, if you'll excuse me, I've got a murderer to catch."

Shirley leapt up and spun round in anger.

I said: "Cool it."

She said: "What's this?"

She crossed to the noticeboard and gazed at her picture.

"Someone's written on my picture in Biro," she said. She turned and faced Tomkins. "I bet it's you."

"Many people visit this office," Tomkins blustered.

Shirley grinned: "I bet you've got handwriting experts here who could tell us who wrote this."

"They're too busy for a trivial..." Tomkins started.

"What does it say?" I asked.

Shirl looked closer. "It's written over my right thigh and it says 'Cor! What a bum!'"

She ripped the cutting from the board. "You're a disgusting pervert."

"That's police property," Tomkins screamed.

"Tell that to the magistrate," Shirl jeered.

I said: "I wouldn't like this cutting to fall into the hands of Mrs Tomkins. There's no telling what she might do."

Tomkins' face was red and his ears twitched. They always did when he was furious.

"Relax," I said. "It could be worse. Mrs Tomkins could already have it."

Tomkins nodded reluctantly. He slumped in his chair. Took out his handkerchief and ran it over his sweating forehead.

I said: "Glad to know that we can count on your help in the hunt for Rosina."

I could barely hear Tomkins' whispered reply. "Anything I can do."

Shirley pointed at the *Daily Mirror* cutting she'd ripped from Tomkins' noticeboard.

She said: "You once told me it's always the small detail that gets the crook busted."

"Yes. He should never have written that tribute to your tush. The handwriting is the giveaway."

"If his missus saw that she'd have his balls for breakfast."

"In an egg cup with toasted soldiers. But we can only threaten to expose his lust for your booty for so long."

"How come?"

"Because eventually, he'll work out that we would never do it. He'll figure that we're not the kind of people who'd break up a marriage. Even if Tomkins deserved it, Mrs T doesn't."

We were in the China Garden restaurant in Preston Street. We'd started with a steamed bamboo basket of dim sum – tasty little dumplings. Now we'd moved on to the Peking duck, deliciously basted with soy sauce and honey.

I took a pancake and forked some shredded duck onto it. Added some strips of cucumber and spring onion. I rolled the pancake up and took a bite. Delicious.

I said: "Besides, the picture is a side issue. We wanted Tomkins to help us find Rosina and Brando. He's not going to lift a finger to help us, despite what he says. We've got to work it out for ourselves."

Shirl filled her own pancake with duck and said: "But where do we start? Rosina could be anywhere in Brighton. In fact, anywhere at all. Even back in Sicily."

I poured some jasmine tea for Shirl into a delicate little willow-patterned bowl.

I said: "I don't think so. After all, we know she fled to England because she knew her father was in trouble."

"And to escape Brando."

"Sure. But I think she'd have come even if the pair had been all lovey-dovey. She didn't know what Sergio's trouble was. But now we do. Somehow, he became mixed up in the theft of the Jules Rimet trophy. The cops think that his murder is linked to his trade in dodgy fags and booze. But I reckon it was his connection to the trophy theft which killed him. He knew too much."

Shirl balanced the willow-pattern bowl daintily between her fingers and drank some tea.

"We won't find the answer tonight," Shirl said.

"I wonder," I said. "If we could find Brando and Rosina together, perhaps we could get some answers."

Shirl put down her cup. "That won't be easy."

"I think Marco Fratelli might know more than he told me last time we met."

"The guy at *Casa Marco*?" Shirl asked.

"I think I might pay another visit."

"That could be dangerous. I'm coming, too."

"No, you're not. And that's my final word."

But Shirley doesn't take no for an answer.

She was on my arm when we walked into *Casa Marco*.

The place was doing slow business compared with my previous visit. The bloke with the big cigar and the penchant for fondling a thigh wasn't at his usual table. Neither was the girl with the thigh.

But Marco was perched on a bar stool. He had a bucket-sized brandy snifter on the bar beside him. He raised it, swirled the brandy, and took a drink as we approached.

He said: "I hope this evening it will not be necessary to call the *vigili del fuoco*."

"The fire brigade," I translated. "Not unless our conversation becomes combustible."

"Should it?" He turned to Shirley. "But who is the *signorina bellissima*?"

"I'm Shirley."

Marco grinned the grin of the wolf. "I could introduce you to men who would shower you with gold just for the pleasure of stroking your cheek."

"I don't do cheek stroking even for gold, buster. Try it, though, and you'll find it comes with a special offer - a knee in the nuts. No extra charge."

Marco turned to me. "This woman is dangerous."

"And also thirsty," I said. "She'll have a Campari soda. You know my poison."

Marco signalled to the barman and ordered the drinks.

He said: "After the problem with the fire, you are a brave man to walk in here." He glanced at Shirley. "But perhaps Shirley watches your back?"

"And other parts of my anatomy on happier occasions."

The barman lined up our glasses. We reached for them.

There was a moment's silence while we savoured the drinks.

Then I said to Marco: "Brando Cavaletto. Last time I called, you hadn't seen or heard of him. Strange for a man with his ear to the ground."

Marco sipped his cognac and said: "When your ear is to the ground, all you hear is the tramp of feet."

Shirl piped up: "What we want to know, buster, is whether any of those feet belonged to Brando."

Marco nodded approvingly. "Spirit. I like that. As it happens, I have seen Brando. He and Rosina came here to ask me whether I could help them find somewhere to stay."

"And did you?"

"I always try to help a fellow countryman. And a woman in need."

"Where are they?" I asked.

Marco smiled. "You know I cannot tell you that. But I can tell you that Brando's ambition is still to kill you."

"Makes a change from wanting to be a cowboy, I suppose," I said.

"Do not treat this with your English humour. Brando is very serious. Taking away a man's wife is a deep offence against a husband's honour. To kill is part of our culture in Sicily."

"When we want violence in England, we normally watch wrestling on the TV."

Marco raised an eyebrow. "There is something else I can tell you. Brando confided in me. He said his father, back in Sicily..."

"The capo," I said.

"The businessman," Marco corrected. "Brando said he wanted to impress his father. To show he could pull off a high-profile job. To prove he has what it takes to rise in an organisation which I will not name. Rosina, too, was keen to see Brando regain his father's favour."

"Don't tell me. Brando has decided to become a missionary."

Marco shook his head. "Brando has obtained some tickets. I cannot say where or how. Or what for. But he will sell them in the street to the highest bidders. There is, it seems, always people who will arrive without a ticket and will pay any amount of money to get one."

"So Brando is going to be a ticket tout," Shirl said. "Doesn't exactly make him Doctor Schweitzer."

"That is true," Marco said. "But in London it will make him a large amount of money. And that will impress his father. And, so, when it is time to choose a new capo, perhaps Brando will inherit the title."

"King Tout of Taormina," I said.

Marco wagged a finger at me. "That is disrespectful. And, now, as the hour is late, I suggest you finish your drinks. It would be wise for you to leave before another fire breaks out."

"Yes," I said. "I can feel the heat already."

Chapter 17

I staggered into the newsroom the following morning feeling like a centre-forward who'd just missed an open goal.

Figgis would want a story on the Parisi murder investigation for the midday edition. And that was a big problem.

I couldn't write about what we'd found in the safe at the café. Neither the notes nor the money we'd found there proved beyond doubt that Sergio had been mixed up in the theft of the Jules Rimet trophy.

If I wrote about the missing Cup Final ticket, I'd land Cyril Hands and Judith Kershaw with criminal charges.

I rolled a sheet of copy paper into my Remington and typed: *To FF, I am following very hot leads in the Parisi murder case. Can guarantee major headlines in the next few days. CC.*

I'd admit to myself that my guarantee was about as strong as one from Emil Savundra, the crooked financier. His car insurance scam had just left four hundred thousand motorists without cover.

With that passing thought, I rolled the paper out of the typewriter and called over Cedric.

He loped up to my desk, smiled shyly and said: "I don't suppose you've got any colour pictures of Shirley wearing that North Korean kit? With the black and white newsprint, the ink comes off on my fingers."

I said: "No, I don't have colour pictures. And a young lad like you should be reading the news columns to improve your mind. Not gawping at cheesecake."

"This is the Swinging Sixties, you know."

"Maybe. But in newspapers you need to watch out for what's swinging your way."

I handed him my note to Figgis. "Give this to Frank," I winked. "But leave it until I'm out of the building."

***

Forty minutes later, I was sitting in the MGB outside Crawley Rovers' ground.

I was wondering whether I'd done the right thing. If I came up with the super-sensational headline I'd promised Figgis, he'd grumble a bit. But he'd accept I'd acted for the best.

But if I wasn't able to deliver a story that didn't merit the *Chronicle's* one hundred and forty-four point headline type, my life would be a misery for weeks.

Figgis would see to that.

I'd find myself sitting in an obscure magistrates' court listening to the dull story of a local worthy who'd driven with defective brake lights.

Or I might hear the pathetic tale of a middle-aged matron who'd shoplifted a pair of knickers from Marks & Spencer – even though the panties were six sizes too small for her.

Or I could be wandering along Brighton's Palace Pier debating whether to get drunk or throw myself into the sea – because I'd been sacked.

I'd driven to Crawley on a hunch.

I felt that if I could interview Vernon Stoker, I'd be able to tease out a new angle on the Parisi murder.

But that meant running Stoker to ground.

My hunch was that Betty Mulligan knew more about the goings-on at the club than she'd so far let on. I thought she'd also be the person who'd most likely know where I could find Stoker.

I climbed out of the car and headed into the ground.

Betty was sitting behind her desk, just as she had been when I'd first called.

She looked up as I walked in. She frowned a bit before she recognised me. But then switched on a smile.

She said: "I didn't expect to see you again."

I said: "That's what everybody says. But they find it's not so hard going the second time around."

Betty blushed. "I'm sure I don't know what you mean. I enjoyed our lunch enormously."

"I was wondering whether you'd heard anything about the missing World Cup Final ticket."

Betty pulled a confused face. "No more than anyone else knows."

"No members of the club or the committee dropped hints they might have something to hide?"

"What could they hide? The ticket vanished on the day of Sergio's murder and hasn't been seen since."

"Except by the person who has it," I said evasively.

Betty mulled over that thought as though I'd just delivered one of the seven propositions of Wittgenstein.

While the thought of pleasant lunches was still in her mind, I asked: "As the club secretary, I expect you keep Vernon Stoker's diary?"

"Mr Stoker is a busy man," Betty said, skilfully not answering the question.

"Busy men usually keep a diary. Often with the help of a secretary."

"I've heard that, too."

"So, do you keep Mr Stoker's? It's a simple enough question."

Betty fiddled with some paperclips on her desk. "Mr Stoker has two diaries."

"Greedy man," I said. "I'm guessing that's one for his football interests and one for his car business?"

Betty nodded.

"I suppose you help him keep the football diary, but don't get a look in on the business diary? And the business one would be kept by Marlene, who works at the showroom?"

Betty's eyebrows gave a little jump at that. "You know Marlene?"

"I've had the pleasure," I said. "I've also met Roland and Sergei. Which wasn't such a pleasure."

"So I've heard," Betty said. And then looked as though she'd rather not have said that.

I said: "So, you know where Mr Stoker is when he's on football duties, but not when he's on car business?"

"Yes. Although sometimes a meeting is entered in the wrong diary."

"But neither you nor Marlene know where he is all the time?"

"I suppose that must be right."

"Could there be times when neither of you know where he is?"

Betty thought about that. Sat stiffly in her chair. "I suppose there are things that don't get entered in either diary."

"That would be down to Mr Stoker's carelessness."

I glanced at the table at the side of the room. The one that held the tea things. There was a packet of custard creams.

I said: "I see you've bought some more biscuits."

Betty relaxed a little. "Where are my manners? You'd like a cup of tea."

"Or coffee, if you have any."

Betty bustled over to the table and busied herself with the kettle, cups and saucers.

I sat in one of the chairs and thought hard. Stoker wouldn't have listed his decision to kill Sergio in either diary. If I was to nail him for the crime, I'd have to find another way.

"Coffee, Mr Crampton," a voice said.

"What?"

"Here's your coffee," Betty said. "You seemed a mile away then. No doubt you've been working too hard."

"Sorry, my mind was elsewhere," I said. "And a custard cream, too. Thank you."

I took a sip of my coffee while Betty returned to her seat behind the desk.

I said: "Does Mr Stoker have any meetings in his football diary today?"

"Mr Stoker's diary appointments are strictly confidential."

"Not to the people he meets." Or the people he kills, I thought. "But you could take a quick peek, surely?" I asked.

Betty took a dainty bite of her custard cream. "As it happens, I know that Mr Stoker has nothing in his football diary today. Which is just as well."

"Why just as well?"

"Because on the days he comes here, he insists on meeting Lennox Slattery, so he can review how ready the ground is for the season. And this morning, Lennox called in to say he won't be here for a few days."

"Is that usual?" I asked.

"Not like him at all. He rarely takes his full holiday allowance and when he does, he always gives at least two weeks' notice."

"Did he say why he was taking time off?"

"No."

"Could it be to do with the World Cup? Perhaps he wants plenty of time to watch the matches."

"There are only three games left."

"True, but the most important ones. I don't suppose you know which team Lennox supports?"

"England, I assume."

"He couldn't be secretly rooting for North Korea?"

"Why should he? But I've read in the papers that a lot of football fans have given the Koreans a big hand for the way they've surprised everyone in the tournament. Anyway, North Korea went out in the quarter-finals."

I remembered the passion I'd seen in Slattery just after the game with Portugal. It far exceeded what I'd have expected from a disinterested onlooker.

I shrugged my shoulders as if I weren't especially interested and said: "As Vernon Stoker isn't here today, I suppose I'll never be able to track him down."

"Oh, I wouldn't go as far as to say that," Betty said. "As it happens, I had to call Marlene yesterday about a diary mix-up and she was in a thoroughly bad mood. It seems the big man was unexpectedly due in the showroom today. Marlene was right fed-up because she'd booked a day off for a trip to the hairdressers. Apparently, she's saved up for one of those Vidal Sassoon cuts – the pixie look, all short and combed, with a big fringe."

Betty had a gulp of her coffee. "It won't suit her."

I found a telephone box outside the Crawley Rovers' ground.

I put a call through to the *Chronicle* and asked for Henrietta Houndstooth.

Henrietta sounded a bit cautious when she came on the line. "Your name is about as popular as the Black Death around here at the moment."

"Don't tell me, Frank Figgis is pining for his favourite reporter."

"If by favourite you mean the one whose backside Figgis wants to kick from here to Shrove Tuesday."

"All part of the rough and tumble of newspaper life," I said. "Henrietta, I urgently need some background on a couple of characters."

"Who are?"

"The first is Lennox Slattery, groundsman at Crawley Rovers, but otherwise a bit of a mystery. I'd particularly like to know if he has any connection with North Korea. Or any history of supporting overseas football clubs."

"Got it."

"The second is Vernon Stoker, chairman of Crawley Rovers football club. Perhaps better known as the owner of a car showroom in Beulah Hill, south-east London. I'd especially like to know if he's ever been involved in any criminal activity."

"That's it?"

"Yes. I'm on my way to interview Stoker now. I'll call you when I've spoken to him."

"Take care."

"Don't I always? And, Henrietta, if you see Figgis, tell him a front-page splash bigger than an ocean tsunami is heading his way."

Henrietta laughed. And the line went dead.

It was late afternoon by the time I arrived at Stoker's showroom.

Marlene was sitting behind her desk. She was studying her face in the mirror of a pink compact she held in her right hand.

I walked across to her and said: "'Mirror, mirror on the wall, who is the fairest of them all?'"

She snapped the compact shut and gave me the evil eye. Not too difficult for her, as the left one was a bit bloodshot.

She said: "Not you again. And don't you start on that 'fairest of them all' crap. I was supposed to be at the hairdressers' today."

I flashed one of my warmest smiles. "I was just thinking how great you'd look with one of those Vidal Sassoon pixie cuts. You know, short, straight and with a big fringe. The shape of your face is just right to make it work. I bet it would drive Sassoon wild with delight just to create such a wonder."

Marlene opened her compact again and had another look. Pushed back the curly locks around her ears to see what it would look like if they'd been scissored off.

"I'd been thinking the same thing. But I wasn't sure. You've decided me." She snapped shut the compact. "Now you can bugger off."

"Only after I've completed my business with Mr Vernon Stoker."

"What business?"

"I've decided to sell my MGB."

"And what? Buy a push-bike?"

I ignored her riposte and said: "I'll select a motor from those on your lot. But I need to see Stoker to close the deal."

"He ain't seeing no one today."

I pointed at a door on the other side of the room. "I bet that's the door to Stoker's office."

Marlene frowned. "How do you know?"

"I can read."

I paused while Marlene worked it out.

"And his name is on the door. Well, you can't go in."

"And you'll wrestle me to the ground to stop me?"

Marlene thought about that for a moment.

"Might just be fun," she said. "But the big man would fire me if he found me rolling around on the floor with you. Perhaps another time."

"Call me when you've had your hair styled. Now, why don't you make a visit to the ladies' room?"

Marlene pouted. "I don't need to go."

"You do. Then you're out of the way when I burst into the big man's office. And you have the perfect reason why you couldn't stop me. You weren't there."

The cogs in Marlene's brain ticked round a couple of notches.

"Makes sense I suppose." She stood up and headed across the room. "And when I've had the hair-do you'll definitely call me?"

"Consider it done," I said.

Marlene vanished down a corridor that led to the back of the building.

I stepped across to the room and opened the door to Stoker's office.

Stoker was sitting on a red leather Chesterfield in front of a glass-topped coffee table.

His head rested on the back of the Chesterfield. He'd propped his feet up on the table. His huge torso filled the gap in between.

It made him look like a barrel propped up against a wall.

He was flipping the pages of *Autocar* magazine.

He tossed the magazine aside and swivelled his head to watch me as I marched into the room. He had rolls of fat around his brown eyes so that it looked as though he was squinting between the slits of a Venetian blind. He had a bulbous nose with a cleft, and thick rubbery lips. His brown hair was combed back in a spiv's haircut which might have looked sharp when he was twenty. Now he was fifty, it just looked cheap. He was wearing a blue pin-striped suit that bulged like a barrage balloon. It would have had the guys at the *Tailor and Cutter* shaking their heads in horror.

He said: "Who the hell are you?"

I said: "Colin Crampton. Drive an MGB. White with a black hood. Four years old. That's the car, not me. And only one careful owner. That is me."

Stoker shifted his bulk on the Chesterfield and the thing creaked and squealed like it was in pain.

"Why did Marlene let you in here?"

"No sign of the girl in reception. Perhaps she'd visited the ladies."

Stoker sighed. "Never hire staff with a weak bladder."

"I'll try to remember that advice. In the meantime, perhaps you could tell me what you intend to do with your World Cup Final ticket?"

"I'll be attending the match, of course."

The fat around his eyes rippled. It looked like he'd just realised he'd slipped up.

"Wait a minute. How did you know I've got a Cup Final ticket? Not that I'm admitting I have."

"I thought you just said you had."

"And who the hell are you anyway?"

I pulled out my press card, stepped closer, and flashed it at him. "Colin Crampton, *Evening Chronicle*."

"Then you can clear off. And leave by the tradesmen's entrance."

"Can I see your World Cup Final ticket before I go?"

I moved across the room towards a large desk. It was a flash item with an inlaid green leather top and fancy brass fittings on the drawers.

Stoker huffed and puffed as he levered himself off the Chesterfield.

He said: "I told you I don't have a Cup Final ticket."

I said: "You must remember. Judith Kershaw, your fellow committee member at Crawley Rovers, gave it to you in return for a deal."

"What deal?"

"That you'd support a new women's football team at the club."

"I made no deal."

"But you took the ticket. And Judith will confirm that."

Stoker scowled at me. But he shrugged. "So, she'll say one thing. And I'll say another."

"And you won't be sitting in the reserved seat at Wembley."

Stoker screwed up his mouth. He hadn't thought of that. If he turned up at the match, it would prove he had the ticket. Perhaps he'd been thinking that among the one hundred thousand crowd no one would notice him. A big hope for a hulk of a man like Stoker.

"Suppose I do have the ticket? It came to me fair and square."

"No, it didn't. It was originally won in a raffle you organised at Crawley Rovers. It was won by another committee member, Sergio Parisi. Why did you fix the raffle so Parisi would win it?"

"Print that in your paper and I'll sue."

"I already know the answer to that question. It was because he'd put the black on you. You'd made him dump a package with the Jules Rimet trophy under a hedge."

"That's a fantasy."

"Sergio didn't think so. He'd have been convinced if he'd realised that you'd admitted as much in a note you'd foolishly included with the pay-off."

Stoker scowled. "You know too much."

"But not enough. Let's get back to the Cup Final ticket. It was stolen from Parisi's café."

"And I suppose you're going to accuse me of that?"

"No, I know who stole the ticket."

"Who?"

"We'll save that information for another time. What I'm more concerned with is nailing poor Sergio's killer."

"Don't you dare accuse me of being a murderer. I don't have to put up with this."

Stoker reached across his desk. He pushed a button and held his finger on it for a few seconds.

"Calling up the cavalry won't help," I said.

"Won't it?"

"I know that you killed Sergio Parisi because you had to. Everything you owned was at risk if the cops even suspected you'd been involved in the theft. Everything, especially your car ringing scam. And I'm going to print the story in the *Chronicle*."

A door behind me opened and a familiar nasal voice said: "I hope the article comes with another great picture of that girl in the football kit."

I spun around. Roland and Sergei had just stepped into the room.

Stoker said: "Mr Crampton is just leaving."

To this day, I reckon I could have taken them one at a time. But they worked a pincer movement on me. Roland coming in from the right, Sergei from the left.

I tried the old one-two manoeuvre my father had once taught me. Swing your fist at one while you aim a kick at the other. I caught Sergei on the shin and he howled – but not enough to stop him. And Roland had grabbed my right arm.

I tried to trip him up but Sergei was on me, swinging a haymaker at my face. My nose exploded with blood and I fell backwards. I hit the top of the fancy coffee table full on and the glass smashed. I hung there, clinging to the table's framework, like a fly that had just been splatted on a window.

I looked down. Stoker would not be pleased. I'd broken his table and there was blood on the carpet.

I scrambled to my feet faster than they expected. Sergei had already started a lap of honour. I got a leg over his ankle and tripped him. He lunged forward and I helped him to the floor with a neck chop from the side of my hand.

Roland stepped over Sergei's body and rushed at me. I stepped aside at the last minute. I aimed a punch at his kidneys as he surged by me. He bent forward and howled with pain. I moved closer and speeded him on his way with a boot to the bum.

I looked at Stoker. He had fear in his eyes.

I feinted a move towards him, but he cowered behind his desk.

Instead, I strolled towards the door.

I said: "Your customer service, Stoker, leaves a lot to be desired."

Then I stepped outside and took a deep breath.

Chapter 18

Somehow, I managed to get myself back to my MGB.

I sat in the seat feeling battered and bruised. I managed to staunch the blood from my nose with my handkerchief.

I felt like I'd gone five rounds with Henry Cooper but, after a few minutes, I was ready to face the world. Besides, I had a story for Figgis – and one that was well worth the roughing-up. I could see the headline now: FOOTBALL CHIEF ADMITS HE HAS MISSING WORLD CUP FINAL TICKET. I'd tell the tale, but for now keep Cyril Hands' and Judith Kershaw's names out of it.

Bloodied but unbowed, I piloted the MGB to the nearest telephone booth in a buoyant mood. I called the *Chronicle* and asked for a copytaker. I dictated the first line of my story: "Vernon Stoker, chairman of Crawley Rovers, admitted today he has the World Cup Final ticket that went missing after the murder of fellow club member and café owner Sergio Parisi."

After I'd finished my copy, I asked the copytaker to transfer me to Henrietta Houndstooth.

She came on the line and said: "Frank Figgis nearly burst into flames when he discovered you'd bunked off from the office."

"Don't worry, I've just dictated a story that will have him purring like a pussy. Anything in the files about those two names I gave you?"

"A thick file on Vernon Stoker," Henrietta said. "But most of them football cuttings. Stoker praises team after win. Stoker gutted by eight-nil defeat. That sort of thing. A handful of references to his car business – but nothing to suggest it's criminal."

"There wouldn't be. Not unless we wanted the libel lawyers to call. What about Lennox Slattery?"

"Now there we do have a mystery."

I felt my body tense up. I took out my notebook and had my pencil at the ready.

"We don't have a file on a Lennox Slattery, groundsman at Crawley Rovers. But we do have a file on Lennox Slattery, aged eight, who was killed in a bombing raid on Eastbourne railway station in 1941. Seemed strange to me, so I did some further research. Apparently, Eastbourne was the most heavily bombed south-coast town in the war. It seems Hitler planned to land troops for his invasion of Britain at Pevensey to the east of the town and Birling Gap to the west. He wanted the town that separated them softened up for the assault – which never came."

I stood with my pencil poised over my notebook hardly knowing what to write.

I said: "If the Lennox who was killed had lived, he'd be thirty-three now. That must be about the age of Lennox, the Crawley Rovers' groundsman."

"Could be a coincidence," Henrietta said.

"A massive one. Two people called Lennox Slattery, an unusual name by any yardstick, are born at about the same time. Was Lennox a popular given name for boys in the nineteen-thirties?" I asked.

"I don't know, but I could check."

"Don't bother, at least not yet. I need to look into this more closely. Thanks for your help, Henrietta. See you in the office tomorrow."

I replaced the receiver.

I pushed out of the phone box, climbed back in the car, and sat there thinking.

I couldn't make any sense of it. Lennox Slattery died. But Lennox Slattery lived.

I boxed my brains until they hurt hunting for a solution.

I felt drowsy. I put it down to delayed shock from my barney with Roland and Sergei. My eyelids felt heavy. It would do no harm to close them for a few minutes before I drove back to Brighton.

I opened my eyes with a start. I glanced at my watch. Half past seven. I'd been asleep for nearly three hours.

I opened the car window and took a deep breath. Shook my head to clear away the effects of sleep.

I fired up the MGB's engine. I was battered and bruised. And now I was confused. I needed some tender loving care. And I knew where to find it.

On the way, I wondered whether Shirley had any football kits I hadn't seen her model yet.

As it turned out, she looked great in Portugal's green and red kit.

But I digress.

Shirley and I spent the evening at her apartment. I used her bathroom to fix up my nose. Then we had a fish and chip supper. Drank a bottle of French Chardonnay. Failed to come up with any sensible idea of where we'd find Rosina and Brando.

Shirl said she'd make some discreet enquiries tomorrow around the Italian restaurants in Preston Street. I said she'd better take the Portugal kit off first.

We were both ready to sleep when we finally hit the sack.

At least, almost ready. Shirley still had the Portugal kit on.

Shirl's alarm clock sounded like the warning bell for the end of the world.

I reached out an arm and clicked it off. I turned over, nuzzled closer to Shirley, and went back to sleep.

A sharp elbow nudged me in the ribs.

"Wake up, big boy. Don't you have a meeting?"

"What?"

"The Widow. Those con-guys are coming to take her cash this

morning. Didn't you say you'd be there?"

My brain switched itself on. I sat up smartly. Rubbed sleep from my eyes.

"Where are my trousers?"

"Where you left them, big boy. Hanging from the saucepan rack in the kitchen."

When I reached Regency Square, I found the Widow in her kitchen.

She was taking out her curlers. She'd plastered her face with powder and smeared on orange lipstick. She looked like Crusty the Clown.

"I must look my best when I meet my financial advisers," she said.

That didn't sound good. If the pair of con artists had become financial advisers in her addled mind, she'd be more likely to hand over the five hundred quid she'd taken out of the building society.

I said: "Your financial advisers plan to take your money and do a runner."

"Do a runner? Who do you think they are? Roger Bannister?"

I was so shocked that the Widow had made a funny, I was stuck for my usual witty riposte.

But that was the last thing on my mind. The doorbell rang.

Before I could say anything, the Widow raced out of the kitchen and down the hall like a whippet out of the traps.

By the time I'd strolled down the hall, the Widow was showing Harvey and Lloyd into her parlour.

Harvey was a tall bloke. Topped me by at least two inches. He had a thin face, all mournful with sad eyes and a droopy nose. He had a small mouth and a weak chin. I'd have put him at about twenty-five, but his brown hair was already receding. Must be the worry of the job.

Lloyd had a pudgy figure as though he'd never been able to

shake off his teenage puppy fat. He had a short neck which made it look as though his head was resting directly on his shoulders. His high cheek bones made his eyes slitty so he couldn't help looking crafty. Must have been a real handicap in his work.

I sauntered into the parlour and the pair gave me a hostile look. A mixture of greed and fear. Was I another punter they could bilk? Or some crusader type designed to save the Widow from ruin?

Harvey said: "Who's this?" He had a smooth voice that sounded like it was greased with chicken fat.

The Widow said: "This is one of my lodgers. Mr Crampton."

No hand extended for a hearty shake. Instead, the pair satisfied the courtesies with a suspicious nod.

I said: "I've heard about the great offer you've made Mrs Gribble. Double her money in less than a week, isn't it?"

Lloyd said: "Sure. Guaranteed. Would you be interested in a slice of the action?"

The slimeball sounded like a pool hall hustler. Perhaps he modelled himself on one.

"My money's all tied up in consols," I lied.

The pair exchanged confused looks. They'd never heard of consolidated stock, government bonds that paid a steady interest rate. If they were financial advisors, I was the Emperor of Japan.

"Too bad," Harvey said. "We offer a great deal."

He turned to the Widow. "Do you have the five hundred smackeroos in a safe place?"

"I've hidden them in the coal-scuttle," the Widow said.

I raised my eyebrows at that one. It was just as well we were having a warm summer.

I said: "Mrs Gribble likes to deal in hot money. I expect you're the same."

Harvey scowled: "What do you mean by that?"

"That you like making a quick buck."

"We're entirely legit," Lloyd said.

"You're as legit as a nine-bob note," I said.

"Mr Crampton, these two gentlemen have come here in good faith," the Widow said. "I have already received twenty pounds from them, the dividend from my earlier investment."

"Yes, the convincer," I said.

Harvey had been standing behind the sofa. "Our investment comes with a written guarantee."

"A guarantee that only stands as long as the envelope is not opened until you return. Which as you're not going to, will be a long, long time," I said.

The Widow had been leaning over the coal-scuttle. She stood up waving a handful of five-pound notes. A fat handful.

"Enough of this argument," she cried. "Here's the money. Where's the envelope?"

Harvey reached into his inside pocket and pulled out a smart vellum envelope. An expensive item from W H Smith, but it was the only thing the Widow was going to get out of the transaction. And it had already been used.

Harvey moved towards the Widow. I moved between them.

"Let me see that envelope," I said.

Harvey scowled at me. But he held it up.

"I've signed across the seal at the back so we know this is the envelope which validates the investment."

"And so you know that it's not been opened," I said.

He stepped sideways to walk around me. I stepped sideways with him.

"I'd like a closer look at the envelope," I said.

Harvey shot an anxious glance at Lloyd.

"If I'm satisfied, I'll recommend Mrs Gribble gives you the money," I said.

"That's my decision," the Widow said.

Harvey and I ignored her.

I held out my hand. "The envelope."

Harvey glanced again at Lloyd. Lloyd gave a reluctant nod. Harvey shrugged and handed me the envelope.

I held it up close to my eyes and sniffed it, like I was inspecting a rare Shakespeare first edition. As I did so, I stepped back and away from Harvey and Lloyd.

Then I ripped open the envelope and yanked out the single sheet of paper inside.

I held it up and waved it about like old Neville Chamberlain did when he came back from his ill-fated meeting with Hitler.

Lloyd rushed forward and tried to grab it from me. Harvey yelled an obscenity. The Widow clapped her hands to her ears.

I shoved Lloyd away and he tripped over the pouffe. He sprawled on the shagpile carpet in front of the fireplace.

Harvey moved menacingly towards me. "I'm going to teach you a lesson, Mr Busybody."

I waved the paper at the Widow. "It's blank," I cried. "The first time around they switched envelopes while you weren't looking. The switch held the name of the team that won and the score. They'd filled it in after the match."

Lloyd scrambled to his feet. "We're rumbled. But we can still grab the old bag's dough and vamoose."

Harvey yelled: "Let me get at her."

The Widow shrieked: "I can hear bells."

Harvey shouted: "Don't kid yourself. You may look like Quasimodo, but there ain't no bells ringing for you."

Lloyd pointed out of the window. "She's right."

I shoved past Lloyd and looked out. Three cop cars were racing around the square.

They screeched to a halt outside the house.

Harvey screamed: "We need to run for it."

The pair dashed for the door and I heard them clatter down the hallway.

The Widow slumped in a chair. Harvey and Lloyd legged it across the square like they were being pursued by King Kong.

The Widow looked up: "Thank heavens I wasn't gullible enough to fall for their tricks. I had their number all along."

I sat down on a chair breathing heavily.

Outside cops poured out of the three cars.

Seconds later, Alec Tomkins strode into the room. He made a courteous little bow to the Widow.

"Sorry to interrupt but we found the front door open. Two gentlemen seemed to be in a hurry."

"How did you know I was being conned, officer?" the Widow said.

"Conned?" Tomkins pulled a confused face. His normal look.

"I know nothing about a con. I'm here on a completely different matter."

"And what matter requires the urgent attention of three cars and ten cops?" I asked.

"Murder," Tomkins said.

I stood up. "Whose murder?"

"Mr Vernon Stoker, the respected businessman and chairman of Crawley Rovers football club."

"Spare me the biography. I know who he is. When was he murdered?"

"Last night. His head battered in. His body was discovered by his secretary this morning."

A couple of uniform plods hustled into the room and stood on either side of Tomkins, like a pair of bookends.

A sinister ghost of a smile passed across Tomkins' lips.

"Colin Crampton, I'm arresting you for the murder of Vernon Stoker. You do not have to say anything, but anything you do say may be given in evidence."

I laughed. "That won't run, Tomkins. This is you getting your own back for all the times I've beaten you in solving the crime."

"Cuff him," Tomkins said.

One of the plods stepped forward with the bracelets. There wasn't any point in resisting.

Tomkins turned to the Widow.

"We're taking Crampton to the police station. He won't be home tonight."

The Widow's eyes stared and her mouth gawped. "If it's not one thing, it's another," she said.

Chapter 19

Tomkins had stitched me up as tight as a nun's knickers.

That was clear as soon as we reached the cop shop. He'd alerted a motley crew of reporters and photographers. They hung around outside waiting for me to show up.

I'd seen guilty types arriving outside police stations and courts with blankets over their heads. It just made them look furtive.

So when Tomkins handed me a scrofulous piece of material, I chucked it back at him and said: "No self-respecting dog would sleep on that."

I stepped out of the police car with a smile on my face and my head held high.

Needless to say, my arch-rival Jim Houghton was at the front of the press pack.

"Anything to say?" he shouted as I stalked by.

"Yes. Spell my name correctly."

Inside the cop shop, it was clear I was the celebrity nick of the day.

Cops who'd normally be in the back-office playing cards or snatching forty winks in the evidence store, milled about in reception. They greeted me with a bit of a snigger and the hiss of a whisper.

I said: "What's up? Haven't you seen an innocent man before?"

Two uniform plods hustled me into interview room one – the room reserved for star turns. The place was furnished with a chipped Formica-topped table screwed to the floor and two chairs. The chairs weren't screwed. Only the prisoners who sat on them.

One of the plods took off the cuffs. I massaged my wrists to make the blood flow back into my hands. I wanted them in top shape in case I needed to slug Tomkins on the snout.

I sat on one side of the table without being invited.

Tomkins settled himself on the other. He made a show of opening his notebook. He arranged his pens and pencils by the side of it.

I said: "I didn't know you could write."

He said: "You can cut the smart-Alec comments. This is a serious interview."

"It became a joke the minute you arrested me for a crime I obviously didn't commit."

"Says you. But we have witnesses that you were the last visitor to see Vernon Stoker alive."

"If I saw him alive, I can't have killed him. Even a kid with his first toy truncheon could work that one out."

"Our witnesses believe you returned later and killed Stoker."

"For starters, belief is not evidence. And, secondly, who are these star witnesses?"

Tomkins consulted his notebook. "Two car salesmen. Roland Pratt and Sergei Bogoff."

"With names like that, they'll be laughed out of court."

"Not when they say Mr Stoker called for them when you tried to assault him. They say that you were so furious they had to restrain you."

"They attacked me when I asked Stoker some awkward questions."

"They have given evidence that you returned later that evening, when no one was around, and killed Stoker because he wouldn't cooperate with your absurd fantasy of a news story."

"If no one was around, how would they know who killed Stoker? But, plainly, someone did."

"Yes, it's you. The medical examiner puts Stoker's time of death at between six and seven last evening. Where were you at that time?"

I thought back. I'd been asleep in the MGB.

"Travelling," I said.

"Where?"

"On confidential business."

"So you don't have an alibi," Tomkins jeered

I leaned forward so Tomkins would know I was serious. "This arrest is a stupid vendetta instead of a proper hunt for the real killer. You want to get your own back because Shirley busted you for writing that comment about her bum."

Tomkins clenched his jaw. I'd got to him.

"That has nothing to do with this case. Besides, I'll have to consider charging Miss Goldsmith."

"For what? Having a shapely bum?"

"Stealing police property. I could make that charge stick."

"Says you."

Tomkins said: "Let's get back to the facts. You wrote in your rag last night that Stoker had the Cup Final ticket which was originally raffled at Crawley Rovers. The same ticket that was stolen from Sergio Parisi, the murdered café owner. How did he get that ticket?"

"Someone gave it to him."

"Who?"

"I can't tell you that. Like any good journalist I don't reveal my sources."

"You can go to prison for that. Like those reporters did in 1963 over the Vassall tribunal."

Tomkins didn't need to remind me. A judge was appointed to discover how John Vassall, a Russian spy, had operated so easily in the Admiralty. Two reporters were jailed when they refused to reveal the sources of their stories. But there were rumours they didn't have sources – and had made their stories up. I hadn't.

I said: "You won't turn me into an old lag so easily."

"Won't I? That ticket is now missing. And you stole it."

"If I was planning to steal the ticket, why should I write in the

Chronicle that Stoker had it? Do burglars normally publicise the item they're planning to nick?"

Tomkins didn't have an answer to that. So I said: "Are you pursuing any other lines of enquiry?"

"That's a police matter."

"Which means the answer is no. You should get out there. The killer is still at large."

"We're convinced we'll find the evidence to remand you in custody."

"What evidence?"

"Fingerprints in Stoker's office. And we know there was blood on the carpet. We'll prove some of that is yours."

"Of course, you'll find my fingerprints. I've told you I was there earlier in the day. That proves nothing."

"There's the blood."

"I've told you Stoker's thugs attacked me. One of them punched me on the nose."

"Their story is that you attacked them."

"Of course, they're Stoker's paid muscle. Or were. They'll need to look for new employment now."

Tomkins leaned back in his chair with a smug grin on his face.

"I believe I've got enough evidence to hold you overnight in custody. You'll appear before a magistrate in the morning. I shall apply for you to be held on remand charged with the murder of Vernon Stoker. Have you anything to say?"

"Yes. Your evidence is as threadbare as the seat of your pants. I want pre-charge bail."

"Denied."

"Then I want to make a telephone call."

"Also denied."

"Then I'll make a formal complaint to the custody sergeant. I'll make sure he logs it in his diary. Then there will be evidence when I take you to court for wrongful arrest. You're looking at early retirement without a pension, Tomkins."

Tomkins shifted uneasily in his chair. "Very well. But just one call. Better hire the best lawyer in town."

Tomkins didn't know, but I wasn't planning to call a lawyer.

After I'd made the telephone call, Reg Barker, the custody sergeant, locked me in my cell.

It had a double bunk – one up, one down – each with a pillow and a blanket. There was a small table and an upright wooden chair. The lavvie was in the corner.

The walls had been whitewashed, but not recently. Some wag had scratched on the wall: *The Count of Monte Cristo was here. The loose brick is under the bunk. Replace it on your way out.*

It raised a smile as I settled down on the lower bunk to consider my position.

I wasn't worried about the court in the morning. Tomkins' case was so threadbare, the magistrates would throw it out. They might even throw Tomkins out as well. But, perhaps, that was hoping for too much.

I was frustrated that I had to cool my heels in the cell while other journos were free to chase the story. Figgis would have heard the news by now and have the paper's night lawyer on the case. But he specialised in libel, not criminal law – so I figured I'd have to blag my own way out of trouble.

The big danger was, that even if I got freed in the morning, suspicion about me would still hang in the air. Unless the true killer could be found. But there was not much I could do about that until I was once again free to roam the land.

In the meantime, I had to count my blessings. At least, I had the cell to myself. There wouldn't be anyone in the top bunk fidgeting, farting and hanging his smelly socks over the edge.

A key rattled in the door's lock. The hinges squealed as the door swung open.

Reg appeared. "Got company," he said.

"I booked a single with bath," I said.

"Too bad. At least you'll have someone to talk to."

Reg turned to a figure I couldn't see. "Come in here," he said.

A small man with untidy brown hair shuffled into the cell. He had piggy eyes and a fat nose. He wore scruffy jeans, a Rolling Stones tee-shirt, and dirty plimsolls.

Reg said: "Meet your cell-mate, Archie Kite."

I groaned inwardly. I'd met Archie before.

"Well, if it isn't Mr Crampton," Archie said in mock surprise as Reg stepped outside and locked the cell door.

"Evening, Archie."

"I didn't expect to see you in here, Mr Crampton."

"I did expect to see you," I said.

I knew all about Archie. He was a professional stool-pigeon. The system worked like this. When the cops had nicked a suspect on thin evidence, they urgently needed a way to get more. The con wasn't talking to them but might share a confidence with a fellow villain. The villain would usually be a low-level con who'd avoid heavy sentences because he was useful to the cops. The rozzers bargained on their suspect sharing secrets with their stool-pigeon.

Around Brighton, Archie was said to be the best in the game. He'd generally pretend to be in on a charge – receiving stolen goods was a favourite – to create a bond with the targeted suspect. The cops hoped the pair would spend the night yarning about their life of crime. And Archie would report back to the cops in the morning.

Archie took a proprietorial look around the cell, like he'd returned to a long-lost home.

"See you've bagged the bottom bunk, Mr Crampton. I'll kip upstairs."

"Don't snore."

"So, what you in for?"

"Murder. You?"

"Er… Receiving stolen goods. Namely, a silver teapot

179

belonging to a maiden lady living in Palmeira Square."

I had to hand it to Archie. He provided the "corroborative detail intended to give artistic verisimilitude to an otherwise bald and unconvincing narrative". They kept the silver teapot in the cop shop's evidence store especially for occasions like this.

The wooden framework of the bunk creaked as Archie climbed up top.

He leant down and poked his head over the side. "Mind if I take off my plimsolls? The old plates of meat are steaming like a Christmas pud."

"I'd prefer you leave them on."

"Suit yourself. I bet you hope to get out of here by Saturday, Mr Crampton."

"I expect to get out of here tomorrow."

"I was just thinking, on Saturday you could watch the World Cup Final. Do you follow the footie, Mr Crampton?"

"Now and then."

"I thought you'd be a fan. Funny thing, you know, every time I'm in here I'm palled up with a cell mate who loves football. Mostly local teams, of course. But I've met 'em all."

I leant back on the bunk and closed my eyes. I couldn't sleep as Archie droned on about the football fans he'd met in jail.

I could read his game – because I play it as a reporter. You share a confidence in the hope you'll get one back.

Archie, the stoolie, knew that, too. "Of course, I've met 'em all... there was Len Burke, whose great-aunt Edith once sat on the seat behind George Best's mother-in-law on the bus... got off without paying for her ticket... Bet you could tell a tale or two about tickets... eh?"

"No."

"Then there was Rowley Theobold... he got hit in the head by a Terry Venables shot at goal that came off the crossbar... Knocked him out... he was out of it for the rest of the match...

Rowley, that is, not Venables... said it was worth the pain... Not everyone gets knocked out by a Venables miss... Anything like that ever happened to you?"

"No."

"Did I ever mention Cliff Hartley...? He was the bloke who ran onto the pitch during the FA Cup semi-final between Leicester City and Sheffield United... would have been 1961... and the third replay... first two ended in goal-less draws... still old Cliff got so excited when Walsh put one in the net for Leicester, he said he couldn't restrain his-self... his missus used to say the same... Bet you could tell me a yarn about cup finals."

"No."

On and on he went...

Twenty minutes later, my eyelids felt heavy.

I was drifting into sleep when...

"Did I ever tell you about Charlie Smith...? He played for Ifield third team reserves... this would have been a couple of years back... well, he nearly got picked for Crawley Rovers' first team... it was all a balls-up... there was a second Charlie Smith ... same name... he met the other Charlie Smith when he turned up for training... but, here's the point... the second Charlie Smith knew the groundsman... Lennox Slattery... from way back..."

My eyelids snapped open. The bunk shook as I shot up.

Archie droned on: "Thought that would get your attention... anyway, the second Charlie Smith reckoned he'd met Slattery in an earlier life... I don't mean like he'd been reborn... just when they were kids... lived in the same street... in Poplar... not a very popular place in the east end of London... if you take my witticism..."

"Get on with it, Archie."

"So, the second Charlie goes up to Slattery and says, 'hello, remember me – I'm Charlie Smith and you're...' and, you know

181

what...? he suddenly realised when they were kids, he wasn't called Lennox Slattery..."

"What was he called?"

"The second Charlie couldn't remember... Thought he might have called him Mike or Mickey... you know, like the mouse... had a good moan about it to the first Charlie... who told me..."

I sat on the bunk with my mind racing. Could Lennox Slattery have changed his name? And, if so, why? It was strange that his name matched that of a dead Lennox Slattery, about the same age, who'd lived in Eastbourne.

"Where can I find the second Charlie Smith?" I asked.

"Dunno. I'd have to ask the first Charlie Smith."

"And where is he?"

"Lost touch a couple of years back. I think he moved to Croydon. Did I ever tell you about...?"

"Archie, enough!" I snapped.

"You don't want to hear about how Sadie Young accidentally put laxative in the half-time teas...?"

"I want to go to sleep. And if I hear another word from you... well, just remember I'm accused of murder."

"Message received and understood, Mr Crampton. I'll bid you a very good night, Mr Crampton."

"Good night, Archie."

I lay down on my bunk. But it was a long time before I fell asleep.

The lock in the cell door rattled and the hinges squealed.

I opened my eyes. Yawned. Sat up and swung my legs over the side of the bunk.

A thin light from a window high in the wall illuminated the cell like a black and white movie.

Reg came in carrying two trays. He handed one to me, the other to Archie.

"Breakfast," Reg said, stepped outside and locked the door.

The tray had three compartments. One contained a thick slice of white bread spread with margarine. One held a mug containing a black liquid. Could have been tea. Could have been coffee. Could have been unrefined oil. One contained a brown thing, like something a hiker might scrape off the bottom of his boots.

"Bacon," Archie said. "If you don't want yours, I'll eat it."

"Have the lot," I said.

Archie scoffed the two breakfasts.

The door opened again.

Reg came in and pointed at Archie. "On your feet."

The pair went outside.

I sat on my bunk. Thinking.

It was ten o'clock before the door opened a third time.

Reg came in and said: "Hope you slept well."

"I'll recommend you to the hotel guide," I said.

"They want you upstairs."

"I thought they might."

We trooped outside. Ted Wilson was waiting to escort me.

Reg hovered around. "No hard feelings, I hope, Mr Crampton?"

He stuck out his hand. I shook it.

"No hard feelings," I said.

I turned to Ted: "Interview room one?" I asked.

Ted frowned. "This morning they're all in the conference room."

In the conference room, they were all sitting around the big table.

On the far side, Tomkins looking like he'd just swallowed a slug.

Next to him, Detective Inspector Dougal Turnbull, from the Met, looking pleased with himself. He had a manila file in front of him.

Ted took a seat next to Turnbull.

Colonel Jonathan Stapleford, the chief constable, sat at the head of the table. His bristling moustache and brisk manner disguised a sharp mind. He had a pile of newspapers in front of him.

Next to him, Shirley, wearing a black-on-white polka dot dress with flared cuffs. She looked like she'd just stepped off a catwalk.

She jumped up as I stepped into the room. Rushed towards me. We embraced and she kissed me. Not a twopenny-ha'penny peck on the cheek, either. This was a guinea's worth of smooch.

Stapleford cleared his throat noisily. "Perhaps time for a full reunion later?"

We broke our embrace and took our seats at the table. Mine next to Shirley's.

Stapleford said: "Now that we're all assembled perhaps, Miss Goldsmith, you could tell us all what you have discovered."

Shirley grinned at me. "Yesterday, Colin rang me from the cells to tell me he'd been arrested on this trumped-up charge."

Across the table, Tomkins' face flushed.

"He suggested a way to prove his innocence. The question was: is there anyone who would have a motive for killing Vernon Stoker? Was he the honest car dealer he made out? Or was he a crook? Indeed, had he been mixed up in the theft of the Jules Rimet trophy?

"Colin had discovered that when the trophy was recovered from under David Corbett's hedge, it was wrapped in some pages of the *Evening Chronicle*. Some of the crossword clues had been completed in a red pen.

"Last night, I managed to see Betty Mulligan, who runs Mr Stoker's office at Crawley Rovers. Colin had previously noticed a pile of old *Chronicles* in the corner of Stoker's office. Betty let me look at them and I found three where the crossword had been started. All in a red pen. They're the papers the chief constable has in front of him."

Stapleford nodded. "Inspector Turnbull, I believe you have the remnants of the newspaper that wrapped the Jules Rimet trophy in your folder?"

"I have, sir," Turnbull said.

Stapleford pushed the pile of newspapers across the table. "Would you compare the crossword clues in the trophy newspaper with these taken from Mr Stoker's office?"

Turnbull whipped out a magnifying glass – a real Sherlock Holmes job - and spent two full minutes examining them all.

He put the magnifying glass away. "Both the same. No doubt about it. Same pen. Same handwriting."

I said: "I think that proves that Vernon Stoker was involved in some way in the unsuccessful theft of the Jules Rimet trophy. And because the plot to steal the trophy ultimately failed – possibly because of Stoker's part in it – there may be dangerous criminals out there who bear him extreme ill-will."

Stapleford nodded. "Very well put, Mr Crampton. Wouldn't you agree, Chief Superintendent Tomkins?"

"If you say so," Tomkins mumbled.

"I do say so. Most emphatically I say so." He turned towards me. "I think that concludes the business for this morning, Mr Crampton." He turned to Shirley and patted her hand. "And you, Miss Goldsmith. A pleasure."

We had been dismissed.

We stood up and headed for the door.

Stapleford spoke before we reached it. "Mr Crampton, I trust there will be no talk of writs for wrongful arrest. Especially as you leave this meeting with what I imagine will be a scoop – is that what you call it?"

I smiled. "I think we understand one another completely."

I took Shirley's hand and we walked out of the room feeling like we'd just won a private World Cup.

Chapter 20

Frank Figgis finished reading the copy I'd handed him.

It described how the murdered men, Vernon Stoker and Sergio Parisi, were implicated in the theft of the Jules Rimet trophy.

He said: "That girlfriend of yours pulled a brilliant stroke to spring you from jail. She's not just a pretty face."

I said: "Alec Tomkins would agree with you. He thinks she also has a shapely bum. Personally, I think she has the inscrutable wisdom of a Chinese mandarin allied to the courage of a lioness defending a threat to her cubs."

We were in Figgis' office. It was two hours after Shirley and I had left the cop shop. Shirl had headed for home. She'd been up late the previous night finding the evidence that had forced Tomkins to release me.

Figgis glanced at his watch, lifted his telephone, and said to whoever answered it: "Tell Cedric to come in here."

He replaced the receiver. "If the subs move fast, we can make the afternoon extra edition."

The door opened and Cedric's face peered around it. Figgis waved the sheaf of copy paper at him. "Take this up to the subs. It's for page one. And tell the splash sub the headline is MURDER LINK TO TROPHY THEFT."

"Right away, Mr Figgis." Cedric grabbed the copy and scarpered.

I said: "You realise my story raises more questions than answers? And that once it's out there, every other journo in the land will be chasing those answers, too?"

Figgis reached for his Woodbines. "Then you better get out there and find those answers before they do. Where will you start?"

"As I see it, there are three main puzzles we still need to solve. The first of these is what part Vernon Stoker played in the trophy theft. We don't know whether he organised the heist or whether he was a fence – hired by the guys who pulled the sting to move the trophy on. It's beyond doubt now that Sergio Parisi was Stoker's accomplice in dumping the trophy when things became too hot. Probably to claim the reward money."

Figgis shook a fag out of his packet and lit up. "Seems a fair theory. Let's weave it into a big backgrounder for tomorrow's paper."

"Sure. But we also need to solve the second puzzle - who is Lennox Slattery?" I told Figgis what I'd learnt from Archie Kite. And what Henrietta had discovered in *The Times*. "Looks like Lennox Slattery, the groundsman, stole the identity of Lennox, the dead boy in wartime Eastbourne," I said.

"There's a simple way to solve that one," Figgis said.

"I know. I ask Slattery whether he was ever known by another name. I'm heading up to Crawley after our meeting to do just that. But there's also a third mystery," I said.

"Shirley and I discovered from Sister Brake that Brando persuaded Rosina to leave hospital on the promise of some money. We found out from Marco Fratelli that Brando was planning to launch his career as a ticket tout. London's theatreland is the tout's usual stamping ground. I wonder whether that's where the money he's promised Rosina is coming from. If so, I'm not sure that Rosina is quite the girl we thought her to be. After all, she kept quiet about the baby until she couldn't hide it anymore."

"So why continue the hunt for her?"

"Partly because I want to know what else she hasn't told us. But mainly because Brando still wants to kill me. I reckon that if we find Rosina, we'll also find Brando's hidey-hole."

Figgis took a drag on his gasper and blew a smoke ring.

"I've got only one question," he said. "With all these puzzles to solve, why are you still sitting here?"

Thirty minutes later, I walked into Betty Mulligan's office at Crawley Rovers.

Betty was sitting behind her typewriter. She was hammering away at the keys, like she hated them.

I said: "Looks like you've got urgent work there. I won't delay you."

Betty stopped typing and looked up. "Urgent? The place is falling apart. Sergio Parisi dead. Vernon Stoker dead. A World Cup Final ticket missing. And now this."

"Now what?"

"Lennox Slattery has left. This time for good."

Betty pointed at me. "If you leave your mouth hanging open like that, you'll catch flies."

I realised I was gawping. But I was staggered. Events seemed to be spiralling out of control.

I said: "Had Slattery given any hints that he was planning to leave?"

"He said he was taking a few days off. But I assumed that was holiday leave. I thought he was part of the fixtures and fittings of this place."

"Did he give any reason for leaving?"

"No. Just pushed a note through the letterbox. Found it when I arrived this morning." She rummaged on her desk and handed over a small sheet of blue notepaper.

The paper carried no address. It read: "I am leaving the job and I won't be back. No need to send anything on. Lennox Slattery."

I handed the paper back. "Short and sweet," I said.

"Short, certainly," Betty said.

"When Slattery first came to work here, did he fill in any application form?"

Betty shook her head. "It was so long ago, I can't remember. Besides, Mr Stoker has never been very keen on paperwork."

"I was just wondering whether Slattery was ever known by

another name."

"What kind of name?"

"Mickey, perhaps. Like the mouse."

Betty pulled a puzzled face. "Never heard anything like that."

"Did he ever talk to you about his earlier life?"

"No. He kept himself to himself. Buried himself in that groundsman's hut and didn't mix with the others. Made a point of discouraging them from visiting the hut. But he did his job well."

"Have you checked the hut since he left?"

"Didn't think there was any point. Besides, Lennox always locked the place with a padlock when he wasn't there."

"And you don't have a key?"

"No."

"Do you mind if I take a look in the hut?"

"Can't see that will do any harm. If you can get in."

I thanked Betty and left. I heard her thumping the typewriter as I closed the door behind me.

There was no one else about as I crossed the ground to the hut, wondering what I'd find there.

The first surprise was that the place was unlocked. The padlock was hanging open over the door handle. I opened the door and walked straight in.

I stood there in the half-light. The place smelt of cut grass, sweet and moist. Remnants of the grass clung to the blades of the gang-mower which stood in the middle of the hut. Slattery had evidently mowed the pitch before he left. Good of him.

There was a cabin trunk and pile of wooden boxes behind the mower. When I'd called on Slattery during the North Korea-Portugal match, the television had been perched on top of them. Now the TV was on the floor. The boxes had been moved so the cabin trunk stood alone.

I moved around the mower and lifted the lid off the trunk. The thick musk of mothballs wafted up from inside. The thing was stuffed with old clothes. Neatly folded. There was a jacket-and-trouser outfit in blue, which looked as though it might be part of a uniform. There was a set of overalls with a medical motif on the front. There was the kind of pin-striped suit you'd see a city banker wearing.

I rummaged deeper into the trunk and came out with a large cardboard box. I opened it. The thing was filled with wigs. Hairpieces. Must have been eight or ten of them. Some with long hair. Some with short. Brown hair. Fair hair. Black hair. You could be a different person every day of the week with them. There were some smaller boxes towards to bottom of the trunk. One held half a dozen pairs of glasses in different styles. Another, sets of false teeth.

I rocked back on my heels trying to make sense of it. Was Slattery into amateur dramatics on the quiet? Or did he have some kind of weird dressing-up fetish?

I turned from the cabin trunk and moved over to the workbench at the far end of the hut. The bench had two drawers in the front and a vice fixed to the side. An Anglepoise lamp sat at the far right-hand side. I switched it on.

Behind the bench, there was a thick board studded with hooks. Slattery had hung his tools over the hooks – knives, scissors, screwdrivers and the like. I checked each hook. Everything seemed to be in place.

I turned my attention to the drawers. One of them had been fitted with a lock. The key was missing. I tried the drawer and it opened.

I peered closer inside. The edges and the corners of the drawer were caked with dust. The kind that comes when you store papers for a long time. It looked like Slattery had taken the papers before he'd scarpered.

There was a black box made out of heavy plastic. I pulled it out and opened it. The inside had been moulded and lined with blue velvet. The hollowed area had been shaped to hold a gun. Could it have been a starting gun? Like the kind used in athletics races. I couldn't tell. Because the gun was gone.

The other drawer had no lock. I heaved it open wondering what horror I would find. There was only one item inside. A wooden baton, about two feet long, and roughly carved from pinewood. One end had been wound with gaffer tape to make a kind of handle. The wood was stained with brown blotches. The edges had flaked away in a couple of places – as though the baton had had rough work to do.

I felt my heart beat faster. I took a deep breath to calm my nerves.

I was convinced I was looking at the weapon that had beaten Sergio Parisi and Vernon Stoker to death.

I returned to the office to give Betty the bad news.

She had a touch of the vapours but then decided the best way to deal with the crisis was to make a cup of tea.

While she did so, I called Ted Wilson to tell him what I'd found. He said he'd be with me within half an hour.

Then I called the *Chronicle* and dictated a story to a copytaker. At least Figgis would be happy.

Betty and I were drinking tea when Ted walked through the door.

He said: "If you're right about this, we'll have a definite suspect." He turned to Betty. "By the way, I take mine with milk and two sugars."

Ted declared the whole ground a crime scene and called in a full forensic team. He promised to call me if they found anything significant.

As I drove back to Brighton, I wondered why Slattery had left the murder weapon to be found. Perhaps he was taunting any cops who came after him. Or, perhaps, he simply forgot it was there.

I wondered whether I'd ever get the chance to ask him. I'd

have to find him first.

Figgis bustled into the newsroom with a proof of the front page a few minutes after I'd returned.

It carried my story under the headline: DOUBLE MURDER WEAPON FOUND.

He sidled up alongside my desk. "We're way ahead of the competition on this story now. Let's keep it that way."

"What would you like me to do? Commit a third murder?"

Figgis stroked his chin. "*Hmmm.* I'll consider that offer."

He bounced off across the newsroom in a high-stepping gait like a dressage pony. A sure sign he'd done up his braces' buttons too tightly again.

I leaned back in my captain's chair and thought about the next steps in the story. There were so many angles, I couldn't be sure which one to take.

The phone on my desk rang. I lifted the receiver and said: "Colin Crampton."

Shirley spoke, her voice taut with tension. "Listen to this. A strange cobber has just rung the doorbell."

"Not one of your photo admirers?"

"This is serious. But, yes, in a weird kind of way."

"Weird how?"

"He's Korean. From North Korea."

"How can you be sure?"

"Because he looks Korean. He speaks reasonable English. But he's told me he's North Korean."

"Why has he come to you?"

"He saw my picture in the *Daily Mirror* wearing the Korean kit. He thought I'd be sympathetic to his problem."

"What is his problem?"

"He wants to defect to Britain."

Ten minutes later, I was in the living room at Shirley's flat.

The Korean – his name turned out to be Kim Tae-won - sat on the sofa drinking black tea.

He stood up when I entered the room, which made me feel like the headmaster at my old school. I waved him down.

He was a small man with a slim figure and an oval face. He had the kind of perfect skin you see in face-cream adverts. He had dark intelligent eyes. I suspected they could be soft or hard depending on the effect he wanted to produce. At the moment, they were soft. His hair was black, cut short, and slicked back across his head. He was wearing a blue suit, white shirt, and a preppy tie. All dressed for the office.

Or, perhaps, for defecting to another country.

I said: "Should I call you Mr Kim or Tae-won?"

"Tae-won is good," he said.

"Why have you come to Shirley?"

"I want to defecate."

"You mean defect."

Kim produced a thin smile. "Apology from me. My English is at work still."

"I know the feeling. But why Shirley? Most defectors go to the police."

Kim put down his cup and saucer and held up his hands. "No police. In North Korea they not good men. In Britain, I don't know. I not trust police. I see picture of Shirley in newspaper. She wears North Korea clothes for football…"

"Kit," Shirley said.

"Ah, kit!" Kim said. "She looks nice in clothes. I think I can trust her. I think maybe she help me detect."

"Defect," I said.

Kim nodded.

"But how did you find out where Shirley lived?"

"I am with the football team from North Korea. But I no play. I speak to the newspapers. I ask them to write nice things about the team."

"Public relations," I said.

"Yes. Pubic relations."

Shirley giggled.

Kim looked embarrassed. But he carried on: "I see the picture and I ask the man from *Daily Mirror* who is this Shirley Goldsmith? He says she is girlfriend of reporter from *Evening Chronicle* in Brighton. I get train to Brighton and then I go into telephone box and look in the fat book of names."

"The directory," Shirley said.

"Yes, the directory, and I find Miss Goldsmith's name."

"You realise life as a defector is not easy?"

"My life in North Korea is hard. We have little food. And no freedom. This is my first time in another country. I see what life can be like. People laugh and smile. And they have full bellies. And they speak without fear. I want that, too. That is why I deject."

"Defect," I said. "The authorities here will want to question you closely. They will want you to give them information."

Kim's gaze flicked anxiously from me to Shirley and back again. "I know much," he said.

"If you tell us, we will help you," I said.

"Colin..." Shirley said. She gave me a serious look.

"The fact Kim has come here already means we're in this," I said. "We might as well know what we're in it for."

Shirley shrugged. "I'd better make more tea."

I turned to Kim. "Can you tell our authorities anything that will encourage them to offer you political asylum?"

Kim took a moment to take that on board. Then he said: "Plenty. I know that our embassy here arranged to steal the trophy, the football prize."

"The North Korean embassy stole the Jules Rimet trophy?"

Kim nodded. "They hire men to do it. But I do not know these men."

"Then how do you know about this?"

"Because of my job. I am told I must arrange a photograph with our football team holding the trophy. The photograph must make it look like we won the trophy. Then the government, they show this photograph on television and in our newspapers. They say our glorious workers' team of good communists have won."

"And the people of North Korea believe it because there is no free press or television in the country," I said. "The government is the only source of information."

"It is what you call propaganda," Kim said.

Shirley came in from the kitchen with a fresh tray of tea. "I heard that," she said. "It's unbelievable."

"Not really," I said. "The country's leader, Kim Il Sung, has form for commissioning paintings which show North Koreans lifting sporting trophies – from Wimbledon tennis to boxing's heavyweight championship of the world. A bit of a stretch that last one – as the bloke pictured winning it was a ten-stone weakling. But most propaganda is ridiculous if you think about it for long enough."

Shirley handed round more tea.

I asked Kim: "I assume the photographs were never taken?"

He nodded. "The cup was stolen. The deal was that the embassy would pay the thieves then. But the embassy didn't have the money the thieves wanted. We are a poor country. No foreign currency. And the thieves took the trophy away."

I said: "We know what happened after that. There was a ransom demand."

"And two murders," Shirley added.

Kim rubbed his hands together and looked at his feet. He couldn't look us in the eye.

I said: "Apart from the theft and the murders, is there anything else?"

Kim looked up. His Adam's apple bobbed as he swallowed hard.

"We... my masters in North Korea... have an agent in this country. He is a slapper."

"You mean a sleeper," Shirley corrected.

Kim nodded. "But he sleeps no longer. He has gone and we believe it is to kill someone important."

"Who is this sleeper?"

"I don't know. I am not so important. But I hear talk about this when I pass a door at the embassy. There is going to be a killing... what do you call it?"

"An assassination."

"Yes, an assassination. Of a very important person. At the World Cup Final. But this is not good. It is what finally makes me know that I cannot live in a country that allows these bad things. It is why I want to live here."

I looked at Shirley. She stared at me wide-eyed.

"A sleeper agent disappears and Lennox Slattery quits his job on the same day," I said.

"I never was one to believe in coincidences."

Chapter 21

Shirley clunked her cup back on the saucer.

"Are you thinking what I'm thinking, mastermind?" she said.

"Lennox Slattery is already a killer," I said. "He topped Sergio Parisi and Vernon Stoker because he couldn't risk the theft of the Jules Rimet trophy being traced back to North Korea. The Koreans would've been tossed out of the World Cup for ever."

"And now it looks like Slattery plans to kill again," Shirley said.

"At the World Cup Final. A kind of grand finale to his killing spree," I added.

My brain was racing at Formula One speed to process the implications of Kim's story. If Slattery was the sleeper agent, could he have been called on to organise the theft of the World Cup? I could see some logic leading to that conclusion. As a sleeper, Slattery would have had little truck with common thieves. So, he'd have had to conduct an undercover search for a crook to carry out the heist. Slattery would have known Edward Betchley. Like Stoker, he was a used car dealer. The pair often sat together in the directors' box at matches. As an agent, Slattery would have known the weaknesses of people around him. He could have discovered that Betchley had convictions for handling stolen goods. To Slattery that would have sounded like a recommendation.

"Betchley's in jail and hasn't grassed on Slattery," Shirley said.

"Slattery must have paid Betchley well. Or, more likely, warned him of the terminal consequences of betrayal," I said. "Parisi's and Stoker's fates would've served as a frightening warning for Betchley."

Kim swallowed the last of his tea and put down his cup. "I would like to go to the room for boys... and men," he said.

"The bathroom," Shirley said.

"Yes, the batroom," Kim said.

Shirley pointed the way and Kim left the room. All shy, like a naughty boy who's been told to stand in the corner.

Shirl said: "While he's out of earshot, we need to discuss what we're gonna do with the guy."

"We can't call the cops," I said. "At least not yet. You can tell he's scared witless at the thought. Besides, I don't think we could keep him here. If he knew the cops were on their way, he'd scram. We're not his jailers."

"What about MI5, the spooks?" Shirley asked.

"They would scare him even more. Especially before the World Cup is finished. If the North Koreans knew Britain held a defector, they could cause an international storm of diplomatic problems. Harold Wilson and his government would hate that. They look on the World Cup as a feel-good boost, just as their term in government starts to get rocky. I wouldn't rule out them handing him back to North Korean diplomats to keep everything quiet."

"That would mean curtains for poor Tae-won."

"And in an especially unpleasant way… *pour encourager les autres*."

"Yeah! He might have to listen to you quoting French."

I grinned. "This is serious. If Slattery is on the loose for a third victim, we need to work out who it is."

"That's a job for the police."

"Can you see Tomkins – or any one of a dozen other coppers - taking this seriously? They'll treat the idea that Slattery is a North Korean sleeper agent as a fantasy. They'll note we don't have a shred of proof that he's a killer. And they'll be able to think of a dozen valid reasons why he should want to leave a dead-end job at a no-hope football club."

"So, like the Christmas turkey, we're stuffed."

"I guess so."

Down the corridor, we heard the lavatory flush.

"He'll be back in a moment, so we need to decide quickly what to do," I said.

"What's the answer, Einstein?"

"The guy I met in the cops' cell, Archie Kite, said he'd heard of someone – a Charlie Smith - who knew Slattery under a different name. If we could prove that Slattery is flying under false colours, the cops would have to take us more seriously."

"Need the name first. How are you gonna find that?"

"How are we going to find it?" I grinned.

"I feel I've just been enrolled in a wild goose chase," Shirley said.

"In the meantime, I think Tae-won will be happy to stay here. Running water and all mod cons."

Kim stepped back into the room. He smiled shyly at both of us.

"Shirley's got some good news for you, Tae-won," I said.

"You can stay here in the spare room," she said.

Kim gave a little bow. "It is great honour. Thank you. I be a good guest."

It took a few moments for us to explain what we intended to do. We told Kim we planned to go out to meet with other people who could help him live permanently in this country. At first, he looked worried... uncertain. But Shirl's winning smile quelled some fears.

And after she'd shown him around the apartment, he was sold on the idea.

I settled him down in a chair and gave him a copy of the *Evening Chronicle*.

"It's good," he said. "First time I see newspaper without picture of Kim Il Sung."

"The man we need to find is the second Charlie Smith," I said.

"Any relation to the second Mrs Tanqueray?" Shirl asked.

.rlie has even heard of Arthur Wing Pinero's play, I'll
.otebook."

'ere in my MGB heading west. I had the car's roof down
and Sᴜirl's blonde hair streamed in the wind. We were heading
for the Franklin Road Trade and Working Men's Club. The
place was in Portslade, a small town that nestled next to the less
fashionable end of Hove.

I said: "In the cells, Archie Kite told me he didn't know where
the second Charlie Smith could be found. But I suspect Archie
knows more than he was telling. The Club will be a good place
to find Archie."

"How come?" Shirl said.

"The venue could more accurately be called the Light Fingers
Club. Most of the drinkers don't work. They're crooks of one
kind or another. If Archie's not there, someone will know where
he hangs out."

I swung the car into Franklin Road.

The club was a few doors away from the Rothbury cinema.
The flea-pit was showing *One Million Years BC*. There was a
huge poster that showed Raquel Welch bursting out of a tiny
animal skin costume. Possibly made from a mouse.

I pulled the car into the kerb and we climbed out.

I opened the club's outer door and stepped into a small lobby.
Shirley moved in behind me.

An old guy was sitting behind a beaten-up metal desk. He
had a toothbrush moustache which made him look like Hitler's
long-lost uncle. His name was Wally. He'd been reading the
Evening Chronicle.

He said: "Can I see your membership card?"

I said: "Certainly. If you go to my flat in Regency Square,
I think you'll find it at the back of my sock drawer, which is
in the cabinet to the left of my bed. Or it may be behind the
toothpaste in the bathroom. I once left it under my mattress to
hide it from my landlady. Could still be there. Alternatively,

instead of making that journey, you could ask yourself whether the management committee would want you to exclude the most gorgeous girl who's ever put delicate foot to scratched linoleum in this den of thieves."

Wally said: "Eh?"

I said: "May I introduce Miss Shirley Goldsmith?"

Shirley stepped out from behind me.

She said: "*Ooooh*, you smouldering hunk of man muscle. You make my ankles tingle. I may need a massage, all the way up my legs. Hope you have soft hands. Can we go in now? Thank you. What a darling man. I may give you a kiss on the way out."

Wally's mouth hung slack. His eyes looked like they were dancing. "Eh?" he said.

We took that as a yes and pushed through the swing doors into the club room.

The room had a high ceiling and walls painted in a dirty brown colour. There was a series of alcoves down one side, each with a table and two or three chairs. A large snooker table dominated the centre of the room. A couple of old boys weren't having much luck at potting the black.

I recognised one or two of the faces that turned towards us as the door swung shut. Over in the first cubicle Eric Binkle, the gas meter grifter, nursed a half-empty glass of Guinness. A couple of tables on Barry Tate, the racecourse tipster, had his nose stuck in the *Sporting Life*. Over the other side of the room, Sly Sidney, the widow's comforter – specialty: parting elderly ladies from their late husband's life insurance - was deep in conversation with a bloke who looked like a bank manager.

Shirley hissed in my ear: "Not exactly the Whisky a Go Go."

"No sign of Archie," I whispered back.

The bar was at the far end of the room. We made our way towards it.

The bartender was a young bloke with hair over his ears and a know-all expression on his face. His name badge said: Freddie.

I said: "Give us a gin and tonic and a Campari soda."

"Can't serve non-members," Freddie snorted.

Shirley bustled up to the bar. "Listen, snot-nose. I come from Oz, the proud daughter of earlier generations of murderers, cut-throats and sheep stealers. You should be down on your knees thanking me for bringing a touch of class to this slop bucket of a joint."

Freddie looked around nervously, like he hoped to find some help.

"I guess I can make an exception," he said.

He reached for glasses and poured the drinks.

I said: "Is Archie Kite in the club?"

"Who wants to know?"

"An old cell-mate."

Freddie's eyes lit up. "Oh, you're the guy who was banged up with Archie."

Evidently the word had got around. Sounded like I was a celebrity among the criminal classes.

"I had that honour," I said.

"Archie can't stop talking about it. Says he's never done porridge with a toff before."

Shirley snorted.

I said: "I'm not a toff. In Archie's eyes, anybody who owns their own socks is a toff."

Freddie put our drinks on the bar and pushed them towards us. I picked up my gin and tonic and had a good pull at it.

Freddie said: "Archie don't normally come in until later on a Thursday on account of he has to report to the police station at eight o'clock. His bail conditions."

I glanced at my watch. It was nearly nine. Perhaps Archie would arrive soon.

I said: "We'll wait."

Shirley and I took a table away from others on the far side of the room.

I said: "I feel this story is in double jeopardy."

Shirl sipped her Campari. "How do you mean?"

"First, it relies on Archie helping me to find the second Charlie Smith. Then, it depends on Charlie remembering what Slattery's other name was."

Shirley patted my hand. "It'll be fine."

But thirty minutes later, we were on our second drinks.

And Archie still hadn't appeared.

Shirl said: "How long do you think we should wait?"

"Until closing time," I guess.

Shirley looked around at the other punters. They didn't look like they planned to move any time soon.

Then the door opened and Archie hurried in.

He looked harassed and upset.

I called out: "Archie, over here." I waved my arm. Felt a bit of a fool when everybody looked around.

Archie stared at me with hard eyes. Turned away and stomped up to the bar.

I said to Shirley: "I'll need your help on this."

We picked up our drinks and hurried over to Archie. Freddie had poured Archie a pint of bitter.

I said to Archie: "Have that one on me."

I handed a ten-shilling note to Freddie and said: "Have one yourself."

Archie picked up the glass like it was a live grenade and said: "I ain't supposed to be drinking with you, Mr Crampton."

"I thought we were old lags together."

"Yeah! Well, that didn't go so well. I got a bollocking from Tomkins." He turned to Shirley. "Pardon my language, your ladyship."

"Don't let it get to you," I said.

"But Tomkins said it might be the end of my little side-line."

"What little side-line?" Shirley asked.

I said: "Archie is a stool-pigeon. He tricks other cons into providing the evidence the cops are too dim to find themselves."

Archie spluttered over his beer. "Mr Crampton, that's not a word you should say around here."

"Don't be ashamed of it, Archie. When you're dealing with hardened crooks – like those who steal from people who can't afford to lose what little they have – a clever stool-pigeon can discover what a squad of detectives never would. You help to put the really bad men away. Archie, you are a prince among stool-pigeons."

Archie drained his beer. Wiped the froth off his lips with the back of his hand.

"Never looked on it like that, Mr Crampton."

"But we need your help. We have to find the second Charlie Smith – the one who knew Lennox Slattery."

"What's in it for me?"

"Another pint."

Archie's crafty eyes glanced at Shirley.

In mock horror, I said: "Archie, you wouldn't take another man's woman?"

"No, no, Mr Crampton. Even the thought of it and the missus would give me what's for. I was just thinking about one of those pictures."

"The one of me in the North Korean kit?" Shirley said.

"And could you sign it? The lads down the cells won't believe I know a real beauty model, like your ladyship."

Shirl flashed a hundred-watt smile. "Consider it done, you lovely man. And I'll even add a kiss."

Archie's lips puckered up.

"With a cross on the picture," Shirley added hastily. "What kind of a girl do you think I am?"

"Now," I said. "Where can we find the second Charlie Smith?"

Shirl and I had much to think about as we drove back to her flat.

Archie turned out to be one of those people who know a lot less than they think they do.

He knew Smith lived in Gossops Green up Crawley way. Or, at least, had three years ago when he last saw him.

He knew he worked as a bus conductor, collecting the fares. But had thought about giving it up because of the shift work.

He knew he had a harridan of a wife called Marje with a tongue on her like a bullwhip. Or, possibly, he'd divorced her.

He knew he drank at a pub called the Windmill. Except when Marje had taken his hard-earned for housekeeping.

I said: "It's not much to go on. But I should be able to track down Smith tomorrow from the files we have in the newsroom."

"And if you can't?" Shirley asked.

"Then we're back to square one. Which, frankly, scares me."

"Not like you to be a cowardly-custard."

"Consider this, o sex siren of the tabloids, if Slattery does plan to kill someone at the Cup Final, who is it?"

"Plenty of big nobs there," Shirl said. "The Queen, for starters."

"I'm not sure Her Majesty prefers to be known as a Big Nob. But I take your point. If Slattery is a sleeper, and North Korea is planning some kind of revenge attack on Britain, it couldn't possibly be more devastating. But there are plenty of other targets."

"I've heard Prime Minister Harold Wilson will be there. He could arrive alive and wind up dead," Shirley said.

"Would anybody notice the difference? Plenty of other big names, too. We just don't know."

"Makes it all the more important we track Slattery fast."

I pulled the car into Clarence Square and stopped outside Shirley's flat.

"I'll leave you with our refugee this evening. I'll need to make an early start in the morning. Can I have a kiss? Or does it have to be a cross on your picture?"

Shirley answered that question with a million-dollar smacker.

I made it to the *Chronicle* newsroom by seven o'clock the following morning.

I wanted to track down Charlie Smith's address before Figgis loaded me up with some other task.

My first stop was the Crawley telephone directory. Several Smiths, but no Charlie in Gossops Green. That didn't surprise me. The paper had carried a story a couple of days earlier. It said the number of households in Britain who owned a phone had risen above four million for the first time. But that meant only one in six families had one. No wonder there were always queues outside phone boxes.

I hit paydirt with the electoral register. Charlie Ebenezer Smith was listed at an address in Cuckmere Crescent, Gossops Green. There was also, I noted with concern, a Marjorie Alice Smith.

I wrote the details down in my notebook.

I was about to quit my desk, when the phone rang.

I lifted the receiver and a voice said: "You'll never guess who this is."

I said: "You're Albert Petrie, news editor of the *Daily Mirror*."

Petrie said: "It's been some time and I thought you'd have forgotten me."

Some chance. Petrie was already a legend in newspapers. And, besides, he'd once offered me a job. Hadn't been able to take it because, at the time, someone was trying to kill me on a cross-channel ferry. But that's another story.

Petrie said: "It's about your call to the sports desk the other day. Lazy buggers have punted it over to me to deal with. We've been impressed with what you tell us about young Christopher Matthews."

"But you can't find a place for him in the press box at the World Cup Final?"

I'd been consumed with a way that Chris could see the match in person. Especially after Stoker had decided to raffle the ticket that could have made Chris' dream come true. I'd suggested to the *Mirror* that the lad should be given a chance to write a piece about the match from the youngsters' point of view. It was a long shot. A very long shot.

And with Petrie on the phone, it looked as though I'd missed the target.

I said: "Well, thanks Albert, for passing on the bad news in person."

"Bad news? What are you mithering about? We want Chris in the press box alongside our sports team. At the big match."

"You do?" I must have sounded like an idiot.

"Of course, we do. But there's a catch."

"Oh?"

"We want you with Chris. It'll be the old formula. Chris will have the big by-line and your name will be small type at the end – 'as told to Colin Crampton'."

I had a grin on my face that made my body feel like it wanted to float into space.

"'Twas ever thus," I said.

"Don't give me that one, Colin" Albert said. "I'm sending a courier with the tickets and the rest of the info."

The line went dead.

I sat there as my heart beat faster and a warm glow seemed to spread all over my body. Like I'd just slipped into the water in a sunny Mediterranean cove.

Then I reached for the telephone and dialled Wayne Matthews, Chris' dad.

"It's Colin Crampton," I said when he came on the line.

"Not more bad news?"

"More?"

"Lennox Slattery has quit."

"I've heard. This is about Chris."

"So is it bad news?"

"Not exactly," I said.

Chapter 22

I left the newsroom with the whoops of Wayne and Chris down the phone line still ringing in my ears.

But they faded as I raced the MGB towards Gossops Green. I had no idea whether bus conductor Charlie Smith would be at home. But I was riding my luck.

Cuckfield Crescent proved to be not far from Ifield Mill Pond. It was a pleasant enough street of modern terraced houses with generous gardens.

I climbed out of the car, walked up a short garden path, and rapped on the door.

The door was opened by a man in his mid-thirties. He had dark hair brushed back from his forehead and big ears. A protuberant nose – but not in the Cyrano de Bergerac class - jutted over thin lips. His bristly chin hadn't seen a razor blade for at least a couple of days. He was wearing a grey cardigan over a green tee-shirt and striped pyjama bottoms. His crafty eyes instinctively looked behind me to see whether I was alone.

I said: "Charlie Smith?"

He said: "Who wants to know?"

"An old friend of Archie Kite."

Smith rolled his eyes. "Not him. You don't look like an old con to me. Not wearing a jacket with a proper buttonhole in the lapel."

"You don't look like you're dressed for a day in court either."

"So what do you want?"

"Some information."

"You haven't told me your name."

"That's right. I'm careful like that. But it's Colin Crampton. I'm a reporter with the *Evening Chronicle*. And I'd like to ask you about Lennox Slattery."

"Who?"

"Lennox Slattery. You may have known him by a different name in London. Archie thought it may have been Mickey. As in the mouse."

"Oh, him."

Smith stuck his head out of the door and looked up and down the street.

"You better come in," he said. "Any more of this doorstep chatter and the neighbours will think I'm being arrested again."

Smith stepped aside and let me into a narrow hall. There was a red runner on the floor and a whiff of last night's herrings in the air.

"We'll go in here," Smith said. "The Old Witch is out, so you should be safe from bodily injury for about half an hour."

We entered a small sitting room. It had two wing-backed chairs on either side of the fireplace.

I took one of the chairs. Smith plonked himself in the other and hooked a leg over the arm.

I said: "I think Archie mentioned he met you in the cells at Brighton police station."

"Yeah! It was all a mistake."

"Same with me. What were you in for?"

"Fraud. The bastards said I'd been pocketing some of the bus fare money and fiddling tickets. It was all a load of cods, of course. They didn't have the evidence, so they had to drop the case. They still fired me though."

Smith looked out of the window as if recalling it all.

"What were you in for?" he asked.

"Murder," I said.

"Impressive. Did you do it?"

"Not this time."

"Yeah! I've had a hankering when the Old Witch is having a go at me over my beer. But, to tell the truth, I worry about what I'd do with the body. She weighs eighteen stone in her undies."

I took out my notebook.

"When did you first meet the man you knew as Mickey?" I asked.

Smith blew out his cheeks while he thought about that. "Must've been around 1941. I was eight. Mickey was the same age. I probably wouldn't have palled up with him, but he were at the next desk to mine in the classroom. That would have been at the school in Poplar, in the east end of London. Or what was left of it after the Nazis had bombed us to buggery."

"During the Blitz?" I said.

"Yeah! Hairy times. Lessons by day. The bombers by night. Amazing we kids got any learning at all."

"What did you know about Mickey?"

"Well, I knew he weren't English. He told me he'd come from Poland. His father had run a small engineering business in Lodz, a town west of Warsaw. When the Jerries invaded in 1939, his dad joined up as a soldier, but died in the first wave of fighting. Rotten luck for the kid. But his mum somehow got herself and Mickey out and they washed up in the east end."

"And that was all he told you of his background?"

"He didn't like to talk about it, and it didn't seem fair to press him. But it was clear he was a fanatical anti-Nazi. Hated them. Would have killed the lot of 'em himself, given half the chance. Never got it, of course. I remember towards the end of the war, when the Russians moved in on Poland, he couldn't have been more pleased. I told him they were communists and were going to take over the country – and how was that different from the Nazis? He got furious with me. Shouting. Red face. Arm waving. The full show. Said the communists were our saviours from oppression. Personally, I thought it was Winston Churchill."

"Did Mickey often lose his temper?" I asked.

"He had a short fuse, and no mistake. I guess that was because of his experience. See your country over-run, your father killed – it's bound to leave scars. Deep ones, too. Yes, Mickey, could get angry quickly. I think he had one of those split personalities.

He were a bit wrong in the head. Carpet didn't reach quite to the top of the stairs, if you get my drift. I felt he could be violent, too. But he always held it in when he were with me."

"Did you keep in touch after you left school?"

"Nah! I was kicked out when I reached fourteen. Never much cop in the reading, writing, 'rithmatic department. Got a job cleaning the buses at the depot in Stratford. Then the family moved down here when the houses got built in Crawley New Town. As far as I know, Mickey stayed up in London with his mum. We lost touch."

"Archie told me you thought you'd seen him when you ran into Lennox Slattery."

"Yeah! That were a queer do. Don't normally stand on the terraces at Crawley Rovers. No-hope side, a bit like Brighton and Hove Albion – marooned for years now in Third Division South. Anyway, Arthur Lanford dragged me round to Crawley one Saturday afternoon. Thought I recognised the bloke who touched up the white lines round the penalty area at half-time. Mickey! Caught up with him as he were wheeling his cart back to his hut. 'Mickey', I says, 'It's your old mucker, Charlie.' He looked at me like I was Old Nick come up from the Underworld. 'Never seen you before,' he says. 'My name's Lennox Slattery. Clear off'. Well, I were so put out I never stayed for the second half of the match. Crawley were going to lose anyway."

"How sure were you that it was Mickey?"

"I was certain at the time. Mind you, I hadn't seen him for twenty years, and people can change a lot in that time. And he were sure he were Lennox Slattery. So, I suppose he must know who he is."

I thought about that for a moment. From the way he'd told the story, I felt Charlie's instinct about Slattery had been right. That he was Mickey. But Slattery had dismissed the idea without a thought. And people can have lookalikes.

I said: "Can you remember Mickey's full name?"

Charlie shook his head. "It were Polish – and I don't speak Polish. Not so hot on English."

"Did you ever see the name written down?"

"I suppose I must have done. At school, we all had to write our names in capitals on the front of our workbooks. Must have seen Mickey's. But never took any interest in it."

I wondered whether the school might keep records of old pupils. But I thought it was unlikely that far back. Especially as it was wartime.

I said: "Did you ever have any photos of Mickey when you were at school?"

Charlie crashed the palm of his hand against his forehead.

"Why didn't I think of that before?"

"Think of what?"

"The class photo. It were taken in our last year at school. Some old bloke with a droopy moustache and an ancient camera on a tripod. Even had a black cloth which he climbed under to take the shot."

"A photo would be interesting but it doesn't help with the name," I said.

"But that's the point," Charlie said. "It does. The names of the kids are printed on the back of the photo."

I felt a flush of excitement surge through me. "And you have the photo?"

"Dunno. If I have, it'll be in the lumber box up in the loft."

I reached in my pocket. Pulled out my wallet. "Two pounds if you can find that photo in half an hour. Five if you do it in a quarter."

Charlie grinned as he leapt from his chair and headed for the door. "Say ten if I do it in five minutes."

I sat in the room and listened to the sounds. A thump as he let loose the door to the loft. A rattle as he moved a ladder into position. Then some scratching, and squeaking, and scraping as he moved boxes around. And, finally, a crash as a heavy box hit the floor.

Then silence.

I waited.

And waited.

It seemed like an hour.

But when I glanced at my watch, it had been only four minutes.

Charlie appeared in the doorway. There was black dust over his pyjama bottoms and a spider's web hanging from his ear.

"Better pay me the full ten," he said.

I pulled a dog-eared photograph out of my inside pocket and laid it on Henrietta Houndstooth's desk.

"Class of forty-five," I said. "Poplar Primary School."

Henrietta picked it up and looked at it. "Poor kids. Look at their clothes and shoes. They look like they haven't three-ha'pence to rub together."

"Pick the Pole," I said.

"They all look the same to me. Poor, tired and worn down by war."

"Turn the photo over."

Henrietta flipped it and stared at the names on the other side.

"I see what you mean," she said. "It's easier to pick the Pole when you see their names. Mikolaj Kowalski."

"Or Mickey to his friends," I said.

"Like the mouse," Henrietta added unnecessarily.

"Don't suppose you'll have a file on him," I said.

"Unlikely, as he lived in London. Our best hope is if he was ever mentioned in *The Times*."

Apart from whole corridors of filing cabinets which held millions of cuttings from the *Chronicle*, the morgue also had a set of annual indexes to *The Times*. And there were copies of *The Times* on microfilm going back to 1945.

I started with the index volumes. Nothing in 1945. Or 1946.

But when I hit 1951, I called Henrietta over.

"Look at this," I said, pointing to an entry. It read: "Kowalski, Mikolaj. Guilty verdict at court martial."

Within a couple of minutes, Henrietta had loaded up the microfilm. It was a small item towards the bottom of an inside page. It was headed: Korean War - Soldier Guilty of Desertion.

The text read: "Private Mikolaj Kowalski of the Middlesex Regiment was found guilty *in absentia* at a court martial of desertion while serving on the Korean peninsula. The court was told the army had no definite knowledge of Kowalski's whereabouts. But other reports suggested he may have absconded to the north."

"No wonder Slattery didn't want to be reminded that his real name was Mikolaj Kowalski," I said.

Frank Figgis leaned back in his chair. It was five minutes after I'd left Henrietta.

"Let's not jump to conclusions," Figgis said. "We know Kowalski deserted, but that doesn't mean he reappeared in Britain as Slattery. The chain of evidence is not complete."

"There's Charlie Smith's identification."

"A couple of minutes at a football game. I expect Smith had had a couple of brown ales. You wouldn't convict on his say-so."

"But there's the name on the back of the photo."

"Again, doesn't prove Kowalski is Slattery," Figgis said.

"What about the fact he's disappeared from his job?"

"Painting lines on football pitches for a living? If I had to do that, I'd disappear."

I fidgeted in my chair. I felt total frustration.

I couldn't persuade Figgis that Slattery was a dangerous foreign agent without telling him about Kim Tae-won. I wondered whether I could swear Figgis to secrecy. But that would be like getting a rabid dog to promise not to bite. Figgis wouldn't be able to resist his lust for a big story.

And, as a reporter myself, I had to respect that.

But, perhaps, I could persuade Figgis to take the story seriously another way.

I said: "Just suppose for a moment that Slattery is an agent intent on murder at the World Cup Final. Who would his target be?"

Figgis said irritably: "Do we have to play pretend games?"

"Indulge me."

"Very well. The Queen would have to be the number one target. But she'll be well protected. No assassin would get near her."

"I'm not so sure. In an exciting football match, everyone's focus will be on the pitch. Even the people who are supposed to keep an eye open for Her Majesty's safety."

"Maybe. But there are other targets. Harold Wilson, the prime minister. Or the team captains."

I said: "We're talking about Slattery's future targets. Aren't we forgetting something? If Slattery is a sleeper agent, he'd be mixed up in the theft of the Jules Rimet trophy. So were Vernon Stoker and Sergio Parisi. And they're both murdered. In my book, that makes Slattery the number one suspect."

Figgis stroked his chin in thought. "I might buy that theory."

"Consider this," I said. "Neither Stoker nor Parisi were involved in the original theft plan. That was something which seems to have been organised by Edward Betchley who is now in jail. Serving his time in silence – and, I would think, looking forward to a big pay-out when he's released in a couple of years.

"It would have been Betchley who got Stoker involved when the caper became too hot for him. They were old football pals, going way back. As a couple of wide boys, they'd have schemed how to make some cash out of the trophy after the North Koreans reneged on the deal. When that failed and Betchley got himself arrested, Stoker would've had to promise him a big pay-off to do his time and keep his lips buttoned. That's when Stoker would have thought up the scam to claim he'd found the trophy and pocket the reward. To pull that off, he recruited Parisi to play the bit part of chucking the trophy under the hedge. I wouldn't mind betting that Slattery was horrified when he found out what was going on.

"So suddenly, the heist's mastermind has two new players in the drama. That's risky enough. But the fact he personally knows them makes the situation intolerable. He can't risk Parisi squealing about his link to Stoker. That could be the weak link that puts the whole chain in jeopardy. So he kills Parisi. Later, when Stoker boasts about his World Cup ticket, Slattery realises he has to be silenced as well."

Figgis nodded. He jotted a couple of notes on a piece of copy paper. "Trouble is, we've got no evidence to support that theory."

I shrugged. Figgis was right.

"Maybe tomorrow will turn up something new," I said.

"It's the day of the big match," Figgis said. "People will want football news – not murder stories."

"Perhaps I can deliver one that has a bit of both," I said.

Figgis turned his head and gazed out of the window.

"I do believe I can see a squadron of porkers performing aerial acrobatics," he said.

I stomped back to the newsroom and slumped down in my captain's chair.

Figgis' crack about pigs might fly had set me thinking. He may have written off the threat of an assassination at the World Cup. But, in my opinion, the porkers were lined up on the runway ready for take-off.

I reached for my telephone and dialled a number at Brighton police station.

***

I met Ted Wilson half an hour later in Prinny's Pleasure.

I said: "You'll need a large scotch for the tale I'm going to tell you."

"In that case, you better add a packet of pork scratchings," he said.

Pigs again! Were they trying to tell me something?

We took our drinks to the table at the back of the bar.

I said: "I've gathered enough evidence to convince me there's going to be an assassination at tomorrow's World Cup Final."

Ted gave his scotch some serious punishment, then looked me in the eye. "Yes, and I've just seen a Gloucestershire Old Spot doing a loop-the-loop over Shoreham airport."

I shook my head in exasperation. "Listen to this," I said.

I told Ted what I'd discovered about Lennox Slattery. How he'd originally come from Poland. How he'd deserted the army in Korea. How he'd changed his name from Mikolaj Kowalski. How he'd stolen the name of a boy who'd been killed in an Eastbourne air-raid. How he'd returned to Britain under his assumed name as a North Korean sleeper agent. How he'd organised the theft of the Jules Rimet trophy. And how he had to be the top suspect for the murder of Sergio Parisi and Vernon Stoker.

Ted rustled his packet of pork scratchings while I described what I knew.

He said: "You have a pile of suspicions a mile high. None of it holds together as a linked chain of evidence. If I took this to Tomkins, he'd just laugh at me. Any other senior detective, too. Anyway, where did you hear all this guff?"

I hoisted my glass and had a good pull at the gin and tonic. I needed time to think about that. Should I tell Ted about Kim Tae-won? It would mean breaking a solemn promise – possibly with dire consequences for Kim.

I said: "I've pieced the story together. And I've seen the inside of Slattery's groundsman's hut. He has a gun."

"You saw it?"

"Well, no. I saw the box he kept it in."

"So you've seen a box, not a gun."

"There was the cabin trunk stuffed with dressing-up clothes and wigs. I think Slattery is used to wearing disguises. He may be disguised tomorrow."

"It's not a crime to wear unusual clothes."

"I'm sure Slattery killed Stoker to get his World Cup Final ticket. An easy way into the ground for him."

"Then you'll know where he's sitting."

"He won't be there. Once inside, he'll disappear into the one hundred thousand people in the crowd."

Ted drained the last of his scotch. "Don't think I'm unsympathetic, but I need more than this. Otherwise, I'm going to look like a plonker down at the station. We need more. Is there anything else you can tell me?"

I put down my glass. "Yes. Those pork scratchings are bad for your teeth."

Shirley snuggled up close to me on the sofa.

We were in her flat. It was a couple of hours after I'd met Ted Wilson. And the evening before the World Cup Final. I'd told her I couldn't persuade Frank Figgis or Ted to take the assassination threat seriously.

She put her arms around me and gave me a long lingering kiss. If it were a painting in oils, I'd have framed it and hung it in the National Gallery.

She said: "I'll be glad when this is all over."

I relaxed a little. Moved closer and kissed her again.

I said: "Personally, I could keep this going all night. And I've got one or two other tricks we can try."

Shirley gave me a playful slap on the arm. "I'm not talking about a smoochy hour, big boy."

"What then?"

"This whole World Cup gig. It's just taken over everything. It broke up our holiday. Stopped you going down on one knee with that proposal act. We don't know where Rosina's run to. Don't even know for sure whether she's with Brando. Guys I talked to in the Italian cafés had their lips zipped. And now I'm landed with an unwanted lodger."

Kim Tae-won had tactfully retired to bed.

I said: "It'll all be over tomorrow."

"Will it? The final match may be over. What will happen to Kim?"

"We'll make sure he's treated fairly by the security services. With the complications of the World Cup out of the way, he'll gain political asylum in this country."

"And then there's Rosina. We still don't know where she is."

"With Brando, it seems, cooking up a ticket tout scam."

"We don't know she's involved in that."

"Perhaps tomorrow we'll get some answers." I glanced at my watch. "It's getting late. I'd better go. I have to pick up Christopher Matthews in the morning. I'm driving him to Wembley so he can perform his stint as a special *Mirror* reporter."

"Take care," Shirley said.

"According to Ted Wilson, I've got nothing to worry about," I said.

Chapter 23

Christopher Matthews sat in the passenger seat of my MGB and stared at the road ahead.

His lips were screwed tight and he looked a bit tense.

It was World Cup Final day and I had my foot firmly on the accelerator as we sped up the London Road towards Wembley.

I said: "You look a bit worried. Is everything all right?"

Chris turned his head and gave me a half-smile. "Yes. I can't believe I'm going to be at the World Cup Final. But I don't know whether I'll be able to write what the newspaper wants."

"You'll be great," I said. "They want to know what kids like you make of it all. They want your view – that's why they've asked you to do it."

"But I don't know whether I'll have any ideas."

"You'll have hundreds of ideas – and impressions – as you watch the match. Just jot down a brief note about each, so you don't forget. At the end of the match, choose the best ones. And there's your article. A lively three hundred words."

"It sounds a lot to me."

"Not as much as you think. There are about twenty words in an average newspaper sentence. So you've got to write just fifteen sentences. You'll do that before you've even realised it."

"I'll do my best," he said. "You've put my mind at rest."

Which was good news for one of us. Because my mind definitely wasn't in rest mode. In fact, it was churning around like a hurricane-whipped sea.

I'd called Ted Wilson before picking up Christopher. Ted had told me he'd had a "quiet word" with other 'tecs about the assassination idea. No dice.

The cops hadn't taken my warning about Slattery seriously. They'd written off everything I'd told them. The North Korean connection. The false name. The suspicions over Parisi's death.

And Stoker's. The dressing-up box. The theft of the World Cup ticket.

The cops had said an assassination at the game was impossible. Killers avoid crowds, they'd said. They lurk in the shadows, they'd said. They simply don't carry out their trade in front of an audience, they'd said.

But wait a minute. The evidence of history suggested that's exactly how they carried out their business. Like Brutus and his pals who did for Julius Caesar in the Roman Forum. Or John Wilkes Booth who shot Abraham Lincoln while he was watching *Our American Cousin* at Ford's theatre in Washington. Or Gavrilo Princip who picked off Archduke Francis Ferdinand waving at the crowds while on his way to visit wounded officers in hospital.

The trouble was, the cops were thinking like cops. Not like assassins. They should have got into the assassin's mind. Role played what he might do. Put themselves in his position. Looked at the problem from his point of view.

I'd tried it myself. Not easy, I had to admit.

I simply couldn't work out who the target would be.

Or how the killing would take place.

And all of the time, I needed to watch my own back.

Marco Fratelli at *Casa Marco* had told me Brando Cavaletto had no greater ambition in life than to end mine. It was an honour thing, Fratelli had said. Deep in Sicilian culture, he'd said. Being a cold-blooded Englishman I wouldn't understand, he'd said.

I understood only too well. And I didn't like it one little bit.

We hit heavier traffic on the South Circular Road. I slowed the car and tucked in behind a red London bus.

I took a quick glance at Chris.

He'd gone quiet and stared out of the window.

"Nearly there," I said.

He turned and smiled. "I know it's going to be great," he said.

***

"I never realised this happened at football matches," Chris said.

We were in the press box at Wembley stadium. We each had a chair with a small table in front of it. There was a portable typewriter on the table. And a telephone with a direct line.

There were rows of seats with the same tables, typewriters and telephones.

It felt like everyone had turned up at a football match with part of their office.

"Most journalists type on sheets of copy paper," I said. There was a little pile of it on our table.

Chris picked a sheet up. "It's quite small."

"About six inches deep. Reporters type up key events in the game as they go along," I explained.

"Like a goal or a penalty?" Chris asked.

"That's right. They'll type no more than two or three sentences on each page. Then, as the end of the match gets near, they can arrange the pages into the order that tells the best story of the match. All they need to do then is bat out an intro to their story – and they're ready to file. That's especially important for evening matches when newspaper deadlines may be only minutes after the match ends."

"And they use this telephone to read it over to their office," Chris said.

"You're catching on fast. We dictate it to a copytaker who will type it out and hand it to sub-editors who will provide a final polish. It's exactly what will happen to the words you write."

"I've never used a typewriter before," Chris said.

"Don't worry. Just write your thoughts in pencil on the copy paper. After all, you're going to dictate it to someone who'll type it out anyway."

I felt a tap on the shoulder. I spun around. Ben Trafford, the *Sunday Mirror's* sports editor, was standing beside me.

"So this is the future editor of the paper on his first

assignment," Ben said with a smile.

He stuck out his hand. Chris took it and they shook.

Ben said: "Now, Chris, we'd like to use your copy in all editions starting with the first UK edition of the paper, which goes to the Channel Islands and Cornwall. The deadline for that is quarter to six. The match might not finish until quarter past five if there's extra time. Think you can file before deadline?"

"Yes, sir," Chris said.

I took Ben aside. "I may need to leave Chris for a bit this afternoon. Can you keep an eye on him?"

Ben gave me a leery look. "What's the story?" he asked.

"Just something personal."

"Why do I feel I'm being shafted?"

"Don't worry, Ben. If it comes to anything, the *Mirror* will have first refusal. After the *Chronicle*, of course."

He arched an eyebrow. "Of course," he said.

He sloped off across the press box in search of a drink.

I glanced at my watch. Quarter past two. Forty-five minutes to kick-off.

I picked up the telephone and called the *Chronicle*.

I said to Chris: "I'll just let the paper know what our number is here in case they need to get in touch. Why don't you take a look around the press box?"

Chris nodded. He stood up and moved slowly along our row.

I got through to Figgis.

He said: "What's happening?"

I said: "Nothing yet. The match hasn't started and the crowd is still coming in. None of the VIPs have turned up so far."

"Any sign of a special police presence?"

"Nothing more than you'd expect for a big match."

"What about Slattery?"

"No show. I'm going to check the seat where he should be sitting in a few minutes."

"He won't be there."

"That's what I'd expect. But the wise man always expects what he shouldn't expect."

"One of your old Chinese proverbs?" Figgis asked.

The line went dead.

I looked over to the other side of the press box. A small circle of journos had gathered around Chris. It looked as though they'd rolled out the welcome mat. One of the journos handed him a Coca-Cola. Another brought in a hot dog.

He'll be fine, I thought.

I glanced at my watch again. Twenty minutes to kick-off. Most of the stadium was full now. It buzzed with anticipation.

Time to check on whether Slattery was sitting in his seat.

I left the press box and headed around a back path to the stand which held Slattery's seat. South stand. Block 29. Third row from the front. Right-hand aisle seat.

I climbed up the staircase into the block and took a good look around. This seating block was on the opposite side of the ground to the Royal Box. That was over the Royal Tunnel in the North Stand.

In fewer than fifteen minutes Bobby Moore and Uwe Seeler would lead the England and West German teams out onto the pitch.

I walked down the central aisle between the seats. I counted the rows back from the front.

Third row. Right-hand aisle seat. Should be empty if Slattery was a no-show.

I stopped. A man was sitting in the seat with his back to me. Slattery? Surely not.

I checked the left-hand aisle seat. A woman sitting there.

I stepped swiftly down the aisle to the front. Turned round like a guy soaking up the atmosphere.

Let my eyes sweep casually over the crowd. Let them come to rest on the guy in the right-hand aisle seat, third row.

It wasn't Slattery.

Not unless he'd had a major surgical procedure since the last time I'd seen him.

Slattery had a thin ascetic face. This man had cheeks like a chipmunk.

Slattery had a body-builder's figure. Muscles the product of years of heavy outdoor work. This man had a prize paunch and muscles that looked like deflated balloons.

Slattery had brown hair, cut short and combed back from his forehead. This man's hair straggled over his collar like it had taken up residence and wasn't going any place.

The man was opening a packet of Maynard's wine gums. He took out a blackcurrant one, popped it into his mouth and sucked.

I stepped up to the man and crouched down beside him.

He turned his head towards me. Suspicious eyes peered at me through rolls of flesh.

I flashed my press card too quick for him to read and said: "Stadium security."

"Anything wrong?" he asked nervously.

Nervous. Good. I'd need to keep him that way if I was going to get the information I wanted.

I said: "Could I see your ticket?"

"Showed it at the turnstile."

"Of course. But they'd have only torn off the stub. You should have the rest of it."

"Suppose so." He swallowed his wine gum and selected another. Orange.

I said more firmly: "I'd like to see your ticket."

"Who are you?"

"Stadium security. I showed you my pass."

"Didn't really see it."

"Would you like to continue this conversation in one of our interview rooms under the stand? It'll be more private but you won't see any of the match."

His piggy eyes beamed a hate ray at me. But he rummaged in his pockets and pulled out the creased remnants of the ticket.

I took it and held it close to my eyes. Sniffed it. Rustled it by my ear. Held it up to the light.

I said: "This ticket was originally stolen."

The man said: "I bought it fair and square."

"But not from the ticket office. Am I right or am I right?"

The bloke scowled and chewed hard on his wine gum. He said nothing.

I said: "I thought I was right. Where did you buy it?"

"From a seller outside the ground."

"A ticket tout?"

"No."

"A guy selling tickets outside the stadium must be a ticket tout."

"Not if he's an ordinary bloke who just wants a different seat."

I thought about that for a moment. "You mean you swapped tickets with a random person? I think you'd better tell me exactly what happened."

The man swallowed his wine gum. He said: "If I do, will you then leave me alone to watch the match?"

I said: "Just tell me."

"Okay. I came here without a ticket hoping to get one from a tout. Some hope. One of the twisters wanted ten guineas for a ticket in one of the standing sections. I ask you, more than a tenner to stand on my own two feet. Anyway, I was arguing with the bloke when this other bloke came up. He said he had a seating ticket and if I wanted it, he'd buy the standing ticket and have it himself."

"Why would he do that?"

"The bloke with the seating ticket said he liked the atmosphere among the real football fans. Well, what was I going to say to that? I grabbed the ticket and legged it in here. Left the bloke to fork out ten quid for the tout's standing ticket."

"What did the bloke look like?"

"The tout or the bloke with the standing ticket?"

"The standing ticket guy."

The man scratched his head. "Didn't really take much notice. I was more focused on the ticket."

"Was he tall or short, fat or thin?"

"Average, I'd say."

"What was he wearing?"

"Ordinary football clothes."

"What are ordinary football clothes?"

"Same as any other clothes. Trousers and jacket. He did have a cap. Don't know whether that's any help."

"Where did you meet the guy?"

"Outside the North Stand. Well, a bit more round to the west side, to be strictly honest."

He peeled back the paper on his sweets and took another wine gum. Lemon.

"Normally get through two tubes of these in a needle match. Got three today, just in case there's extra time."

I straightened up and headed back up the aisle with a black thought.

The match was about to kick-off. Slattery was hidden among the standing spectators.

And planning to kill.

Chapter 24

I ran through a few hard facts on my way back to the press box.

There were eighty-seven spectators' blocks - seats or standing room - in Wembley Stadium. A surging crowd of ninety-six thousand football fans filled them.

Slattery was in that crowd – in any one of the blocks. I could start at Block One. But the match would have finished before I was anywhere near Block Eighty-seven. It was an impossible search. Wine-gum man had no idea which block the tout's ticket occupied. Other than it was a standing block.

But, in my book, that meant nothing. If Slattery had swapped his ticket once, he could have done it again. He could now be sitting comfortably waiting for the match to begin. Waiting for the moment when he made his move – and his victim died.

And, after that, he could slip away through any one of the stadium's one hundred and four exits. Silent. Unnoticed. While nearly a hundred thousand fans cheered their team on to victory.

I re-joined Chris in the press box just as a huge roar from the crowd filled the stadium.

Bobby Moore and Uwe Seeler led their teams down the Royal Tunnel and out onto the pitch.

Chris was reaching for a sheet of copy paper and a pencil. I tapped him on the shoulder to let him know I was back.

He turned round and grinned. "You were right. When something happens, I do get ideas about it." He wrote furiously on his paper.

As the teams started their warm-up kickabout, I took a look around the stadium. The Queen and her party were in the Royal Box. Harold Wilson and other members of the government were in the boxes behind. There were guests from the West German Federal government.

If I had a sight with crosshairs, I could have put any of them in the centre of it.

Perhaps Slattery would.

A sharp blast on the ref's whistle brought the captains to the centre of the pitch for the toss. The coin flipped into the air and Bobby Moore called it right.

The teams took their positions. Another whistle blast. Another roar from the crowd.

The match was on.

Chris was on the edge of his seat. He leant on the desk and pushed himself up for a better view.

I sat back and tried to take an interest in the match. But every time a move by England got my attention some black goblin in my mind crushed it.

There was going to be an assassination. But nobody believed me. And I wasn't even sure that I believed it myself.

The minutes ticked by.

In the twelfth minute, Sigfried Held sent a cross into England's penalty area. Helmut Haller picked up the ball from a Ray Wilson mis-header. He fired at the goal. One-nil to West Germany.

Chris wrote more notes on copy paper.

The minutes ticked by.

No gun shots were fired. No one died.

In the eighteenth minute, Bobby Moore took a free-kick. He lifted the ball into the West German penalty area where Geoff Hurst was waiting. Hurst leapt towards the ball. Got his head to it. One all.

Chris wrote notes on copy paper.

The minutes ticked by.

Half-time came.

Half-time went.

No gun shots were fired. No one died.

In the seventy-seventh minute, Alan Ball passed to Hurst. He managed to deflect the pass to Martin Peters. Peters took the final shot. Two-one to England.

Chris wrote more notes on copy paper.

The minutes ticked by.

No gun shots were fired. No one died.

In the eighty-ninth minute England were penalised for a Bobby Moore foul on Uwe Seeler. Lothar Emmerich fired a hard shot at a wall of English defenders. The ball deflected across the goal mouth. Silence fell on the stadium. Wolfgang Weber struck the shot. Two-all.

The referee blew a long blast on his whistle.

The end of full time.

No gun shots had been fired. No one had died.

I should have felt relief. But the tension mounted in me.

On the pitch, the players' bodies slumped. Their thoughts focused on the reserves of strength they'd need to find for thirty minutes of extra time.

Chris made more notes. He arranged his sheets of copy paper into a new order. He made some edits.

The minutes ticked by.

No gun shots were fired.

The phone on our table rang.

I lifted the receiver.

Frank Figgis said: "There's been an important development."

"What?"

"I've got Charlie Smith on the line."

"The first one or the second one?" I asked.

"The only one I know."

"What does he want?"

"He says he's remembered new information about Lennox Slattery. Says it might be important."

Time stood still.

I said: "Frank, switch Charlie through to me."

There were some clicks. A buzz. And a final clunk.

Charlie said: "Is anyone there?"

I said: "Colin Crampton, Charlie. I'm in the press box at Wembley Stadium."

"Lucky bleeder. I'm in the public bar at the Fox and Hounds. And the blooming telly's just packed up. But not before it reminded me of something about Slattery. Or Mickey. Or whatever his bleeding name is this week."

"Time's pressing, Charlie. What is it?"

"Well, it was that foul Bobby Moore committed on the German captain."

"Uwe Seeler."

"If you insist. Personally, I didn't think it was a foul. No free kick. No German goal. We'd have won by now. But I suppose you have to take the rough with the smooth."

"Get on with it, Charlie."

"Well, Mickey as I knew at Poplar was always funny about that."

"Funny about what?"

"Having a foul or penalty awarded against him when we were playing football. I remember one occasion when the ref said he tripped the other team's centre forward just as he were lining up for a shot on goal. Mickey was furious. Yelled and shouted that it was a genuine accident. The ref was having none of it. So Mickey went up and kicked the ref right up the Khyber Pass, if you get my drift. Apparently, he couldn't sit down for a week. Of course, Mickey was sent off and banned from the team after that, but always raged when he thought a free kick or penalty was wrongly given against his team."

"Raged?"

"Well, more than that, actually. He usually threatened revenge. You could tell from his eyes that he meant it, too. I often suspected he had a screw loose. The bloke was two pork pies short of a picnic. Especially when there was a foul at footie and Mickey thought the ref was wrong. Most blokes would let the ref have a few well-chosen four-letter words. Not Mickey. He wanted to hang, draw and quarter the poor blighter."

A shiver passed through my body. Like a lizard had just crept down my spine. I felt cold. My hand gripped the telephone like a claw.

And, at last, I knew who Slattery planned to kill. Perhaps already had. But, if not, I knew where he would deliver his *coup de grâce*.

Charlie said: "Are you still there, Mr Crampton?"

"Yes, Charlie."

"Only I could hear you breathing heavily. I thought you might have that girlfriend with you. She'd get me breathing heavily, no worries. No offence intended, Mr Crampton."

"None taken, Charlie. Thanks for your help."

I replaced the receiver.

Chris tapped me on the arm. "Is everything all right?"

I forced a smile. "Yes, Chris. I've just had some news."

"Good or bad?"

"Important. I may have to leave you for a few minutes during extra time. Think you can cope?"

"Everyone here is so helpful."

I gave the lad a pat on the shoulder. I headed up the stairs and out of the press box.

Lennox Slattery, sleeper agent and serial killer, had referee Manfred Ashburton in his sights.

Ashburton had refereed the quarter-final match between North Korea and Portugal. He'd awarded two penalties against North Korea. Penalties which Slattery had fumed against. Penalties that would have left the match a draw at full-time if they'd not been given.

I had watched as Slattery had raged against Ashburton's decisions.

I had heard him vow: "That ref will not sleep soundly in his bed again."

And now Slattery was ready to take his revenge.

To take Ashburton's life.

But how?

And where?

Slattery would have known that Ashburton would have a seat at the final, like other tournament officials. He'd know that his chance of killing Ashburton in his seat would be remote. He simply couldn't get close enough. And, if he did, he could never hope to escape.

So he would have to lure Ashburton away. I thought about how Slattery would do that as I hurried towards the tournament officials' seats. Perhaps Slattery had tried and failed. Perhaps he was now frothing with rage somewhere. I hoped so. For Ashburton's sake.

A steward stopped me at the entrance to the officials' section.

"Reserved seats," he said.

"I don't want to sit down." I flashed my press card. "It's a quote thing. Is Manfred Ashburton around?"

The steward consulted a list on a clipboard.

"He left at half-time."

"With whom?"

"No one. I think he said he'd received a note to meet someone important."

I rocked back on my heels. So that was how Slattery had decoyed his sucker.

"And he's not come back?" I asked.

He ran his finger down the list. "Nope. Crazy. He's missing the best final ever. Must have something better to do."

I didn't tell him it was dying.

I hurried to the back of the stadium. Looked down at a huge oval of people jammed together. Almost one hundred thousand of them. In what? Perhaps fifteen acres. Must be the densest crush of humanity anywhere on the planet.

Denser than London's Waterloo station in the rush hour. Or New York's Times Square on New Year's Eve. Or India's Kumbh festival when thousands gather on the banks of the Ganges.

Nowhere to run. Nowhere to hide.

But Slattery was hidden somewhere.

What had he told me?

"You'll always find a haven of peace in the groundsman's hut."

No groundsman's hut at Wembley. Too grand for that. But there was a groundsman's workshop under the east stand.

I hustled round the back of the stadium towards it.

I didn't know what I would find. Perhaps Slattery taunting Ashburton before killing him. Perhaps Ashburton already dead.

I thought about calling the cops.

But those in the stadium were too intent on watching the match. And, while I wasted minutes convincing them of the danger, Ashburton could die.

I heard the roar of the crowd as extra time kicked off.

I tensed my body and strode towards the workshop.

Behind me, a hundred thousand voices cheered their teams to victory.

The notice on the door of the groundsman's workshop read: "Stadium staff only. Strictly no admittance."

I opened the door and stepped inside.

The space was big. And black.

It was like walking into a cave. One of those tropical ones where bats hang from the roof.

Except that it wasn't a cave. And there weren't any bats hanging from the roof.

I looked up and couldn't see a ceiling. And then I realised the ceiling was the underside of the banked seating of the stadium. Highest on the outside. Lowest towards the centre.

The roar of the crowd sounded like the rumble a train makes

as it slows down before a station.

I searched along a wall near the door and found a light switch. I pressed it.

Fluorescent lights, hung by wires from the ceiling, flickered into life.

The place was huge. It stretched fifty yards from side to side. Perhaps eighty yards to the far wall. A forest of steel pillars – I guessed ten yards apart – supported the weight of the ceiling and the banked seating above.

Thousands of people were in those seats. Just yards away. But I'd never felt so lonely. So exposed. More in danger.

Now the lights were on, the pillars cast long shadows. They loomed across the floor. They criss-crossed one another. They created strange shapes. And they seemed to move, like they wanted to hide from the light. I looked up. The fluorescent tubes swayed in a hidden draught.

I couldn't see Ashburton anywhere. Or Slattery.

To my right, a roped-off area held a gang-mower and three motor mowers. The kind where the driver sits on an elevated seat at the back and the grass cuttings spray into a hopper at the front.

There was a small tractor. And a couple of trailers. There were machines for marking white lines on pitches. And trolleys for moving bins from one place to another.

I moved slowly further into the workshop. There was a bench along the left-hand wall. There were machines for drilling things, and cutting things, and bending things. There were hammers and wrenches and bolt cutters and something with a handle and a hook on the end.

At the end of the bench, there was a huge hopper. It overflowed with footballs. No doubt spares if the match ball became deflated.

No sign of Ashburton. Or Slattery.

I stepped around one of the pillars. To my right, a partition had been erected to screen off part of the area. I tiptoed silently towards it, like I was playing grandma's footsteps. I peered cautiously around the edge of the partition. I half expected to find Ashburton dead on the floor.

He was there, all right.

Chained to a pillar.

Still alive. But looking like he wanted to be dead.

His body had slumped against the pillar. His head was hanging over his chest. There was a smudge of blood on his left cheek.

The shadows of the other pillars gathered around him. Like ghosts at a funeral.

I checked out the area behind the partition. Couldn't see Slattery.

I stepped towards the pillar. No more grandma's footsteps. Ashburton's head came up as I approached.

His eyes were dull with defeat. His body tensed with fear as I moved closer.

He said: "Have you come to kill me?"

I said: "No. But you're clearly into injury time."

He let out a low moan. His body relaxed against the chains.

I said: "Where's Slattery?"

Ashburton nodded towards the far end of the workshop. "There's an office over there. It's in a kind of windowless cabin. Slattery's in there. I don't know what he's doing. He's mad. Raving. Says I've ruined the honour of his country. He says he wants to kill me. But wants me to suffer first. I don't know what to do. I just referee matches."

"How did Slattery get you here?"

"I received a note. Looked like official Football Association notepaper. Signed by Joe Mears, the chairman. The note said the Association wanted to make a presentation to me after the match, for services rendered. Joe wanted to have a quick word and asked me to come to the groundsman's workshop where we could speak privately. The note was obviously forged. Slattery coshed me when I came through the door."

Ashburton's voice started to echo around the place.

I said: "Keep quiet. I'll get you out of here before Slattery comes back. There are some bolt cutters on a bench over there. I'll get them and it'll be Hercules Unchained all over again."

I hurried over to the bench. Rummaged around in the tools. There were so many. I'd forgotten where I'd noticed the bolt cutters. Whoever looked after this place didn't believe in putting things back in their rightful place.

It felt like minutes, but was only seconds, before I found the cutters. Hefted them in my hand to test their weight. Hummed and hawed a bit over whether they'd cut the chains. Decided they'd do the job.

Made my way back. Passed the mowers. Around the pillars. Into the partitioned-off area.

Slattery was waiting for me.

He stood next to Ashburton. He had a gun. The barrel followed me as I dropped the bolt cutters and crossed the floor between us.

When I was ten feet from him, he snapped: "Stop!"

I said: "What's the problem? Am I off-side?"

"You're in the killing field."

"That's what I wanted to talk to you about. I was thinking a nice friendly conversation. With no guns."

"Power comes out of the barrel of a gun."

I said: "It's the bullets that worry me. But is this any way for a distinguished football club groundsman to end his career?"

"How better than in defending the honour of the greatest country on earth?"

"Great Britain?"

"North Korea," he said. "From the moment I headed north across the thirty-eighth parallel back in 1951, I knew I had found my true home. They welcomed me with rice and flowers."

"I'd have rather had a gin and tonic."

"You are disrespectful."

"I know. I think it must be a medical condition. I'll get it seen to."

"Your attitude will ensure you are also killed."

"In the end, we're all dead. But I reckon I have a few years to go yet. I'd like old Ashburton here to have a chance to pick up his pension, too."

"Ashburton is an enemy of the people."

"Just because he punished a couple of pretty obvious fouls against Portugal?"

"They were not fouls. The glorious people's team of North Korea plays by the rules."

"The rules don't mention a gun. Put it down. I'll take Ashburton back to his place in the stadium and we'll say no more about it."

"You will set the running-dog police onto me."

I turned to Ashburton: "He's got all the chat, hasn't he?"

Ashburton groaned.

Slattery said: "You must both die."

I said: "If we have to die, answer some questions first."

"Why should I?"

"Because your answers may show how clever you are."

Slattery preened himself a bit. "You are right. You should see how strict discipline and Marxist thinking is the route to a good life."

I said: "It wasn't much of a route for Sergio Parisi. He only played a bit-part in the Jules Rimet trophy caper. Why did you have to kill him?"

"Parisi was greedy. A hyena of the capitalist system. He wanted more than his fair share. He was stupid. I had to teach him a lesson. It had to be a final lesson."

"And what about Vernon Stoker? Did he deserve a final lesson, too?"

"Stoker was a useful fool. He had no idea of the great socialist plan to steal the trophy and use its image as an inspiration for the workers. But, when I decided to liquidate Ashburton, I needed Stoker's ticket in order to enter the ground in disguise. His life was a fitting sacrifice to the triumph of the proletariat."

Above us, a huge cheer went up. It was followed by applause and feet moving.

I said: "They've reached mid-point in the extra time. It's still a draw. They'll change ends and play another fifteen minutes."

Slattery moved across the floor and rattled Ashburton's chains.

Ashburton straightened up a bit. But I could tell from his body language that he'd given up. If he was going to die, best get on with it. For the poor bloke, life had turned into a penalty shoot-out that never ends.

I moved towards Slattery: "There's still time to change your mind."

Slattery waved his gun to indicate he wanted me to move away from him. I took a couple of steps back.

Slattery said: "I shall kill you first. Ashburton can watch. It will heighten his fear as his own end approaches."

He flicked the gun at me again. "Move over there – about ten yards away. I shall shoot you in the heart. And if I miss, I shall shoot you again."

"*Non sparerai a nessuno finché non lo dirò io,*" a voice said from behind us.

We spun around.

Brando Cavaletto was standing by the partition. He had a gun which pointed at us.

Slattery looked at me with a blank expression.

"You'll shoot no one until I say so," I translated. "Better do as he says," I added.

Chapter 25

Brando swaggered towards us and mimed three shots from his gun.

Pow! Pow! Pow!

Fake shots. Real gun.

A loud cheer erupted above us. The crowd in the stadium had greeted the second half of extra time.

Brando ignored the roar and lined up his weapon on Slattery. He said: "You don't kill Crampton. He's mine. He helped my wife get away. In Sicily, a wife is a man's most valued possession. After his gun, of course. And his dog. When I lost Rosina, I lost face. I lost respect. I can't have that. I get back my good name by killing Crampton."

Slattery pointed his gun at Brando.

He said: "Join the queue. Crampton is a capitalist crony who has sabotaged the work of the Democratic People's Republic of Korea. He has been tried by a People's Court – me - and found guilty. Sentence: death by a single shot. To the head. Or possibly the heart. It's just one decision after another. But I shall administer the sentence."

"Like hell, you will," Brando said.

"Try and stop me," Slattery spat.

I moved between them. "Don't I get a say in this?"

Over by the pillar, Ashburton groaned.

Brando said: "Who's the guy chained to the pillar?"

"A football referee," I said.

"I often wondered what happened to them after the match," he said.

"This is a special case," Slattery said. "Ashburton is also a lackey of the ruling classes and guilty of sabotage. Of the glorious victory of our football team. There can be only one consequence of that."

241

"A replay?" Brando asked.

"Death."

This was way out of hand. I had to try and keep them talking until some help turned up. That wouldn't be before the end of the match.

I'd do it by asking questions. The first one was obvious. How had Brando pitched up in this football farrago?

I turned to him and said: "How did you find me?"

His lips twisted into a vulpine grin. "I had business outside. Tickets to sell."

Of course, I'd forgotten. Marco Fratelli had mentioned that Brando had moved into the ticket tout racket. I'd assumed they'd be tickets for *The Sound of Music* – or whatever was pulling audiences in the West End. Not a football match.

"A tout," I said.

"A salesman," he said. "I saw you arrive with the *giovanotto*."

"The young man."

"Yes. The young man. He will be going home alone."

"What I can't figure is why you're here. Shouldn't you be with Rosina? She's gone back to you. You persuaded her to leave the hospital."

"Yes, I made her an offer she could not refuse."

I couldn't help raising my eyebrows in exasperation at that. Wherever did he pick up these expressions?

Brando was a clown. But a dangerous one.

He said: "Rosina says she will love me even more now she has returned. But if you lost a dog and then found it again a few days later, you would always wonder where it had gone. And what it had been doing. It is the same with a wife. Perhaps worse with a wife. That is why I must kill you."

"What does Rosina think about that?"

"She will understand when I tell her. As an act of reconciliation, I will allow her to send flowers to your funeral."

"No lilies, please. They smell rank when they fester."

Slattery stamped a foot. "What is this talk of flowers? If there are any flowers on Crampton's grave, they will be the mountain magnolia, the national symbol of North Korea. And they will be there because I have executed him according to the laws of Marx."

"Would that be Karl or Groucho?" I asked.

Slattery raised his arm and levelled his gun at me. "We are wasting time. Turn around and I will put one bullet in the back of your head."

Brando yelled: "Don't you dare, commie bastard. I'll shoot Crampton through the heart. In fact, I'll shoot you first to make sure I get to do it."

I held up my hands. "If you both shoot at the same time, you'll never know which bullet croaks me. You'll go to your own graves wondering whether you were a hero or a zero."

Slattery and Brando exchanged a quick glance. The outstretched arms with the guns wavered.

Brando said: "He could be right."

Slattery said: "Bullets from the People's Republic travel faster. Mine will kill him."

Brando said: "He's standing closer to me. It's distance rather than speed that counts."

I piped up. "Why not settle this another way?"

"What way?" Slattery asked.

"*Si, che modo?*" Brando said.

"A sporting way," I said. "Like real football fans."

The pair lowered their guns.

"Settle the matter with a penalty shoot-out," I said.

They exchanged puzzled looks.

I don't know why I said it. I just blurted it out. But I had to say something. I was dealing with two angry guys. Fired-up guys with loaded guns. Any moment now they planned to use those guns. On Ashburton. And on me.

"What's a penalty shoot-out?" asked Slattery.

"We played it at school," I said. "Each player takes it in turn to score a penalty. The player who scores the most wins. One of these days, they'll use penalty shoot-outs in the World Cup when there's a tied match."

"Over my dead body," said Ashburton.

"If we don't try it now, your body may be dead faster than you think."

"My football boots are in the groundsman's hut at Crawley Rovers," Slattery said.

"We kick for goals?" Brando asked with a puzzled frown. He scratched his forehead with the barrel of his loaded gun. Not something recommended by the manufacturers.

I said: "I don't mean kicking the ball into a goal. I mean a real shoot-out. With guns and with footballs as the target."

"Which footballs?" Slattery asked.

"The footballs in that large hopper over there. We won't use all of them. We'll make the winner the best of six."

I had no idea how many bullets they each had in their guns. But in the westerns I used to watch as a kid, the cowboys always talked about their six-shooters. If I could con Slattery and Brando into using their shots on footballs, perhaps Ashburton and I would get out of here alive.

I said: "I'll get the footballs. I'll line them up on the workbench over there and you take it in turns to shoot one out."

"But that will destroy the balls," Slattery said. "That's vandalism. It's a crime."

"So is murder. But that doesn't seem to bother you."

"Afraid I'm going to beat you?" Brando jeered at Slattery.

Above us, a big cheer went up from the crowd in the stadium.

"If we fire our guns down here, they will hear us," Brando said.

"That didn't trouble you when you were planning to kill Ashburton and me. Besides, there's so much noise up there, they won't hear anything down here. If they do, they'll think it's a car back-firing outside the stadium."

I hoped that wouldn't be the case. If someone heard, surely they would come to investigate.

Brando said: "Very well. I will do this. I will win this contest. And then, I will kill you."

"You must beat the People's Republic of Korea first," Slattery sneered. "And we are invincible."

I said: "We should release Ashburton. We need a professional ref for a contest this important."

Slattery and Brando exchanged worried glances.

"Suppose he runs away," Brando said.

"Why would he run away?" I said. "He's got an important match to referee. It would be a dereliction of duty to quit. He'd be kicked out of the ref's union and have his whistle confiscated."

Slattery and Brando exchanged wary looks.

Their gaze travelled back to me. They each gave a reluctant nod.

Slattery moved across to Ashburton and unlocked the padlock holding the chains.

Ashburton breathed out deeply. He shook the chains free and stepped away from the pillar.

I said: "I'll set up the footballs in a row now."

I strolled over to the hopper and made heavy work of selecting the balls. The more time I could take up, the more likely it was that rescuers would come.

"Hurry up," said Brando. "I must leave this place soon. Rosina will be waiting for me. And when she hears how I have exacted revenge, she will make passionate love to me."

"Don't let the thought of it put you off your game," I said.

I set up the footballs on the workbench. A nice neat line of them. Each ball six inches from the next.

I said: "I think we should let Ashburton decide the penalty spot that you'll shoot from."

"I think it should be that oil stain on the floor," Ashburton said. "It's about the same distance as a real penalty spot from the goal."

He jogged on the spot like he was warming up to referee a big match. He seemed to have got over his ordeal. With the prospect of some authority to chuck around, he was getting into it.

Slattery and Brando walked over to the spot and stared at it. They still held their guns at the ready.

Slattery said: "An oil stain is a symbol of capitalist expropriation."

"Get over it," Brando said. "In my world, we get oil stains where we've run a roadside heist. Lifted cash off a rich *signore* in an expensive car. Perhaps a Maserati. Or a Lamborghini. Plugged a hole in their petrol tanks with a bullet. Oil stains have happy memories."

Slattery said: "After I've beaten you, oil stains will have bad memories." He made a get-on-with-it gesture with his gun. "You can fire first."

Brando's eyes narrowed. He raised his gun. Waved it about a bit. Pointed it at Slattery.

"Who said anything about me shooting first?" He turned to Ashburton. "Say, ref, did you say I should fire first?"

Ashburton shook his head. Looked worried. "Perhaps we should toss a coin."

"*Lasci perdere!* Forget it!" Brando snarled at Slattery. "You're the home team. You should kick-off."

"Fire-off," I said.

"I'm not a home team. My heart is in Pyongyang."

"*Sei uno stronzo,*" Brando spat.

"What does that mean?" Slattery asked.

"You don't want to know," I said.

"It means you must shoot first," Brando said.

"Loosely translated," I said.

Slattery stomped up to Brando. Waved a gun in his face.

He said: "Nobody speaks to an agent of the People's Republic of Korea like that."

"I just did," Brando said. "And if I were *stupido* and shot first, you'd kill Crampton while I was doing it. And then me."

"I am a man of honour," Slattery yelled. "I understand the people's cause."

"*Non hai capito una sega*," Brando shouted.

"Gentlemen, gentlemen," Ashburton shouted above the din. We all fell silent. Looked around in case any gents had just wandered in.

"I am the appointed referee and I will toss a coin. I have a penny here." He held up the coin. "I am going to toss it in the air. If it comes down heads Mr Slattery will shoot first. If tails, *Signor* Cavaletto will step to the penalty spot."

Slattery and Brando stepped forward with guns raised in protest.

But Ashburton had already tossed the coin. High above our heads it spun.

Over and over and over.

Then, as if in slow motion, it hung in the air – and started to descend. Still it spun.

Over and over and over.

I glanced at Slattery's face. His eyes stared hard. His lips parted in fear.

I flipped my gaze to Brando. His eyes blazed with anger. His chin jutted forward.

And as I watched, his arm moved, like a serpent striking towards its prey.

He raised the gun and fired. The explosion filled the place. My eardrums felt like ripe grapes in a wine press.

A loud *ping*, like the snap of a harp's string, cut through the echoes of the explosion.

The bullet had hit the spinning penny.

The coin shattered like shell shrapnel. Tiny specks of metal cut through the air.

They zinged off the pillars.

They dinged off the floor.

Instinctively my hands went to my head. And I crouched low. But I looked up.

Slattery had turned his gun on Brando.

I shouted: "Brando, look out."

Brando spun round. Saw Slattery aiming his gun. Brando's gun arm swung towards Slattery.

Slattery settled on his aim and fired.

Less than a second later, Brando's gun exploded with a shot.

I scrambled to my feet. Brando was standing by a pillar. He had a smile on his face. Job well done. But then the smile faded. His eyes turned upwards into his scalp. His mouth lolled open. His gun arm dropped by his side. With a clatter, the gun fell to the floor. Brando's left leg collapsed, like it had been kicked from under him. He slumped against a pillar. Held there for a moment. Then slid, ever so slowly, to the floor. His head hit the concrete hard. His lips twitched again. Perhaps it was a smile. It was certainly Brando's farewell to the world.

I turned towards Slattery. He was gripping his gun with both hands in front of his chest. Like he wanted to lift it to his lips and give it a kiss. But the arms dropped from his chest. And the gun tumbled to the floor. A red bloom, like a carnation flowering, blossomed on Slattery's chest. He opened his mouth as though he wanted to scream. But there was no yell of pain. Just a deep gurgle. His head drooped forward. He braced his right leg to support himself. Then the strength gave way and he collapsed to his knees. For barely a second, he knelt looking at me. As though he was in prayer and I were a saint. And then his eyelids drooped closed. He fell face-forward onto the floor.

Ashburton stood immobile, his hand to his mouth. His eyes misted with disbelief.

And then a roar erupted above us. In the stadium, one hundred thousand people yelled in triumph at the tops of their voices.

The roar built like a great wave of noise.

Like the rush of a river racing over a giant waterfall.

It fed on itself, growing louder and louder.

As though it wanted to fill the whole world with its joy.

"It sounds as though England have won the World Cup," I said.

Chapter 26

Chris Matthews sang the World Cup Willie song all the way home to Crawley.

My MGB rocked with joy as we sped down the road from London.

I said: "You could make a record to rival Lonnie Donegan's version."

Chris grinned. "It's been just the best day ever!"

I'd kept the grisly details of events in the groundsman's workshop from Chris.

Indeed, few people outside the cops and the security services – the spooks from MI5 – knew what had happened. I intended to change all that in the first edition of the next day's *Evening Chronicle*.

The noise of the shots had brought the cops running and they'd sealed off the place.

It was an hour before I made it back to the press box. Chris was at his seat dictating over the last of his copy. The *Sunday Mirror's* Ben Trafford was sitting next to him.

Ben raised a quizzical eyebrow when I returned. He'd heard rumours that something had happened, but didn't know what. But he didn't press me in front of Chris.

Besides, just as Chris finished his dictation, a familiar figure had appeared alongside him.

Chris replaced the receiver, looked up and gawped. "You're... You're..."

"Bobby Moore," said Bobby Moore. He was holding a football.

He said: "I've just run up from the dressing room to give you this. It's one of the kick-about balls we've used in practice, but all the team have signed it. The guys heard what you've been doing and thought it was the least we could do."

Chris's eyes were like dinner plates as he took the ball.

"Yes, that's Nobby Stiles' signature you're looking at," said Bobby.

"Thanks... thanks..." Chris stammered.

"Can't stop. Interviews to give and a celebration party to attend."

"Thank you, captain," I said. "You're a winner off the pitch, too."

Moore nodded a farewell and took the steps to the exit two at a time.

After that, there wasn't much to say.

Chris croaked out a last chorus of the World Cup Willie song as I dropped him outside his parents' neat semi-detached house in Three Bridges, on the outskirts of Crawley.

Football was coming home. And so were we.

But to what?

Chris had shown that he had the makings of a real reporter in him. I could see him in the newsroom. Or in the press box at Brighton and Hove Albion's Goldstone Ground in years to come.

But what about me?

And what about Shirley?

This whole saga had begun with me about to propose marriage. On one knee. With a ring in my hand. But we weren't engaged. And the ring wasn't on Shirley's finger. We'd sold it.

And now I didn't know what my next step should be.

I reached the newsroom at the *Chronicle* the following morning with a fat pile of copy paper.

After dropping off Chris the previous evening, I'd headed for Regency Square. I'd kept the Widow's other tenants awake as I'd hammered out a story on my portable typewriter.

I handed the copy to Cedric and asked him to take it to

251

Figgis. Then I sat in my old captain's chair and busied myself by checking out messages that had come in.

Fifteen minutes later, my phone rang.

I lifted the receiver and a voice said: "Come in here."

I said: "Trailing clouds of glory."

"Leave the clouds outside my door."

I stepped up to Figgis' door, tapped lightly on it, and went in before he could bellow "Enter."

Figgis was sitting behind his desk with a proof of the first edition's front page.

He said: "Sit down and take a gander at this."

I sat and gandered.

The page was dominated with a piece by Phil Bailey about World Cup celebration parties. Phil had dotted his piece with banal quotes from half-drunk merrymakers about how the result was the best thing in the world. *Et cetera.*

I said: "Where's my story? I've written a piece about the double killing of a secret agent and a Mafia don. I'd added that the agent had already murdered twice – Sergio Parisi and Vernon Stoker. And the Mafia don's smuggling network will now be wound up by the cops. Since when has soft-news fluff had the drop on a granite-strength hard news story?"

Figgis reached for his Woodbines and said: "There are problems about your story."

"What problems?"

Figgis shook a fag out of the packet and lit up. "For starters, the cops are saying Slattery's and Cavaletto's deaths were accidental. The spinning coin stuff confused them and Cavaletto fired at the penny by mistake. That confused Slattery who thought Cavaletto was going to kill him. And when Cavaletto saw Slattery with his finger on the trigger, he jumped to the wrong conclusion. They both fired by accident."

"You know that's nonsense."

"The cops can't admit Slattery killed Parisi and Stoker without revealing his background as an agent. So they'll be added to the unsolved crimes file. And, as for the smuggling network, who'll even notice that's gone?" Figgis had a drag on his gasper. "The point is, the cops have been leant on."

"By the security services?"

"Whisper, who dares?"

"Because MI5 doesn't want to admit it's had a sleeper agent under its very nose for fifteen years. Too embarrassing."

"True."

"But it won't mind claiming that it's got an agent from the other side. Kim Tae-won."

I'd told Special Branch cops about him after the shooting at Wembley. They'd collected him from Shirley's flat the previous evening.

"They won't want to turn the spotlight on him. He'll be in a safe house with a butler and a cook and a couple of handlers," Figgis said. "They'll drain him dry of everything he knows about North Korea. They won't want the press poking their noses in."

"What about Ashburton's kidnap? Slattery planned to kill him."

"Without Slattery's testimony, pure supposition," the cops say. "Could all be a mistake."

"How often do football referees get chained to pillars?"

"Couldn't say. Beyond filling in my weekly Littlewoods coupon for eight score draws, my knowledge of football doesn't stretch that far."

I ran my hands over my hair in frustration. It didn't help.

I said: "We still have an accidental death story."

"Possibly," Figgis said. He sounded about as enthusiastic as if he'd been asked to bring out the paper in Cyrillic type. "But Cavaletto doesn't come from our circulation area, so he's of little interest."

"Slattery does."

"Yes, but how newsworthy is a small-town football club's

groundsman? I suppose we might manage three paragraphs on an inside page. Towards the back of the paper, of course. And no mention of sleeper agents."

"And that's it?" I asked. "I could resign from the paper and take this story somewhere else. I know the *Daily Mirror* is interested."

"You'd meet the same problems. Neither the cops nor MI5 will confirm your version of the story. Without that, it's down among the rumours where there's no independent evidence."

"What about Ashburton?"

"He's been told to keep his mouth shut if he wants to don the black shorts and referee more international football."

"You've forgotten about Rosina. Brando Cavaletto's abused wife. And now widow. She may speak."

"I can't see a dutiful widow doing anything other than singing his praises."

Figgis may have been right. But there was still a mystery about Rosina's apparent reconciliation with Brando. I was determined to unravel it.

I picked up the front-page proof. Took another look at it. There was nothing I could do to change it. I tossed the proof back to Figgis.

Figgis took a last drag on his fag and stubbed it out. "There is another possibility," he said.

"I'm listening."

"In recognition of past service, the paper is willing to offer you a five hundred pounds bonus. And some holiday leave. I've had a word with His Holiness. He agrees."

Gerald Pope, the paper's editor, was putty in Figgis' hands.

I thought about the offer. Nothing could replace the thrill of a scoop. But five hundred pounds might ease the pain.

Especially if it came with sun, sand, sea – and Shirley.

"I'm owed four weeks holiday," I said.

"Why not take two of them?" Figgis said.

"You're all heart," I said. "And don't forget to sign and date the cheque."

A solution to the mystery of why Rosina went back to Brando took a step nearer after I'd returned to the newsroom.

My phone rang.

I lifted the receiver and Shirley said: "Listen up, big boy. I've tracked down Rosina."

Shirl sounded like she'd just won first prize in a boasting competition.

"I'm impressed. How did you do it?"

"Thought of something you hadn't, you old lame-brain."

"Amaze me."

"When a patient is discharged from hospital, they have to give a forwarding address. It's in case the hospital needs to get in touch with them again about their treatment. I went round to the Royal Sussex and found this guy in the records office. Persuaded him to tell me which address Rosina had given."

"Hospital records are confidential. That's why I hadn't tried that."

"But you hadn't been pictured wearing the North Korean kit. He had the cutting with the photo on his wall. Let's just say I made his day."

"You brazen strumpet!"

Shirl giggled. "You horse's arse."

"Anyway, I called and caught Rosina at home. She'd heard the news about Brando."

"How has she taken it?"

"You know that opera – *The Merry Widow*. She could take the lead role. But she's agreed to come to the pub tonight to tell us more."

"Prinny's Pleasure?"

"Where else? Seven o'clock. Don't be late. See ya!"

The line went dead.

***

Rosina, Shirley and I gathered around the corner table at the back of the bar.

Shirley had a Campari soda and I nursed a gin and tonic. Rosina sipped a glass of Chianti.

Her face was pale and her eyes were lowered. I thought it was probably the nearest she ever came to being embarrassed.

"I felt I owed you two an explanation," she said. "After you'd rescued me from Italy and everything."

"Yeah! Don't forget the everything, kiddo," Shirley said. "You had some of that at my apartment."

Rosina twirled her glass nervously. "I had to make an instant decision."

"What instant decision?" I asked.

"When Brando cornered me in my hospital bed."

"What happened?" Shirl asked.

"He said he'd come with some good news. He said he'd been in touch with his family with news of the baby."

"How did he know about the baby? It's your lover Ricardo's. I thought you'd kept it quiet."

Rosina lowered her eyes. "When I left Taormina so suddenly, I forgot to bring a letter from my doctor with me. It confirmed I was pregnant. Brando found the letter. With typical arrogance, assumed he was the father. It was one of the reasons he was so keen to pursue me to England. And, now, he will never know the truth."

"How did Brando's family take the news?" I asked.

"He told me they were thrilled. Especially his grandfather. Lorenzo Cavaletto. He's the old man. The head of the family. Nobody moves or breathes without his say-so."

"He's the local Mafia capo?" I asked.

Rosina nodded. "He controls everything on the east side of Sicily around Catania. Anyway, Brando told me Lorenzo was delighted he was going to have a great-grandson – as if he had the right to order a baby boy. But he was pleased to have an heir, a future capo. He was going to give Brando and me five thousand pounds so the kid had everything he needed. The trouble was, Lorenzo had arranged for a lawyer here to draw up papers which we both had to sign. Brando wanted me to come to the lawyer's office right away."

"Why the rush?" I asked.

"It was something about moving money through an international bank account. Had to be done in less than twenty-four hours. Obviously crooked. But what could I do? If I didn't sign, I couldn't get the money for the baby. Besides, I knew once the money was in Brando's bank account, he would spend it on himself. I had to find some way to get the money – and I couldn't do that in hospital."

"You signed the papers?" I asked.

"Yes. And the money was transferred into a bank account with both our signatures. But the next day, I discovered that Brando had transferred all the money into his own account."

"The snake," Shirl said.

"But you weren't prepared to leave it there, were you?" I said.

Rosina had a nervous gulp of Chianti. "What do you mean?"

"I think I know," I said. "When you were both at *Casa Marco* with Fratelli, you played on Brando's low reputation with his own father. You suggested that Brando should pull off a World Cup ticket scam that would raise his reputation in his father's eyes. And you suggested that as it could be dangerous, Brando should carry a gun. You planned to tip off the cops so that Brando would be arrested. And the fact he was armed would mean he'd go away for a long sentence. But you didn't bargain for the fact that Brando saw me – and decided killing me would give him a higher status in his father's eyes."

"I never wanted that to happen," Rosina said.

Shirl piped up. "The best-laid plans of mice and men… kiddo. Even mice and women…"

"What will you do now?" I asked.

"I've got two deaths to deal with. My father's as well as Brando's. I'm his sole heir. So, when they're over, I'll collect the five-thousand pounds and anything else Brando has stashed away. I'll sell my father's café. And then I'll move far away. Far, far away. I've often had a hankering to see Canada."

Rosina swallowed the last of her Chianti.

"You've had a tough life, kiddo," Shirley said. "Don't get mixed up with any more of the wrong men."

"I won't."

Rosina stood up, nodded shyly to us and headed for the door.

I called after her: "And don't bother to keep in touch."

She looked over her shoulder and grinned: "I won't."

"Where does that leave us?" Shirl said.

"Needing another drink," I said.

I signalled to Jeff to bring refills.

We sat in silence while Jeff poured the drinks.

"No more Chianti?" he asked.

"Our guest left."

"Never liked the wine," Jeff said. "But the bottles make great table lamps."

He shuffled back to the bar.

I raised my glass and took a good pull at the gin and tonic.

I said: "We were interrupted."

Shirl grinned. "We sure were. You were gonna go down on one knee."

"Can't do it now. I haven't got the ring."

"You sold it to buy Rosina's air ticket. That worked out well – I don't think."

I smiled. "I've got a bonus cheque for five hundred pounds. Could buy a big diamond ring with that. You know what Marilyn Monroe says?"

"'Diamonds are a girl's best friend.' But I don't think I agree with Marilyn this time."

I raised an eyebrow at that. "Oh?"

Shirley moved closer and linked her arm through mine. "I think you have your life-long friend when your two hearts are beating as one."

"Two souls linked in life's journey," I said.

"Two hands clasped in eternal friendship," Shirl said.

"Two minds that think alike," I added.

Shirl grinned. "I bet I know what your mind's thinking."

"How did you guess?"

Shirley took a sip of her Campari soda. "Instead of a ring, I'd rather have a holiday."

"Me too. Where shall we go?"

"Everywhere. Let's travel the world until our money runs out."

"Done. We'll leave tomorrow."

"So, the World Cup mystery is over?" Shirley asked.

"Not quite," I said. "Who sent that World Cup Final ticket anonymously to Crawley Rovers?"

"I guess we'll never know," Shirl said.

As it happens, after we'd returned from our holiday, we did find out...

EPILOGUE

Dateline: Brighton 15 September 1966
WORLD CUP TICKET MYSTERY SOLVED
by Colin Crampton

The mystery of how a free ticket to the World Cup Final came to be sent anonymously to Crawley Rovers football club has finally been solved.

The ticket was sent by Mr Bert Hodgkinson, 83, a long-time Crawley Rovers supporter. Mr Hodgkinson forgot to send his covering letter with the ticket.

The letter was found yesterday by Mr Hodgkinson's daughter, Mrs Tracy Bunce, 58, folded inside a library book. Mrs Bunce was returning Mr Hodgkinson's books following his death from a heart attack two weeks ago.

In the letter, Mr Hodgkinson explained he had saved up for a World Cup Final ticket from the moment he knew the competition was coming to England. But a week before the final, Mr Hodgkinson was told by his doctor that the event would be too exciting for his weak heart.

Mrs Bunce told the *Chronicle*: "My father was a forgetful old cuss. He was always putting things down and forgetting where they were. He probably used the letter as a bookmark while he got the cat's supper."

In the run up to the World Cup Final in July, the ticket was linked to two murders.

In a postscript to his letter, Mr Hodgkinson wrote: "I'd been looking forward to the match, but I hope sending you the ticket so close to the final doesn't cause any problems."

Read more Crampton of the Chronicle stories at:

www.colincrampton.com

Author's note and acknowledgements

I've mentioned before that any Crampton of the Chronicle adventure couldn't appear without help from many people. Barney Skinner has designed the cover and typeset and formatted the book for both the e-book and paperback editions. Barney is also the designer behind the Crampton of the Chronicle website. Members of the Crampton Advanced Readers' Team read the manuscript and made many helpful suggestions and corrections. The members of the team who helped are (in alphabetical order) Jaquie Fallon, Andrew Grand, Jenny Jones, Doc Kelly, Amanda Perrott, Mark Rewhorn, Christopher Roden and Gregg Wynia. Thanks to you all! Needless to say, any errors that remain are mine and mine alone.

Much of the information about the 1966 World Cup in this book – such as the match scores and goals - actually happened. But the events at Wembley Stadium are fictitious – as is the activities of the imaginary Crawley Rovers.

Finally, a big thankyou to you, the reader, for reading this book. If you've enjoyed it, please recommend it to your friends! In these days of internet sales, online book reviews are very important for authors. So, if you have a few minutes to leave one on Amazon and/or Goodreads, I would be very grateful. Thank you.

Peter Bartram, October 2021

About the author

Peter Bartram brings years of experience as a journalist to his Crampton of the Chronicle crime mystery series. His novels are fast-paced and humorous - the action is matched by the laughs. The books feature a host of colourful characters as befits stories set in Brighton, one of Britain's most trend-setting towns.

Peter began his career as a reporter on a local weekly newspaper before working as an editor in London and finally becoming freelance. He has done most things in journalism from door-stepping for quotes to writing serious editorials. He's pursued stories in locations as diverse as 700-feet down a coal mine and Buckingham Palace. Peter wrote 21 non-fiction books, including five ghost-written, before turning to crime – and penning the Crampton of the Chronicle series. There are now 14 books in the series.

Follow Peter Bartram on Facebook at:
www.facebook.com/peterbartramauthor

Follow Peter Bartram on Twitter at:
@PeterFBartram

More great books from Peter Bartram...

HEADLINE MURDER

When the owner of a miniature golf course goes missing, ace crime reporter Colin Crampton uncovers the dark secrets of a 22-year-old murder.

STOP PRESS MURDER

The murder of a night watchman and the theft of a saucy film of a nude woman bathing set Colin off on a madcap investigation with a stunning surprise ending.

FRONT PAGE MURDER

Archie Flowerdew is sentenced to hang for killing rival artist Percy Despart. Archie's niece Tammy believes he's innocent and convinces Colin to take up the case. Trouble is, the more Colin investigates, the more it looks like Archie is guilty.

THE TANGO SCHOOL MYSTERY

Colin Crampton and girlfriend Shirley Goldsmith are tucking into their meal when Shirley discovers more blood on her rare steak than she'd expected. The pair are drawn into investigating a sinister conspiracy which seems to centre on a tango school.

THE MOTHER'S DAY MYSTERY

There are just four days to Mother's Day and crime reporter Colin Crampton is under pressure to find a front-page story to fit the theme. Then Colin and his feisty girlfriend Shirley Goldsmith stumble across a body late at night on a lonely country road...

THE COMEDY CLUB MYSTERY

When theatrical agent Daniel Bernstein turns up murdered, any of five comedians competing for a place on a top TV show could be behind the killing. Colin and Shirley take on identical twin gangsters and tangle with an unlikely cast of misfits as they set out to solve the mystery.

THE POKER GAME MYSTERY

Colin discovers nightclub bouncer Steve Telford murdered – but can't understand why five cards of a poker hand are laid out next to the body. The tension ratchets higher when the life of a young girl is on the line. Colin must win a poker game with a sinister opponent to save her.

THE BEACH PARTY MYSTERY

Brighton is about to host its most exciting beach party ever – with the world's biggest name in rock music headlining the show. It seems a world away from the work of Evening Chronicle crime reporter Colin Crampton. But that's before fraudster Claude Winterbottom is beaten to death. The climax explodes on a pirate radio ship moored off the British coast.

THE MORNING, NOON & NIGHT TRILOGY

The adventure starts in *Murder in the Morning Edition*... when crime reporter Colin Crampton and feisty girlfriend Shirley Goldsmith witness an audacious train robbery. (Free on my website when you subscribe to the readers' group).

The mystery deepens in *Murder in the Afternoon Extra*... as the body count climbs and Colin finds himself hunted by a ruthless killer.

The climax explodes in *Murder in the Night Final...* when Colin and Shirley uncover the stunning secret behind the robbery and the murders.

Read all three books in *The Morning, Noon & Night Omnibus Edition* or listen to them on the audiobooks available from Audible, Amazon and iTunes.

Printed in Great Britain
by Amazon